New York Times and *USA Today* best-selling author **Helena Hunting** lives outside of Toronto with her amazing family and her two awesome cats, who think the best place to sleep is her keyboard. She writes all things romance – contemporary, romantic comedy, sports, and angsty new adult. Helena loves to bake cupcakes, has been known to listen to a song on repeat 1,512 times while writing a book, and if she has to be away from her family, she prefers to be in warm weather with her friends.

@HelenaHunting
www.helenahunting.com
www.facebook.com/helena.hunting

THE GOOD LUCK CHARM

HELENA HUNTING

piatkus

PIATKUS

First published in the US in 2018 by Forever, an imprint of
Grand Central Publishing, a division of Hachette Book Group, Inc

First published in Great Britain in 2018 by Piatkus

1 3 5 7 9 10 8 6 4 2

A CIP catalogue record for this book
is available from the British Library.

ISBN 978-0-349-42143-8

Printed and bound in Great Britain by
Clays Ltd, Elcograf S.p.A.

Papers used by Piatkus are from well-managed forests
and other responsible sources.

Piatkus
An imprint of
Little, Brown Book Group
Carmelite House
50 Victoria Embankment
London EC4Y 0DZ

An Hachette UK Company
www.hachette.co.uk

www.littlebrown.co.uk

To my very own good luck charms,
Hubs and Kidlet

ACKNOWLEDGMENTS

Endless love for my husband and my daughter, who give me the time, love, and support to pursue this incredible dream and live it with me; and for my parents and sister, who are the most amazing cheerleaders in the world.

Pepper, one day we'll write books side by side in Florida. Until then, FaceTime lunches will have to do.

I have an entire village of people who help me take a story from a kernel of an idea into the book you're holding in your hands. Kimberly, you are such a joy to work with and so much more than an agent. Thank you for being awesome times a million.

Sarah, you're truly one of a kind; I'm so fortunate to have you running my team. Hustlers, thank you for being my safety net.

Huge love to Leah and my team at Forever for making this project so incredibly rewarding.

Nina, I'm so glad we get to keep doing this together, one book at a time. Jenn, you're a special brand of wonder woman, and there aren't enough tacos in the world to express my love for you.

Beavers, you are amazing and I love you to bits. Thank you for always sharing the excitement with me and for taking chances on new worlds.

I have so much love for the incredible women in this community who are my friends, colleagues, teachers, and cheerleaders: my Backdoor Babes, Tara, Meghan, Deb, and Katherine; Tijan, Marty, Teeny, Susi, Erika, Shalu, Kellie, Ruth, Kelly, Melanie, Leigh, Karen, Marnie, Julie, Laurie, Kathrine, Angela, Kristy, my Pams, Filets, Nap girls, Holiday's. Thank you for being you and dealing with my crazy.

Thank you, readers and bloggers, for all your support and for believing in happily ever afters.

THE GOOD LUCK CHARM

chapter one

GHOSTS

Lilah

The curdled cream in my coffee should've been the tip-off that today was going to be craptastic.

Because I couldn't start the day without a caffeine kick, I stopped at a lovely little café on my way to work—only to get to the counter and realize my wallet wasn't in my purse and I had no way to pay for the overpriced latte I felt compelled to order.

So I ran back out to the parking lot and managed to scrounge up enough spare change to pay. Of course, by the time I went back to claim my drink, my latte had been scooped up by someone else and I had to wait an extra ten minutes because seven more people were now ahead of me in line.

Fortunately, work wasn't far and even with the delay, I would still be early. I'd hoped to have half an hour before my shift to do some reading in preparation for my upcoming statistics class. But no problem. I could fit that in during lunch instead of being social.

Just one more course after this and I'd have all the admission requirements for the master's of nursing program at the University of Minnesota, where I'd applied for next fall. I'd been working as a nurse full-time for four years, and now, at twenty-six, I was ready to go back to school and further my education.

Latte in hand, I stepped outside into the drizzle that had begun during my wait. Ominous dark clouds loomed low as I rushed to my car. Setting my coffee on the roof, I rooted around in my purse for my keys. The light rain quickly became a downpour, soaking my hair and plastering my scrubs to my skin, and still, I couldn't find my damn keys.

Which was when I lost my grip on my purse. The contents scattered over the parking lot, and my keys rolled under my Corolla. I had to get on my hands and knees to retrieve them, mashing my chest against the ground right into a puddle of dirty rain water.

By the time I finally managed to get all my things together—apart from my lipstick and a compact that had rolled into a sewage grate—I was approaching officially late status. And I had a staff meeting at nine thirty. In my frazzled state, I forgot about the coffee on my roof, which miraculously stayed in place—until I hit the first stoplight, where the coffee promptly dumped all over my windshield.

I made it to work with little time to spare, looking like a

drowned rat and completely uncaffeinated. Thankfully, I had an extra set of scrubs in my locker for just such mishaps.

Discombobulated but determined to keep it together, I managed to semidry my hair with the hand dryer in the women's bathroom, although the time I'd spent with the flat iron this morning was completely wasted.

I was on my way into the conference room for the morning staff meeting when an attractive man in a suit, wearing glasses—I'd always had a bit of a weakness for men with glasses—called my name.

Turned out he was from my husband's lawyer, sent to deliver the final divorce papers. After nearly six years of marriage, the asshole didn't even have the common courtesy to bring them to me himself, or schedule a time for us to meet and sign them. I hadn't realized we'd reached this kind of communicationless impasse.

I spent the entire meeting trying to hold back tears—of embarrassment, of anger, of frustration.

A pervasive feeling of emptiness clung to me like climbing vines, making the day drag. But I didn't want to go home, aware my only company would be my dog, Merk, and as much as he was a good listener, I needed more than that right now.

I didn't think my day could possibly get any worse.

I was horribly wrong.

At the end of my shift, I make my customary final stop at the nurses' station to review end-of-day paperwork. Ashley, who works the reception desk, is staring up at an MRI brain scan, her hands on her hips.

"What's this?" I ask, moving to stand beside her. The shadows on the scan don't look particularly good.

"Stroke. Came in less than an hour ago." She glances over her shoulder at me. "You on your way out?"

"Yeah." My gaze snags on the name at the bottom of the scan. The clipboard slips from my hand and clatters to the floor. "Oh God."

"Lilah? You okay?"

I shake my head, unwilling to believe what I'm seeing. This can't be happening. Not today.

Ashley puts a hand on my shoulder. "Do you know him?"

I nod, swallowing back a terrified sob before I can respond. "Yes. What room?"

"Let me check." She rushes to the board, finds the room number, and repeats it twice. "Do you need me to come with you?"

"No. I'm fine." That's not even close to true. The man I love like a father has suffered a stroke.

I wish I'd never gotten out of bed today. I wish there were no today.

I race to his room, heart in my throat, body humming with adrenaline. But when I get there, I don't find Martin Kase's wife, my second mother, as I expected. No, sitting in a chair next to the bed, head down and looking lost, is their son. My stomach fills with concrete as I take in not *a* ghost but *the* ghost from my past. *Ethan*.

My mouth goes instantly dry. My legs feel suddenly wooden and weak at the same time. I can't seem to take a full breath. Or get a handle on the sudden, violent rush of emotions that paralyze me. I feel raw, as if my nerve endings are all exposed, and the air makes my skin feel like it's on fire.

This is all too much. I've already taken too many punches to the heart today. And in this moment I feel like I've barely recovered from the punch he delivered eight years ago. My heart aches exactly the way it did the night he called to tell me it wouldn't work anymore. *We* wouldn't work anymore. That all the years we'd been together—through my dad leaving when I was just a child, all of high school, every single first-time experience, prom, helping him pack for college—all of it meant nothing. He needed to focus on hockey, on his career in the NHL, and I was a distraction he couldn't afford.

Ethan pushes up from the chair, his massive body unfurling. Good God, he's filled out. Sure, there have been pictures on social media, and I've caught glimpses of him on the ice when I've accidentally turned on a hockey game—any time he plays I've made a point to turn it off. But nothing could ever prepare me for being this close to the man who took my heart, crushed it, and gave it back to me in pieces.

He's still uncommonly beautiful, more now than he was when we were teenagers. I swear his shoulders are twice as broad as they were a decade ago. I can barely hold his eyes without being submerged in a deluge of memories I thought I'd buried long ago. I'd nearly forgotten how arresting his eyes are—okay, that's untrue—but it's been a long time since I've been hit with the full force of them. The vibrant blue with a halo of amber edging the iris, the burst of gold that colors nearly a third of his right eye draws me in and briefly holds me captive, just like it always did when we were younger.

"DJ." It's just my name. Two small syllables. But the effect of his voice is bone jarring. I feel the grit of his pain like sandpaper on my heart.

I fight to keep my voice even. "I go by Lilah now." The words leave my mouth before I can call them back and find a different, more appropriate greeting. I shift my gaze away, anywhere but him. Martin looks frail in that hospital bed, and I wish Jeannie were here, a lifeline I can cling to, something to keep me from being torn apart from memories I don't have the strength to handle. After all, the present is already crushing me under its weight.

"I didn't realize Martin had been admitted until a few minutes ago. How long have you been here?" I lock down the emotion and switch gears to professional mode. This I can do. This I am good at. I read through the chart at the end of the bed, then cross the room to check the monitors—though my mind barely registers the numbers.

"I don't know. Awhile, I guess. I just got into town and then... this happened." I can feel Ethan's eyes on me. I self-consciously touch the end of my ponytail, having given up on wearing it down by lunch. My scrubs are a size too big, and my running shoes are old and scuffed, my good ones still soaked from this morning. I look as bad as I feel, and I hate that I care about the way he perceives me and that it's even a thought, with Martin hooked up to monitors, his prognosis uncertain.

"His vitals are good, but we won't know anything long-term quite yet. Where's Jeannie?"

"Mom stepped out to get some coffee." He rubs the back of his neck, as if he's trying to ease the tension. "So you're a nurse here?"

The fact that he has to ask, that it's not something he knows, feels like another shot to the chest. Maybe he's making small talk, but it still hurts to be reminded that he knows nothing about my life.

I look down at my scrubs, as if they hold the answer to his question—which in a way they do, considering the hospital name is emblazoned on the pocket over my heart. At my silence he clears his throat. "I thought you were at Mercy in Minneapolis."

"I transferred a while ago." I've been here since just after the New Year. The last time Jeannie mentioned Ethan was two weeks ago. She'd said something about hoping he'd come for a visit before the hockey season started, not that it would make a difference to me since he never made an effort to see me when he blew in and out of town.

A very small part of me is happy he's here—for Jeannie and Martin. But the bigger part, the part that he discarded so carelessly all those years ago, is hurt that this is what it's taken to get him in the same room as me for the first time in almost a decade.

He shoves his hands into his pockets, then withdraws them, smoothing them over his thighs. "I figured you'd be working on your residency by now."

I can't tell if it's a dig, or if I'm interpreting it that way because this day has been full of them. "Sometimes we have to readjust our goals."

"Yeah. Don't I know it," he mutters.

I don't have a chance to ask about the deeper meaning of that, or stoke the already awkward fire raging between us, because we're interrupted.

"Delilah!" Jeannie's holding two coffees, one in each hand. When our eyes meet, I see every worry and question. From her fears about Martin to my interaction with Ethan—all of it passes in the few seconds before she opens her arms for me. Like a mother would. Like she's always done.

And I fall right into that offered solace, because I feel as though I'm a ball of wool, unraveling into a darkness that doesn't seem to end. I wrap my arms around her, seeking comfort, not just for Martin, but for everything that's happened today.

The possibility that I could lose the man I've come to see as a father—after my own dad left my mom, me, and my five siblings behind in search of a life that didn't include us—is excruciatingly untenable. Even after Ethan and I broke up,

Martin was the one who helped make sure I wasn't getting ripped off when I bought my first car, taught me how to fix my leaky sink, and always had a smile and a hug whenever I came over to visit. I don't know if I can handle this—not with the way the rest of my life seems to be falling apart, too. Especially with Ethan standing here, hints of the boy I once loved hidden behind those arresting eyes. It took me long enough to finally get over him disappearing from my life and now I wonder if I ever really did get over him at all.

I have years of pent-up frustration, resentment, and disappointment churning in my head and in my heart, and all I want to do is throw it all at Ethan. But there are more important things going on right now.

"It's okay. Shhh, Delilah; he'll be all right," Jeannie says quietly, rubbing slow circles on my back.

I realize I'm crying soundless, body-shaking sobs that I'm unable to control. I'm embarrassed and angry with myself that I'm falling apart like this when clearly it's Jeannie who needs the support.

When I manage to pull myself together enough to release her, I ask brokenly, "What can I do for you? Why don't I go to the house? I just finished my shift; I can feed Flower, bring you a change of clothes and anything else you might need for tonight." My offers are clearly unnecessary, especially with Ethan being here. I don't like this feeling, like I'm not needed. I've always been the one Jeannie comes to when she needs something.

"I thought Flower ran away," Ethan says from behind me.

It's such a normal question in such an abnormal situation.

"Turns out the new neighbors across the street put in a cat door and Flower took to sleeping in their basement, until they discovered the raccoons in the area were using it, too." Jeannie touches my arm. "Remember when the babies got into their fridge while they were away for the weekend?"

"Their entire kitchen was a mess!" We giggle and then Jeannie brings her hand to her mouth, stifling a sob.

"Martin helped us clean it all up before they got back," I say softly.

Jeannie turns to Ethan, who I've been trying desperately not to look in the eye, and says in a wavering voice, "What if he's not okay?"

Ethan steps up and pulls her into his broad chest. "I'll be here to help, no matter what happens."

I don't understand how he can do that when he's living in Chicago, but maybe he's placating.

"I'm so glad you're coming home," Jeannie says.

My stomach dips and then flips. I finally meet his gaze again. Raw emotions make him look older than twenty-seven. My questions must be evident in my expression.

"I've been traded to Minnesota," he explains.

I feel like I'm taking slap shots to the heart left, right, and center today. And this might be the one that finally does me in.

chapter two

LONG NIGHTS

Lilah

Y ou're coming home." It's a soft whisper filled with a range of emotions, not the least of which is anger.

"I am."

I look away as Ethan envelops Jeannie in a hug, murmuring soothing words. He's her anchor in an otherwise turbulent sea of uncertainty.

I focus on Martin's unconscious form, feeling as if I'm intruding on a private moment, unsure of my role. Usually I'm Jeannie's shoulder and she's mine, but Ethan's presence changes everything. As does his permanence.

Jeannie's burst of emotion dissipates on a deep exhale. She turns to me with a small smile. "I'd like to stay the night. Do you think the hospital will allow that?"

"I could—" I'm about to offer to stay with her, but I pause, then force the corners of my mouth to lift and approximate a smile. I'm not needed with Ethan here. "I'm sure I can get clearance. I'll see about having a lounger brought in so you don't have to sleep in one of those chairs." I motion to the one beside the bed.

Ethan squeezes Jeannie's shoulder. "I'll stay, too."

Jeannie's hand covers his. "You don't have to do that. You can go back to the house."

"I'm not leaving you."

Those four words feel like a serrated blade sliced across my heart. He promised me that once, too. It meant something, until he went back on it. "I'll have to get clearance for a second person. The hospital may not allow it." My anger makes it come out snappy rather than a soft caution, and I immediately feel bad. This isn't about me; it's about Martin and Jeannie having support.

"I can stay in the waiting room if I have to." He tries to meet my gaze, but I can't hold his without potentially breaking down again.

"I'll try my best." I direct the comment at Jeannie. She's wearing her favorite apron, one Ethan and I picked out almost a decade ago as a Mother's Day present. I need to get out of here, away from all the memories that come with his presence. "I can stop by the house and get you something more comfortable to wear."

"That's so kind of you, Lilah. You're always so helpful." Jeannie looks down, smoothing her hands over the worn cotton. Her eyes go wide with panic, and she looks to Ethan. "The pie! I left it in the oven!"

"I took it out before I left," he reassures her.

I'm 100 percent sure the house will smell like apples, cinnamon, and butter. Apple pie has always been Ethan's favorite, and Jeannie is the kind of mom who would make it because he's come home for a visit, or to stay, as seems to be the case.

"I could pick up things for you, as well, Ethan, if you'd like." His name feels sharp and bitter on my tongue.

Jeannie pats his chest. "Or you could go together."

"No." I don't mean to shout, but I can't be alone with Ethan, closed in a car with his scent and his voice and a million memories I can't hide from. I clear my throat and try again. "I'd feel a lot better if you weren't alone, Jeannie."

Ethan's expression is impassive. I'm sure he's as relieved as I am not to be in a confined space with me for any length of time. "I have a duffel in the basement bedroom."

Another shot of relief hits me. Before I moved into my town house earlier this year, I stayed with Martin and Jeannie for a couple of months in Ethan's old bedroom. I might have left a few things in there, and the last thing I want is Ethan finding my pajamas in his dresser.

"I'll bring the bag back, then." No way am I going through his luggage. I switch into helpful, action-oriented mode, something I excel at when faced with stressful situations. "Jeannie, I'll grab your favorite yoga pants and a sweatshirt. Anything else you think you might need?"

"That would be wonderful. My travel bag is in my bedroom

closet, and maybe you could bring my crossword book in case I have trouble sleeping?"

"On your nightstand?"

"Or the living room. The usual spots."

"Okay. I'll be back in a bit. Text if you think of anything else. I'll talk to someone about getting a lounger brought in and about having two people stay the night." I don't honestly think it will be difficult to get approval for Ethan, but it makes me feel marginally better to envision him trying to get comfortable in one of those tiny chairs in the waiting room, which is petty considering Martin's current state.

Jeannie steps up to hug me again. "Are you sure you don't want Ethan to go with you?"

"It's better if he stays with you, don't you think?"

Jeannie steps back, holding my shoulders as her eyes move over my face. "We'll get through this together. Everything happens for a reason, Delilah." She lets out a pained sigh and presses her hand to her chest.

I pat her hand and smile, but say nothing. I can't understand the reason behind Martin having a stroke, my almost ex-husband having apparently lost his balls entirely, and my first-ever ex-boyfriend, and once best friend, returning to Minnesota all in the same day, unless I've done something horrible to warrant this kind of hellish karma. "I'll be back as soon as I can."

I make a right out of the room and speed walk down the hall, exhaling a long breath. I need to keep it together until

I'm in my car. I stop at the nurses' station and put in a request for two lounge chairs and two overnight family members for Martin. Fairview is a smaller hospital, people know each other, and my connection to the family allows me some leniency in what I can reasonably ask for.

Just as I finish filling out the paperwork, Ashley, the receptionist, pokes me with her pen. "I know you've had a bad day, so I'm going to do you a favor. Do not turn around right now, but there's an EFF at three o'clock. Wait, three for me and nine for you. Be nonchalant when you look." I roll my eyes and suppress a grin. EFF is Ashley code for Extra Fine and Fuckable.

She wags her eyebrows. "Have a good night."

"I have an errand to run. I'll be back in an hour." I tap the desk and turn in the direction her eyes keep moving.

I should've known her EFF would be Ethan.

He takes a step toward me, then stops and shoves his hands in his pockets. "Are you sure you don't want me to come with you?"

I grab my purse and step away from the desk. "Did Jeannie send you out here to ask again?"

I move toward the exit, absently waving to Ashley, who I'm sure will be all over me with questions when I get back.

Ethan falls into step beside me. "I thought it might give us an opportunity to talk."

I speed up, heading for the employee parking lot and the fresh air I seem to need so badly. It's hard to take a full breath again. "You mean about Martin? We won't know anything until he's awake and they do more tests in the morning." I know that's not what he wants to talk about, but I'm not going to give him the satisfaction.

Warm summer air does nothing to cool my already heated skin as I push through the doors.

"DJ, wait."

I close my eyes, taking a deep breath so I don't snap. I'm raw. This day has been too hard, and I'm not ready for this kind of conversation with him. Especially not now, when his father's health is so uncertain and our emotions are all tied up in the potential for loss. Because no matter what happens, there's a chance Martin won't be the same man he was before the stroke.

"Please, DJ." His fingers wrap around my wrist.

I don't want the sensation to be electric, but it is. I don't want the warmth that floods my veins at the foreign familiarity of his touch. I don't want my body to react in any way to him, but it does. My heart remembers that he broke it, but the rest of me seems to have forgotten.

I jerk away. "I told you, I go by Lilah now." It's so stupid, a pointless thing to be stuck on, but it's the only place I can put focus so I don't break down.

"Sorry. I'm not used to it." He runs an unsteady hand through his hair, sending the thick dark strands into disarray. "I could drive?" His tone is layered with regret and remorse. Emotions that do me no good, not this long after the fact. Not when they only exist because of all the other things happening to him.

"I don't think that's a good idea tonight."

"I just want to apologize, D—Lilah."

I exhale a breath, trying to remain grounded, to keep the simmering anger from bubbling over and pouring out. But I'm so tied up inside, so broken by the events of the past twelve hours and the piece of my past standing in front of me, splintering me apart all over again.

"What do you want to apologize for?" I ask on a whisper.

"For the way I handled things."

"Handled things?" I echo.

He drops his head, peeking up at me through long lashes. "When I was drafted."

My father was the first man to walk out of my life, and then the dominos began to fall in succession. Ethan was the next to go, then my husband, Avery, and now I might stand to lose Martin, depending on how he comes out of this. I don't want to lose another man I love, or be faced with heartbreak all over again.

I run my fingertip from the center of my forehead down the bridge of my nose, working to find some calm. "Neither one of us is prepared for this conversation tonight."

"I know you're upset, but—"

I hold up a hand. "You're not hearing me. I can't do this with you right now. *I* can't handle this conversation, and *you* can't handle the things I want to say to you."

"I made a lot of mistakes." His voice is soft and sad, which only fuels my anger.

"Mistakes? You abandoned me. You weren't just my boyfriend, Ethan; we grew up together. You were my best friend, and you disappeared from my life for eight years. The only reason I'm seeing you after all this time is because of Martin. Do you know how hurtful your silence has been? Every time you came home and never called, did everything you could to avoid seeing me, talking to me? I can't forgive you for that."

His voice cracks. "Not ever?"

"I don't know. I don't have an answer for that now. Not after all these years of nothing. Not with all of this going on."

He nods slowly, a crease forming between his eyes. "Right. Okay. You're right. It's just . . . I just . . . I didn't ever want to hurt you."

"But you did. I mean it when I say you're not ready to hear what I have to say, and frankly, I'm not ready to say it. This is too much for both of us. Too much is happening. Can we just deal with your dad being in the hospital? I think that's enough."

"Can I at least walk you to your car? Make sure you're safe?"

"I'm right over there." I motion across the lot. "You should be with your mother. She needs you." Unspoken words hang between us like a noose waiting for a neck to tighten around. The implication is there, even if I'm unsure whether it's true. *I don't need you.*

"Okay. You're right." Ethan's defeat makes my heart ache even though it shouldn't. I was always too soft for him, too quick to fold.

Before I can leave, Ethan takes a step forward, closing the distance between us. I don't have time to react, to protest, to do much of anything before his body is pressed against mine, his thickly muscled arms wrapped around me.

I feel simultaneously protected and vulnerable.

As much as I want to push him away, I return the embrace instead, aware that he's struggling, and despite my anger, I'm someone familiar he can lean on. I know better than anyone how tumultuous his relationship with his father has been, and what a shock this must be for him. We all believe our parents are invincible until we find out they're not. So I give in, allowing his touch to soothe and ignite. I absorb the feel of him, the memory of him made real again. For one beat, my fractured heart feels deceptively whole.

Stubble brushes my cheek, Ethan's lips at my ear. "I'm so sorry."

I push on his chest, desperate to hold on and escape at the same time. "I'll be back in a bit. Jeannie can message if she thinks of anything else she needs."

I rush across the lot, hands shaking as I start the car and pull out onto the street. I drive around the corner before I pull over and put my face in my hands. "Why? *Why, why, why?*" I give myself one song on the radio to break down. I need to keep it together for Jeannie. When it ends, I wipe my eyes on

my sleeve, find a tissue in the bottom of my purse to blow my
nose with, take the hazards off, signal, and pull back onto the
road.

The route to Jeannie and Martin's house is one I could almost drive in my sleep. When my almost ex-husband, Avery,
and I couldn't work things out and the fighting became unbearable, I opted to stay with Jeannie and Martin. I could've
stayed with my sister Carmen, but she's not the neatest person.
I would've driven her nuts with my cleaning.

I pull into the Kases' driveway beside a fancy pickup filled
with boxes. It must be Ethan's. As always, the door is un-
locked. I step inside and inhale the scent of cinnamon and
apples. Before I go upstairs to pack a bag for Jeannie, I head to
the basement. Occasionally, Ethan and I used to sneak down
here during one of our lunch breaks when his older brother
Tyler was away at college. If Jeannie came home while we
were in the middle of something we didn't want her seeing,
we'd climb out the basement window undetected.

The basement has been redecorated—sort of. All of Ethan's
trophies from high school line one wall, along with the team
pictures for each year—his parents' shrine to their unexpected
miracle. Their Ethan. My Ethan. At least he was then.

I stop in the doorway of the wood-paneled bedroom.
Ethan's hockey quilt covers the double bed and more of his
high school memorabilia litters the room, including a picture
of us at his senior prom. I'd spent so much time as a teenager
sprawled across that comforter, trying to make Ethan study for

tests. He was easily distractible back then. I grab his duffel from the bed and turn off the light before I head back upstairs. Getting lost in the past isn't a constructive use of my time.

I find Jeannie's yoga pants, a sweatshirt, her toiletries, and an extra change of clothes. I throw in a pair of pajamas for Martin, as well as his toiletries.

Before I make the trip back to the hospital, I stop in the kitchen and throw a few snacks in the bag, along with some bottled water. The pie sits on the counter. It looks like it had just gone in the oven before they left. I might be able to take it home and save it. Apple pie for breakfast would make for a nice surprise for them tomorrow morning.

I'm grateful that Jeannie is in the room with Ethan when I return to the hospital. I don't want to be alone with him. Maybe he wants to apologize to alleviate his conscience. I have no idea. What I do know is a conversation or an apology isn't going to change anything.

He can never unbreak my heart.

chapter three
ENDS AND BEGINNINGS

Ethan

Ethan?" My mother puts her hand on my arm after DJ dropped off our bags and bolted from Dad's room. "Are you okay?"

Isn't that the question of the week? I glance at my mother, wondering how much better she knows DJ than I do, everything she's seen in the past eight years that I missed. "She's stayed close with you and Dad, hasn't she?"

"We were always her family, and aside from her sister Carmen, everyone else moved away." She sounds apologetic.

"I'm glad that didn't change." I run my hands down my thighs. My jeans are still damp from running into the lake to pull my dad's boat in to shore. I don't think I'll ever be able to erase the memory of finding him like that, disoriented and afraid, my own panic merging with his. And on top of what's happening with my dad, now I have to face the woman I left behind. "She's still very angry with me."

"She has a lot going on, Ethan. Give her some time. This is hard on her, too." She roots around in her overnight bag and finds the blanket from the living room couch, shaking it out.

"She said I abandoned her." My mom pauses to look at me, deep sadness making her eyes glassy. "I think she's right. That's not what I meant to do, but that's exactly what happened, wasn't it?"

"You did what you thought was best."

"I did what Dad thought was best." I close my eyes and let my head drop against the back of the chair. "Sorry. This isn't a good time to talk about this. I just didn't expect to see DJ, or for any of this to happen." I gesture toward my father.

She sighs. "I know you and your father haven't always seen eye to eye on things, Ethan, especially where your career and Delilah are concerned, but he's only ever wanted what's best for you."

I glance at my father, hooked up to machines, his future as uncertain as my own, and I worry that this animosity I feel toward him will never be resolved. It's selfish and unfair, but I don't know where else to put my anger.

My phone rings and I check the screen. It's Josh Cooper, one of my former teammates from LA who was traded to Minnesota a few years ago. I told him I'd be in town tonight, and we'd talked about getting together while I was here.

"It's a teammate. I'll be right back," I tell my mom, then leave the room so I can take the call.

"Hey, man, how's it going?" I say to Josh.

"Good! Me and some of the guys were thinking about heading out for a few beers. You wanna join us? I talked to Coach this morning; he thinks he can get us some ice time on Sunday."

"That sounds great, but uh, I've got a family thing going on right now."

"Oh no—is everything okay? You've only been in town for a few hours. You and the old man have one of your pissing matches already?"

I wish it were that simple. I fill him in on the situation with my dad.

"Fuck, Kase. I'm sorry. What a shit thing to come home to. We'll put off ice time until you know what's doing with your dad, yeah? And if you decide you just need to gear up and get out some frustration, you let me know."

"Thanks for that. I'd like to be on the ice before practices start."

"They're not mandatory for a couple of weeks, so you don't have to worry about it."

"I'd like some time to get comfortable with the team, you know?"

"Yeah. I hear you. They're good guys, though; you'll mesh easy."

I sure as hell hope so. It's hard to get my head around any one thing right now. "Thanks, Josh. I'll keep you updated."

"Just call if you need anything."

The next morning two nurses come to take my dad for more tests, but unfortunately DJ isn't one of them. My dad is disoriented and a little aggressive until he realizes where he is. His speech appears to be affected by the stroke, sounds rather than words the only thing he seems to be able to manage so far. We can only hope it's not permanent.

We follow the nurses until they wheel him into a restricted area. I'm about to suggest we get coffee before we go back to the room to wait, when DJ comes around the corner. She's carrying a bag and a tray of coffees. Her hair is pulled back in a smooth ponytail. She looks tired but she smiles, eyes sliding over me and coming to rest on my mother. "Is Martin already in for tests?"

"They've just started." My mom pulls her in for a quick hug.

"I tried to get here before he went in but there was a line at the coffee shop. I brought you breakfast so you wouldn't have to endure the crap they try to pass off as food here." She looks around to make sure no one has overheard her slam on the health-care system's subpar food options.

"That was very sweet of you, Delilah—wasn't it, Ethan?"

"Very sweet," I agree. DJ doesn't seem to be able to look at me for more than a second or two.

"It's nothing really. I left your coffee black, Ethan. I wasn't sure if you still took it with a pound of sugar and cream or if your taste buds had matured since high school."

"Apparently my taste buds are still as immature now as they were back then," I reply with a wry grin.

Her cheeks flush and she turns her attention to my mom. "I have to start my shift, but I'm around if you need anything. All you have to do is ask for me and someone will find me."

"Thank you, Delilah, but I don't want to interfere with your job."

"It's not interfering. I'm here to help."

My mother hugs her again and then she's off, ponytail swinging as she walks down the hall.

My mom and I take a seat in the waiting room and she unpacks the bag. Inside is the pie from last night, a little dark around the edges, but it smells delicious. Neither of us had dinner, and the last time I stopped for food was around noon yesterday. A small container of whipped cream and another of sharp cheddar slices accompany the pie. The cheese is for me. DJ used to make fun of me when we were younger for liking cheddar with apple pie.

My mom sniffs. "She's such a lovely, thoughtful girl."

I put an arm around her. "She always has been." I hope one day she can forgive me and maybe I'll get to know her again.

It takes more than two hours for them to complete the tests for my dad. His recovery is going to be long and challenging, but possible. My father's stubbornness is both a blessing and a curse.

We'll be looking at months of appointments, therapists, and assessments, and my mom is already overwhelmed, as am I.

Returning to Forest Lake isn't just going to be about a new team anymore.

Once my dad is settled in his room again, I suggest that my mother and I go back to the house, shower, and grab some lunch. She doesn't want to leave my father alone, even though he's asleep, so she sends me with a list of things to pick up.

As I'm on the way down the hall, my phone rings; it's Selene. I utter a quiet curse and debate whether to answer it. I have no idea what I'm going to tell her. We've only been seeing each other for a month.

None of our conversations have revolved around family or the details of my personal life. Mostly it's been fun and sex, with some nice dinners as a precursor to the fun sex. Typically, I'd assume I'm not a high enough profile player to be much of a concern for the media. My trade from Chicago won't be announced until Tuesday, so I have some time to figure out how to approach this conversation, but I don't know if waiting is the best idea. It might be better to rip off the Band-Aid.

Before I pussy out and the call goes to voicemail, I answer. "Hey." I push through the front door and head for the nearest empty bench.

"Hey! I'm glad I got through! I wanted to firm up plans for dinner this week, if you're still interested."

I rub the back of my neck. "Yeah, about that... I took an impromptu road trip to Minnesota."

"Minnesota? That's a pretty long road trip. What's all the way out there?"

"My family." It says a lot that I've never even bothered to share those trivial details with Selene.

"Oh. Wow. How didn't I know that? Are you there for a while?"

"At least a few days." Maybe I should've put this conversation off until tonight. Or never.

"Right. Is everything okay?"

Awkwardness creeps in now, hers and mine.

Mine is the kind that results from deciding how much personal information I'm willing to share. "Not really. My dad's in the hospital."

"Oh God! I'm so sorry, Ethan. That's terrible. What happened?"

"He had a stroke."

"A stroke? Isn't he too young for that?"

"He's in his seventies, so..."

"Oh, I didn't realize. Is it serious? I mean, I guess a stroke is always serious." She laughs nervously. "I'm so sorry. Will he be okay? Is there anything I can do?"

The last part seems to be reflexive—the help people offer when they run out of standard apologetic and sympathetic phrases. "That's sweet of you, but we're managing. It's just about devising a treatment plan."

"Okay. Well I'm glad he's going to be okay."

That's not exactly what I said, but I don't bother to correct her. "Yeah. Me, too."

"So I guess it's kind of up in the air as to when you'll be back."

"Yeah. I want to wait until he's out of the hospital and set-tled first."

"Of course. That makes sense. At least season training is still a ways off, right?"

She's opened the door and I have no choice but to walk right through it. "I have something else I need to tell you." My stomach knots. I hate this more than usual, maybe because of my recent interactions with DJ.

"It sounds like more bad news." Another nervous laugh follows.

"I wanted to tell you this in person, but with my dad in the hospital and me here for a while . . . They're going to an-nounce it soon, and I don't want you to hear it from anyone but me."

"Announce what?"

"I've been traded."

"Traded? You've only been with Chicago for a year, though."

"My contract was up, so I'm going to a different team."

"I didn't realize that could happen so close to the beginning of a new season." She sounds shocked and then a little uncer-tain when she says, "Uh, I guess congratulations? Is the trade a good thing?"

"It would've been nice to stay in Chicago, but Minnesota wanted me, so that's where I go." She doesn't need to know about the pay cut, or that if I don't pick up my game this year, my entire NHL career is probably over. Being traded three times in as many years is bad enough, but being sent to this team is pretty much the kiss of death.

"Minnesota? That's where you are now."

"It is."

"Right." After a brief pause she says, "So that means you'll have to move there, doesn't it?"

"It does." God, this is awkward, but not particularly painful, which is a good thing. "I'm sorry I had to do this over the phone. I was going to tell you when I got back to Chicago to finalize some things, but now that I'm here for a while..."

"Yeah. No. Of course. I totally understand. These things happen, right?" After another beat of silence she asks, "Should I let you go?"

"Yeah. I have to run a few errands." It sounds lame, even if it's true.

"Of course, Ethan. I'm sorry about your dad. I guess we'll talk? Maybe I'll see you around?"

"Sure. Thanks, Selene."

We say goodbye and I end the call. Tipping my chin up I stare at the sky. I don't know if that qualifies as ending things or not. We don't have personal effects at each other's places— it never got that far, but I still feel like I left things up in the air.

In all fairness, after the way I broke it off with DJ, I promised myself I'd never be that kind of asshole again— the one who breaks up with a girl over a text message or a phone call.

"Ethan?"

I look up to see DJ standing a few feet away. Scrubs are shapeless and purely functional, but somehow she still manages to look beautiful in them. "Hey."

"Everything all right?"

I don't have a real answer for that, so I lift a shoulder and let it fall.

"I saw the test results," she offers. "There's a good chance he's going to be okay."

"But still a chance that he won't be."

"There's always a chance of that, but Martin is stubborn and healthy. Those things both work in his favor." She nods at my phone. "Have you talked to your brothers yet?"

"Dylan called this morning—he's catching a flight as soon as he can—and Tyler's doing the same. At least it's not life-threatening anymore, but it'd be good to have the extra support for Mom."

"And you."

"All of us, I guess." I give her a half smile. "Thanks for the apple pie this morning. It meant a lot to my mom and me."

"Like I said, it was nothing. Gave me an excuse to eat pie for breakfast to make sure I didn't ruin it." She rolls her eyes at herself. "Anyway, are you here permanently now, or are you still between here and Chicago? I can always be available when Martin's released if Tyler or Dylan can't stay long."

"You have your own life, D—Lilah. I don't want to put this on you."

"You're not putting anything on me. I wouldn't make the offer, otherwise. Just . . . if there's anything I can do, I will."

"I appreciate that, and I know my mom does, too." I give her what I hope is a grateful smile. "I'm going to the house and then I'm stopping to pick up lunch."

"Jeannie's not coming with you?"

"She doesn't want to leave Dad. I could grab something for you, too."

"I brought a lunch. I'm good." She turns to walk away.

"Not even a Cosmo Special? Extra pickles on the side? Coleslaw?" It was her favorite back when we were in high school.

She narrows her eyes. "I ate pie for breakfast. I should probably stick to salad for lunch."

I give her a lingering once-over. The scrubs hide her curves, but she hasn't changed that much since high school, at least not on the outside. "Why?"

"Can't be ruining my girlish figure, especially now that I'm pretty much divorced." She cringes at the bitter tint to her words. "Forget I said that. It makes me sound petty and vain."

My brain gets stuck on one word in particular. "Divorced?"

She gives me a look I'm all too familiar with. It's her get-off-it face. "Come on, Ethan—Jeannie must've told you by now."

I give my head a slow shake. "This is the first I'm hearing about it. When did this happen?"

"We've been separated for a while. I got the final divorce papers yesterday morning."

"Yesterday? And I thought my day was shit."

"They weren't unexpected."

"Still. I'm sorry." I note for the first time that she's not wearing a wedding band. "He better not have cheated on you."

She barks out an incredulous laugh. "Fidelity wasn't the problem. We just want very different things out of life, so it was better that we go our separate ways." She sighs and looks at the sky. "Anyway, I have rounds, so I should go."

Obviously there's more to the story, but she has no reason to share it with me. I wonder why my mom never told me about the separation. Maybe because I would've been tempted to reach out to her. Maybe because knowing this makes me wonder if being traded to Minnesota is some kind of omen. The only problem is I'm pretty sure I'm on the short list of people DJ's not too fond of, so I don't know if it's good or bad.

I can work on fixing that, though. Starting with lunch. "Why don't I bring you back a panini?"

"I have a lunch. It's fine."

"So save it for tomorrow. How can you say no to Cosmo's?"

She sighs but relents. "No raw onions, please."

"So we can make out later?" I raise a hand in immediate apology. "Sorry. That was inappropriate. I didn't mean— It just came out. I wasn't thinking."

She raises a brow and huffs a little laugh. "On second thought, lots of raw onions." She turns and walks away, but I can see her reflection in the glass door as she pushes through it, and she's smiling.

I don't want to get ahead of myself, or let the superstitions rule me, but all of this—the good and the bad—seems like fate is throwing us back together again.

chapter four

PROGRESS

Ethan

"I'm sorry I can't stay longer." Tyler sits beside me on the porch swing with a beer in his hand. He has to go back to Buttfuck Nowhere, Alaska, at balls o'clock tomorrow morning. He should probably be sleeping, but instead we're sitting outside, drinking beers and shooting the shit, since we haven't had much time for that over the past week. Or over the past few years, really, since both of us travel a lot for our jobs. I've missed him.

"Don't be. I'm here and I'm not going anywhere. Besides, Dad hates all the coddling, and it's just a matter of waiting. There's nothing we can do to speed up his recovery."

Dylan returned to Seattle yesterday, after we got Dad settled at home. He stayed long enough to help us convert the main-floor office—which had been a storage space for all of my dad's old files—and move the living room furniture around so it's accessible for a crotchety man stuck in a wheelchair and resistant to using a walker.

At a week post-stroke, some of my dad's speech has returned, but it's slow and slurred, like he's drunk, and his mouth
is frozen as if he's been to the dentist.

"I'm looking for a place in Forest Lake, maybe one with a
pool house that can be converted or something."

Tyler raises an eyebrow. "You want to stay here? Why not
live in Saint Paul and be closer to your team?"

I shrug. Under other circumstances, Saint Paul would make
sense, especially considering the sometimes tense relationship
I have with my dad. He calls me the accident child, and my
mom calls me the miracle baby, which says a lot about perception. "Makes sense to stay near Mom and Dad, especially with
how much support they need."

"Right." He's quiet for a moment. "It wouldn't have anything to do with the fact that DJ lives in Forest Lake, would it?"

I glance at him out of the corner of my eye. "She's getting
a divorce."

"Yeah, Mom mentioned that. Said it was just the paperwork
or whatnot left and then it was done. You were pretty much
together all through high school from what I remember. You
thinking about reconnecting?"

"I dunno."

"Well, you should consider it. She's hotter now than she
was when she was in high school, that's for sure."

I punch him in the shoulder. "What the fuck were you
doing checking her out when she was in high school, you
dirty perv?"

"OW! Fuck, Eth, calm your shit. She practically lived in our house when you were kids. Besides, she's in her twenties now. It's totally reasonable for me to check her out."

"She's not for you."

He snorts. "I'm just making an observation. You still have one hell of a boner over her, don't you?"

"What're you, twelve?"

"Come on—look at you and look at me. I'm a thirty-four-year-old environmental engineer. My best assets are my glasses and my beard. You're an NHL player in your prime. I'd kill to spend a day in your shoes, banging my way through your groupies."

It's my turn to give him a raised brow. "I don't have groupies, and my career is halfway in the shitter. Being me isn't all that awesome at the moment."

"Jesus. Since when did you become such a pessimistic shit? You're getting more and more like Dad."

I punch him in the shoulder again.

"Dude, seriously. What the hell? I'm a delicate flower. I bruise easily."

"Don't compare me to Dad."

"You're living the dream. I know you like to be the best at everything all the time, but you've had the better part of a decade in the NHL. It doesn't matter that you're not the number one player or the captain of a team; it's still a big fucking deal and something to be proud of."

"Are you done with the pep talk?"

Tyler rolls his eyes but changes the subject. "How much longer are you going to stay with Dad and Mom?"

"Until I find my own place, I guess. I can't handle that basement for too long, but I don't want to leave Mom to deal with him on her own yet."

"Maybe DJ's got a spare slice of mattress you could crash on." He wags his brows.

"You're fucking creepy, you know that?"

"I'm just saying. I see the way she looks at you when you're not paying attention. She wants to ride your hockey stick."

I snort. "That was literally the worst pun ever. And she doesn't want to ride any part of me. She barely even talks to me." Our conversations mostly revolve around my dad, his progress and what he needs. So far all of my attempts at a real, meaningful conversation have been shut down.

"I noticed that. I thought it was awkward sexual tension. What exactly is the story there, anyway?"

"Dad pushed me to break up with her when I was drafted."

"But you didn't and you fucked it up with one of those hockey bunnies?"

"No." I shoot him a glare. "I took his advice and broke it off."

"Wow. Since when do you listen to Dad?"

"It was pretty much the first and last time."

"Ah. I'm guessing that breakup didn't go well."

I take a swig of my beer, thinking about how adamant my

dad had been. "Not really. Remember the weekend I came home right after I was drafted?"

"Yeah. I bought you all kinds of booze and told you I'd kill you if you ratted me out." He smiles at the memory.

"I kept my mouth shut. Anyway, Dad pulled me aside and asked me how I was planning to deal with DJ. I was riding the high, right? But then he laid into me, told me if I was going to throw away a scholarship and a career in medicine, that I better be focused one hundred percent on hockey and I couldn't do that with a girlfriend halfway across the country."

"Sounds like something Dad would say. Always pragmatic about things, right?"

"Yeah." I look up at the sky. It's cloudy tonight, keeping the stars hidden. "I told him she was going to move to LA with me when she finished high school."

"I bet he didn't like that."

"Not at all. I thought I had it all planned out, but then he started talking about what would happen if I got traded to a different team. What would DJ do? Transfer schools? She'd have no one but me and I'd be on the road half the time. He kept hammering it in that I couldn't string her along and mess with her life like that. She needed stability and I wasn't going to be able to give her that. It sure wasn't what I wanted to hear."

"Did you end up breaking it off that weekend?"

I shake my head. "Not right away. I kept thinking maybe

I could make it work, but the more I thought about it, the more I realized Dad was right, even though I didn't want him to be. I couldn't take her away from everyone and then leave her alone half the time. It wouldn't be fair."

"That's a heavy realization to come to at that age."

"I was so fucking mad at Dad for a while. I think I probably still am, to be honest. The night I'd finally broken it off with her I'd spent a good hour on the phone with him, listening to his rationale as to why it needed to be done before I left for LA. So I called her and finally ended things."

"Over the phone?"

"Like an asshole."

"Christ."

"That was the last time I talked to DJ until Dad had the stroke. Well, I tried to call her a couple of times after we broke up, but it didn't go well, so I left it alone."

"Well, that sure as hell explains the tension between you."

"Yeah. Pretty sure any vibes you're picking up off of her are more along the lines of her wanting to beat me with a hockey stick, not riding mine."

Tyler rubs at the space where his beard meets his neck. "I don't know. I mean, you can be mad at someone and still want to screw them, right?"

"I guess."

"There's no guessing. She might want to beat you with a hockey stick, but I'm pretty sure she'll ride yours when she's done, too. Maybe you need to let her angry fuck you. Get all that negativity out of her system." His grin is barely visible through his beard.

"It's a real surprise you don't have a girlfriend," I deadpan.

"Whatever. I'm just telling it like it is, and the ladies love this." He strokes his beard affectionately.

"It's a great place to store snacks." I drain the rest of my beer. "You want another one?"

"Nah. I should go; my flight is stupid early tomorrow."

"You sure you don't want to stay here and just leave for the airport in the morning?"

"In your old room? Not unless that mattress you used to sleep on has been burned."

"Mom redecorated the room. It's all girly now."

"So it's pretty like you?"

"Fuck you." I flip him the bird.

"I'm glad you're home, not just because of this stuff with Dad, either. It'll be nice to have you around, now that you're not an annoying little shit." He pushes up off the swing and becomes serious for a moment. "You'll keep me updated on Dad, though? If he doesn't get better, I'll find someone else to finish the project in Alaska."

"Between me, Mom, DJ, and all the medical staff he has access to, I'm pretty sure he's going to be fine."

"I hope so, for Mom's sake, anyway. She's the one who has to put up with his miserable ass the most."

ᶜ⁓

The next morning a loud noise wakes me. It's a little after six. I stayed up long after my brother left, drank half a dozen more beers on the porch by myself, and leafed through old photo albums. It was pretty pathetic. At least there were no witnesses. Although I'm not sure if I got rid of the beery evidence.

Another thump prompts me to get my ass out of bed. Dressed in only boxers, I rush upstairs, hoping that the noise hasn't woken my mother, who's been sleeping like shit. Not that I've been sleeping all that well. Between managing my dad and preseason training ice time, I'm pushing my limits. Beyond that, the mattress in the basement is ancient and there's a dip in the middle. I'm pretty sure DJ and I were the cause of that.

I flick on a lamp in the living room, blinking as my eyes adjust. The room is empty, which isn't a surprise considering the early hour. A few more thumps and grunts come from where my dad sleeps these days.

The office is big enough to fit a double bed, but not much else. I find him in his wheelchair, angled awkwardly. He has something in his hands, and he's concentrating on whatever it is, so he doesn't hear me when I approach. The curtains are drawn tight, so only light from the living room illuminates the small space. I flip the switch, blinding us both.

He grunts his surprise and swears. Something warm and wet hits my shins.

I look down at my legs and then back up at him. In one

hand he's holding an oversize mug, the handle big enough for him to grasp fully.

"What the fuck, Dad? Are you pissing in that cup? Did you just piss on me?" I don't know why I'm asking—it's clear that's exactly what he's doing and what he's just done.

His eyes are wide, at first with absolute horror, and maybe a little embarrassment at being caught relieving himself into a mug. Although, I have to appreciate the lengths he'll go to in order to maintain some level of independence. We have walkie-talkies for those middle-of-the-night occasions when he needs to make a trip to the bathroom, or requires a water refill, or whatever really, but it appears he wanted to do it on his own. Based on his indignant glare and the awkward positioning of his wheelchair, I assume he got stuck, couldn't reach the walkie, and decided this was the most dignified option.

His gaze darts down to where he's holding himself. "I'm a grower," he slurs.

My shock and mild disgust over the fact that I've been peed on—by my father—disappear in the wake of this unnecessary, cheeky-as-fuck revelation. I bark out a laugh. "Like father like son—is that what you're saying?"

A lopsided grin breaks across his face in return; his shoulders start to shake, a low chuckle bubbling up. The mug he's holding shakes perilously. I grab for it before its contents can slosh over the edge and make even more of a mess.

"I'm going to rinse this out and put your coffee in it later."

"Fuck you," he slurs, still smiling.

"You pissed on me. Fuck you back."

His laughter deepens. It's the first time I've heard that sound since I came back to Minnesota.

"You're an asshole, you know that?" We're both still laughing, though. "Next time walkie me."

"I did. Four times." He gives me what used to be his stern eye, but the stroke has softened his features, so it's lost some of its impact.

"Ah, shit. Sorry, Dad. Tyler and I were up late last night talking."

He waves me off, then tips his chin toward the bed. "Help me."

He tries his best to hold his own weight as I shift him back into bed, but it's clear it's taken most of his energy to manage getting his ass into the wheelchair and peeing into the cup. Once he's settled I dump the contents of the mug in the toilet next door. I consider tossing the mug, but I'm not that nice. Instead I throw a capful of bleach in there, fill it with hot water and soap, and leave it to soak. Then I fill a bucket of warm, soapy water so I can wash the floor, grateful it's hardwood and not carpeted.

"Sorry," my dad says as I drop to my knees and wipe away the evidence.

I glance up. He's lying in bed, eyes slits, looking at me. "For the mess I have to clean up or peeing on me?"

It takes a while before he responds and the words are hard to get out. "Don't tell your mother."

"That you pissed on me?"

He reaches for the closest object, which happens to be the walkie-talkie. I grab it before he can get it. "So you're gonna throw shit at me now, too?"

"What if I . . ." He gets stuck on the words for a while. "I can't . . ."

I know where he's going with this. I know what he's afraid of. I take his hand and squeeze, forcing him to squeeze back reflexively. "Remember when Mom got pregnant seven years after you had a vasectomy?"

His brow furrows.

"Even your balls refuse to cooperate with science. You think the rest of your body is going to bow to a stroke?"

He squeezes back, so I keep squeezing, forcing him to put as much effort into it as he can. "My hands are covered in your urine," I say quietly.

He shoves on my chest, hard enough that I stumble back in surprise. "You gettin' your fight on?" I tease.

He smiles again, then drops back against the pillow. It's hard to see him so uncertain of himself, but in some ways it's as enlightening as it is sobering. My dad has always been an I-know-more-than-you kind of man. But now, in this situation, he's just as scared as the rest of us.

"You want me to shut the light off? You gonna try to sleep some more?"

He nods and I turn to leave the room.

"Eth."

I glance over my shoulder.

"Thank you."

"I won't tell Mom." His gratitude is the last thing I see before I turn the light off.

I take the opportunity for what it is and head down to the lake for an early morning swim. It's already muggy with the promise of heat later today. A fine mist lingers on the glasslike surface. The sun hovers above the trees, burning off the last of the nighttime cool, the lemon glow reflected on the smooth surface below.

Still dressed in my boxers, I take the dock at a jog and dive in. The cold water is a welcome shock. I push out, kicking hard, staying under as long as I can. Breaking the surface with a sharp inhale, I flip onto my back and float for a while, watching the sun rise higher in the cloudless blue sky. I wish this stroke hadn't happened to my dad. Not because it's an inconvenience, even though there have been moments when I've thought this and felt guilty for it. But because of the strain it's going to put on my mom, and how difficult it is for my dad to be unable to do things for himself and her.

chapter five

NEEDS AND WANTS

Lilah

It's just after seven in the morning when I pull into the Kases' driveway. Normally I wouldn't stop by this early, but last night Jeannie mentioned needing a few things when I called to check on Martin, so I picked them up for her and figured I could drop them off before work.

Besides, in my head, I rationalized that since both Tyler and Dylan have gone back to their respective homes, and Ethan must be busy with preseason practice, my assistance would be helpful. It has nothing to do with seeing Ethan. That's what I keep telling myself, except I was up before six this morning and the effort I've put into my appearance tells a different story.

While it's nice that Ethan is here for his family, it's somehow displaced my role. I'm used to being the one Jeannie comes to when she needs help, and his presence makes me feel less necessary.

My sister Carmen thinks I need to get over it and talk to him. I keep assuring her I am talking to him—I just find being in his presence safer with the buffer of his parents. It's very twelve of me.

I grab the grocery bin from the passenger seat and head for the back porch. Splashing draws my attention toward the lake. Hands appear at the edge of the dock, a head following after, then thick, broad shoulders. In a smooth, seamless surge, Ethan pulls himself out of the water. It's been a very long time since I've seen Ethan Kase without a shirt. But I can say with absolute certainty that he has grown into his height. The lanky build of his youth has given way to a body lined with heavy muscles and incredible definition that can only be achieved with countless hours of disciplined workouts.

For a moment I envy Ethan. Not because he's a specimen of near physical perfection, from the powerful thighs to the trim waist, six-pack abs, defined chest, and a gorgeous face— that despite his career and the potential for scars and damage, he's even more handsome. I'm not envious of his beauty— although I can certainly appreciate it. I'm envious of his determination to fight so hard for his dream, for the one thing he loved more than anything. More than me. The last thought pricks my heart.

Until he showed up a week ago, I thought I'd gotten over the loss of him, but clearly that's not the case. And it's a big part of the reason I'm avoiding spending any real time with him. I fear my heart remembers loving him more than it remembers how he broke it.

He lifts a hand in a wave and I realize I've been spotted, and also that I've been staring. I nod in acknowledgment since my arms are full, and move toward the screen door—quickly so I can get inside the house before Ethan corners me. The last thing I need is a close-up of all that gorgeous. He still has the ability to make me lose my head and to send my hormones into a tailspin. Or maybe that time of month is coming and that's the reason for all the tingles in my sensitive places.

"Hey, DJ, wait up—let me help with that!" He jogs quickly toward me, his wet body glistening in the morning sun. It really is unfair that he looks this good, and here I am dressed in scrubs with a llama pattern all over them. It's my day of rounds in the pediatric unit, and the kids like the fun prints.

I shift the shopping bin of groceries to my hip and reach for the door handle, but it's heavy, so I have to readjust when the bin slips. By the time it's safely tucked against my side, Ethan is in front of me, not even out of breath despite having run all the way from the dock. He grabs the handles of the bin, and my immediate reaction is to hold on tighter.

He tilts his head, a small smile tugging at the corner of his mouth, possibly at my resistance. Eventually I relinquish the bin; otherwise, I'm going to make an awkward situation even more uncomfortable.

Ethan is mostly naked. I'm trying not to gawk, but dear lord he looks amazing, so I'm not above ogling. Seeing him like this, fresh from the lake, hair dripping, water beading across his chest, reminds me of a time when life was so much simpler. Back when the most complex decision was whether we studied first and made out after, or vice versa. More often than not, making out took first priority. Otherwise Ethan found it hard to keep his hands to himself and the studying suffered.

Except he's a man now, with an incredible career and a body to match, and I'm an almost-divorcée who abandoned my dream of becoming a doctor. Instead, I settled for the man who I thought could fill the hole the one in front of me created.

"Everything okay?" Ethan ducks his chin a little, bringing his face closer to mine.

"Huh?" I shake my head, realizing I've been staring at his chest. Again. "Oh yeah, fine. Jeannie asked me to pick a few things up for her." As if that wasn't obvious based on the bin he's holding.

"She could've asked me so you didn't have to go out of your way."

I shrug and keep my eyes on the contents of the bin. "I was already at the store, so it wasn't a big deal; besides, I wanted to check in anyway. Jeannie mentioned you have to head back to Chicago."

"Yeah, for a couple of days. I have to get my house on the market and tie up a few loose ends." I hold the door for Ethan, glancing at his ass as he steps onto the welcome mat. He's wearing boxers, not swim shorts, which is odd, but I'm not opposed to their see-through quality or the way they cling nicely to his sculpted glutes.

I follow him inside and startle at Jeannie's suddenly stern reprimand. "Ethan! Are you wet? Do not trek through the house like that!"

Ethan takes an automatic step back. I mirror his movement, but the door's already closed, so I have nowhere to go. I raise my hands in an attempt to prevent being pinned against the door. My palms connect with wet, cool skin. The sensation is reminiscent of licking a nine-volt battery on a whole-body frequency. Heat hits me, pushing through my skin, electrifying me. Ethan goes still and stiff.

"Is that Delilah behind you? You're crushing her! Let her past!" Jeannie barks.

Ethan steps to the side but stays on the mat so as not to drip all over the floor and risk being yelled at again. I slip around him, fingertips dragging across his skin as it pebbles, and a small shiver causes the muscles under my fingers to quiver.

"Sorry," I mumble and attempt to take the bin, fingers wrapped around the edge next to his.

"I got it," he says quickly. "It's heavy."

"I can handle it."

"No really, it's fine." His eyes are wide. They dart down and back up a couple of times, so I follow them, not understanding why he won't let me take the bin. And then he lowers it enough so that I can see exactly what the issue is. And what an issue it is. Ethan has a hard-on tenting his wet, nearly transparent boxers, and all that damp fabric is clinging to the contours, giving me a very clear view of said issue.

I pry my eyes away—it's a lot more challenging than I want it to be—and motion to what he's hiding behind the bin. "What the hell is that about?" I hiss lowly.

His cheeks flush a little, but he's still smirking, probably because my face is on fire. "You were just touching me, and your boobs were against my back," he whispers.

He's not looking me in the eye—instead his gaze is trained on the part of my body he's just referenced. The cotton is wet from his back, drawing more attention there. I'm halfway to cupping them for protective measure, considering how my nipples are responding to his stare, when he raises his voice and asks, "Would you be able to grab me a towel, please?"

"Right, yes! Of course!" I'd do just about anything to get some space. I take the stairs two at a time and disappear down the hallway. The image of Ethan's erection pushing against the wet fabric seems to have seared itself into the backs of my lids. I don't remember him being that ample, but then it's been almost a decade since I've seen Ethan's hard-on, bare or covered with fabric. I shake my head as if it will erase the image like an Etch A Sketch. It doesn't help at all. All of my sensitive places are begging for some kind of friction.

I take a few more deep breaths, grab a towel from the linen closet in the bathroom—it's pink with a rose print—and head back downstairs, taking my time on the descent.

Ethan's standing where I left him, still holding the grocery bin. I drop the towel on top and grab the handles along the side with what I hope is a placid, collected smile.

Ethan tips his chin, that infuriating smile I know so well making the dimple under his right eye pop as he relinquishes his shield and takes the towel. "Thanks."

"You're welcome." I step back as he shakes it out at crotch level, then laugh when I realize it's a hand towel.

He lifts a brow. "Not sure this is going to do the job."

"You can make it work." I turn away and cross through to the kitchen, where Jeannie is slicing a loaf of fresh bread, very glad my own physical response to Ethan can remain hidden. Her eyes are rimmed with dark shadows, betraying too little sleep and too much stress, but her smile is real.

"Thank you for picking those things up. You always know just what I need. I'm so scattered these days." I accept her embrace, absorbing the affection she gives so willingly. "Do not even think about traipsing through the house in that dripping suit!" Jeannie calls over my shoulder.

"I wouldn't dream of it, Mom," Ethan replies.

Jeannie releases me on a gasp. "Ethan Martin Kase!"

"I'll hang it up once I'm changed!"

He appears in my peripheral vision; that tiny floral printed hand towel covers just the part that matters. He's left the wet boxers on the mat by the door, so I catch a glimpse of his bare ass as he disappears down the stairs to the basement.

"That boy," Jeannie says, but there's a smile fighting for play on her lips.

"He probably would've done well in a nudist colony if the whole career in hockey hadn't worked out."

"I'm sorry you had to see that."

"Nothing I haven't seen before." Although it wasn't quite so defined back then.

Jeannie barks a laugh, and I cringe at how inappropriate that was.

"Anyway—" I turn my attention to the bin of groceries and start unpacking. "I picked up those chocolate and strawberry meal replacements so Martin can get the calories in like we talked about."

"I appreciate that and I'm sure he will, too," she murmurs.

"Everything okay?" I ask as she passes me the chopping board and berries so I can hull them and make a smoothie for Martin. He's picky about smoothies and I seem to be the only one who can do them "the right way."

"I don't think he slept that well. He's having an off morning."

That means he's in a mood. I've experienced Martin's crankiness plenty of times over the years. This isn't the same, though. Before the stroke he could find ways to manage the anger or frustration. He could take off in his boat and go fishing for hours, or tinker on his old Chevy in the garage, or work on one of his little projects. But now all he can do is stew inside his own mind, unable to verbalize his frustrations without succumbing to further irritation. It's an unending cycle that will take work to break free of.

As we finish loading the blender, Ethan appears at the top of the staircase, hair still wild, shirt still missing, but wearing a pair of dry shorts, carrying a T-shirt and what I assume is his toiletry bag.

I glance at his fly. I wonder if he took care of his situation while he was in the basement.

"Ethan, put a shirt on!" Jeannie scolds.

"I have to shower." He drops his T-shirt on the back of the couch, which has been moved to make it easier for Martin to get around. I think he's parading around shirtless on purpose, because he keeps running his hand over his pecs like he's feeling himself up, or trying to draw attention to his bare chest. Which he doesn't need to do, because it draws enough attention without his assistance.

Once the smoothie is made and it's passed Martin's taste test, I glance at the clock. "I should probably head to work." It's only a little past seven thirty and my shift doesn't start until nine, but I don't think hanging around with a shirtless Ethan is particularly smart.

"Do you have time for a coffee?" Ethan leans on the counter, the muscles in his arms flexing deliciously.

"I just finished brewing a fresh pot. Why don't you grab a cup? I was about to make some scrambled eggs and toast. Have you had breakfast?" Jeannie says.

They're both looking at me with hopeful expectation. I suppose I can't avoid Ethan forever. At the very least, we can clear the air and put the demons of the past to rest.

"I can stay for coffee."

Ethan's smile melts my icy heart the tiniest bit.

He pours us both a coffee and hands me a steaming cup. "Wanna sit on the porch?"

"Okay. Sure." We used to sit on that swing, long after his parents had gone to bed some nights, and watch the stars.

I nab his shirt from the back of the couch and follow him outside. I toss it at him as he holds the door open for me. "Put this on."

He grins but doesn't comment. I take a seat on the porch swing and watch every muscle in his torso flex as he draws the shirt over his head and covers his cut chest and rock-solid abs. He collects the empty beer bottles scattered on the porch floor and sets them on the railing before taking the spot beside me.

I motion to the row of empties. "Who'd you get sauced with last night?"

"Me and Ty had a couple of beers."

I raise a brow. "That looks like more than a couple."

"I kept going after he left."

I glance at him. Beyond the morning scruff and his disheveled appearance, he looks tired. "Everything okay?"

"Just a lot on my mind these days."

I nod as if I understand, and I guess in some ways I do, because it's been the same for me.

"Martin's already making great progress. He's too stubborn to let this get him."

He nods. "Yeah. It's not just that, though." He reaches over and runs his finger along the edge of one of the photo albums sitting on the table beside him. I recognize them as ones from high school. I've looked at them countless times over the years.

"You're worried about the new season?" I know that's not what he's referring to, although I'm sure it's one of the things on his mind.

"Maybe a little."

"Is it hard, getting used to a new team?" I don't know anything about this part of his life anymore.

He nods. "Yeah. I want to mesh with them, perform well, show the coach he made a good call on the trade, but with my Dad, it's a lot of pressure, most of it brought on by me. Being home is challenging for a lot of reasons. But it'll be what it'll be, I guess." He shifts so he's facing me. "That's not really what I meant, though."

My chest feels suddenly tight, and panic sets in. I fight the urge to get up and run. The inches separating us seem to disappear and the tightness in my chest moves up to my throat. "Oh?"

"I don't think it's a coincidence that I've been sent home."

"Ethan—" Always with the superstitions. They ruled him when we were teens, sometimes to the point of obsession. Back then I'd either laugh it off or find it endearing, apart from the putrid lucky socks, anyway.

"Just hear me out for a second. I know I made a lot of mistakes when it came to you, and I can't take back the hurt I've caused, or change the past, and I definitely don't expect things to be anything like they were, but maybe we can start by being friends again."

A light breeze has picked up, causing the surface of the lake to ripple gently. "Friends?" I don't like the sharp sting of the word, a fresh blade across my already aching heart.

"It's a place to start, isn't it? If you want to." He runs his fingers over a knot in the wood a few inches from my leg. "I mean, I get it if maybe you don't, but it's been a long time. We have all this history. You were such a huge part of my life, and you're still very much part of this family. I didn't realize how much I was missing this until I came back, you know? I don't want to force my way into your life, but maybe when you're ready, I can apologize and we can talk about what happened between us. You could maybe give me a chance to try to earn your forgiveness. Then we could move forward from there."

"I don't—"

His smile is sad, pleading. "Please don't say no, Lilah. Just think about it. I know I hurt you, but it was complicated. I was going to come back for you. I wanted to come back for you."

He says it so quietly I'm not sure if I heard him correctly. "What? Come back for me when?"

Ethan rubs the back of his neck, eyes fixed on the lake in the distance. "After my first season in LA, Minnesota wanted me. I was going to take the deal. I knew you were in Minneapolis for college. I thought maybe I could find a way to fix things, but then I found out you were engaged, so I stayed in LA instead."

I feel like I've been backhanded in the face.

"I don't know what to say." And I really don't. What would my life be like now if he had come back? If I had never dated Avery right after high school and accepted his proposal in my first year of college? Would I have broken off my engagement for Ethan? Would it have mattered? We'll never know, because we never traveled that path. And it doesn't change anything now.

"Maybe I shouldn't have said anything." He lifts a hand, fingertips sweeping under my eye.

I startle at the contact and the realization that a tear has slipped free. I look away. "You broke my heart."

"I know, and there's nothing I've ever regretted more. I just want a chance to have you back in my life in whatever way you'll allow me."

I remain silent for long seconds, absorbing this new truth, unsure how I feel about it. Just when I thought I was getting used to having him around again, he turns everything upside down.

"I promised myself I wasn't going to push myself on you, and here I am doing it anyway," he says.

"We can try out the friends thing."

"Yeah?" His tentative smile is a ray of sunshine after a thunderstorm.

I need to lighten this mood, alleviate the tension between us and give myself time to process. "On one condition."

"Sure. Okay. You name it."

"You can't parade around shirtless in front of me."

His smile becomes more of a smirk. "Too overwhelming?"

I laugh. "Stow the ego, Kase."

His lips flatten, but his eyes still glint with humor. "Okay. A shirt must be worn at all times. Anything else?"

"Not that I can think of, but I'll update conditions as they come to me."

"'Kay." He stretches his arm across the back of the swing, fingers skimming my shoulder.

I feel a slight tug on my hair and wonder how good I'm going to be at this "friends" deal. I fear I have too many memories wrapped up in this man, and long-dormant feelings are waking up with his return to my world, especially on the heels of this unexpected revelation.

"Can I give you my number?" he asks quietly.

"What?"

"So we can chat and stuff while I'm in Chicago?" He chews on the inside of his lip.

It's a nervous habit that he clearly hasn't lost. I instinctively pinch his bottom lip between two fingers and tug it free from his teeth, something I used to do all the time.

His eyes flare, and I snatch my hand away. "I don't know why I did that. Sorry."

His reflexes are far superior to mine, and he latches on to my wrist. "It's okay. You're okay."

I give my head a little shake, trying not to get too caught up in the feel of his skin on mine. This morning has been intense. "Has your number changed?"

"Huh?" His attention is focused on where his fingers wrap around my wrist, thumb smoothing along the pulse point.

"Do you still have the same phone number?" At his blank stare, I prompt. "From high school?"

"Oh yeah. It's the same. Is yours?"

I nod.

He roots around in his shorts pocket and retrieves his phone. Keying in his password, he scrolls and then types, looking up as my own phone chimes in my pocket.

I don't know how to feel about the fact that we've been a text message away from each other all these years. It never dawned on me how easy it could've been.

"Just because I left doesn't mean I ever forgot you, Lilah."

My head says I can try to be friends with this man, but my heart isn't so sure it's that simple.

chapter six

FAVORS

Lilah

Hey, what's up? Are you back in town? Is everything okay with Martin?" It's Monday evening and I'm in the locker room at work. Ethan took full advantage of our new "friends" status by texting me constantly over the weekend while he was in Chicago. He also sent flowers to his parents' house, not just for Jeannie, but for me as well, which was unexpected but sweet.

Since I'm alone, I put the call on speaker so I can change out of my scrubs and into the pair of jeans and the T-shirt hanging in my locker.

"I walked in the door half an hour ago. Dad's fine. Annoyed that he has to use a walker and that he's not ready to run a marathon this week, but fine otherwise. And Mom is asking if you're coming by in the morning to make him a smoothie since apparently hers still aren't good enough."

I laugh. "There's no magic in mine. I just press a button."

"Your fingers were always magic."

I cough at that.

"Sorry, that was . . . Did I catch you at a bad time? Do you have a minute?"

"It's not a bad time, and sure, I have a minute."

"Okay. Good."

I wait for more, but there's silence as I shimmy into my jeans. "Ethan?"

"Yeah."

"Is there something you need?"

"What're you doing right now?"

"Um . . . leaving work. Why?" I pull the zipper up.

"Are you changing?"

"Huh?"

"Are you wearing jeans?"

"What? How—"

"I knew I heard a zipper." And here I thought he was trying to censor himself.

I quickly pull my shirt over my head, as if he can see me in my bra. I stuff the scrubs in my bag and slam my locker shut, take the phone off speaker and bring it back to my ear. "Did you call to talk about zippers?"

"No, but now I'm wishing I'd come to see you in person."

"Um, yeah. There's no way I'd be getting changed in front of you. Friends don't get naked in front of each other."

"Untrue. You used to run around naked in my backyard all the time."

"I was six and I was wearing bathing suit bottoms."

"I think you were seven, actually. Is partial nudity an acceptable compromise? I'm more than happy for you to run around topless in front of me if you want."

"I'm going to hang up on you."

"No! Wait. Sorry. I wanted to talk to you about coffee. About getting coffee. With me. Or whatever kind of beverage you'd like to consume with me. What's your work schedule like? Do you have a free night this week?"

I don't expect the question, so I flounder. "I'll need to check my schedule." That's a lie. I typically work the same hours every week, and in a few weeks, I'll have class on Mondays and Wednesdays in addition to yoga, which I already have on Tuesdays. But the flirty conversation and the coffee feel like more than I'm ready for, especially given how much I seem to like the idea.

"I can wait."

"Can I get back to you about it?"

"It's just coffee with a friend, Lilah."

"I know."

"Am I pushing you too much?"

"Yes. No. I don't know. You just caught me off guard."

"What're you doing tonight?"

"Carmen and I are going for dinner."

"And after that?"

"I don't know. Probably reading a book and going to bed."
The butterflies in my stomach are a problem.

"I could come over and you could read to me. Remember when you used to read chemistry textbooks to me in your phone-sex operator voice? I used to love that—not sure it helped me retain much information, though."

"Ethan." It's a warning.

He sighs. "Okay. When you have a chance, let me know what your schedule is. I missed you while I was in Chicago this weekend."

I close my eyes and bite back a smile. "You're too much. I'll talk to you later."

We seem to be bypassing *friends* and heading down a road I'm not sure I'm prepared to travel yet, not with so many loose ends and unsaid things hanging between us. I'm terrified that if I let him back into my life, I'm going to fall for him again and he's going to break my heart a second time.

I pack up the rest of my things, stop at home to take my dog, Merk, for a quick run, and then walk over to meet my sister at our favorite boardwalk restaurant. Mondays we typically have a standing date unless Carmen has to show a house—which happens on occasion since she's a real estate agent. Although we'll have to rearrange it once my course starts.

Of my five older siblings, Carmen is the one I'm closest to, in part because she's only a few years older than I am, and also because our brothers are scattered across the country. One by one they found someone to love and disappeared. The age gap was significant, so I was never close to any of them. They were more like pseudo–absentee fathers, too busy with college and girlfriends to really be bothered with me.

Ever since I was young, I think it was when my father left, I'd been the one to make sure everything was taken care of, that Mom never had to worry about anything. I was always tidying up, making sure there was milk in the fridge and cereal in the cupboard since my brothers were already all but out of the house by then. My memories of them are vague, limited to requests for a ride to the store if we ran out of something important. They didn't have a lot of time for me, and Ethan's family became my refuge.

So when I moved into Avery's condo and she knew I wouldn't see her as often, my mother decided to go to one of my brothers', where she could be a grandmother to their children. In some ways it felt like I lost another parent, but I understood why she moved. Besides, I had Avery, and he needed me in much the same way.

"Can you stop looking at your phone for five minutes? You're worse than a teenager. Who is that, anyway? Wait—" Carmen holds up a finger. "Let me guess. It's Ethan."

"He just got home. He's updating me on Martin."

She scoffs. "Uh, yeah, that's, like, the biggest load of bullshit ever in the history of bullshit. You were at the Kases' this morning, and you talk to Jeannie pretty much every day and have since you were six."

"He's been gone a few days. He might see progress we don't."

"Still not buying it. So what's going on there, anyway? Is

this a trip down memory lane for you two? Are you going to compare his previous skill set in bed to his skill set now? Do you think he can still go forever? I mean, he's a professional athlete. That has to translate into a superior bedroom experience."

"Carm!" I glance around the patio, but the music is loud and the tables closest to us are more concerned with their menus than my sister's inappropriate, but potentially accurate, hypothesis.

"What? You two used to screw like bunnies."

"How the hell would you know that?"

"Oh, come on. We were forever getting phone calls from the school that you'd missed second period, which I intercepted—you're welcome very much. I'm sure you and Ethan used that time to study human biology. Besides, all teenagers screw like bunnies."

"We're just friends, and I'm not going to sleep with him."

Carmen raises an eyebrow. "Seriously? Just friends? So all those text messages are about his dad?"

"I've just finalized my divorce and I'm about to start a course that's going to eat up all my spare time. I don't need to add another complication to my life, especially not with Ethan."

"That's a pretty convenient excuse, and don't think I didn't notice how you sidestepped my question."

"He already broke my heart once. I'm not all that interested in letting him do it again."

She takes a sip of her margarita and motions me to go on.

I sigh. Carmen is persistent. "He wants to go for coffee, or drinks, or whatever. Just spend time together as friends."

"As friends, huh?"

"Yes."

"With benefits?"

"No."

Her eyebrows lift when my phone buzzes again. "If you say so."

I put my phone on airplane mode and shove it in my purse without checking it this time.

⁓

The following evening Carmen's number appears on my phone minutes after I arrive home from work. We don't have plans tonight, and usually she sticks to texting instead of phone calls, so it must be important.

"Hey, Sis, everything okay?"

"Hey, hi. How's it going?" The honk of a horn tells me she's in traffic.

"Did you call me while you're driving?"

"It's hands-free. Don't worry—I'm obeying the rules of the road." I can hear the smile in her voice. "Are you still at work?"

"I just got home. What's up?"

"You have yoga tonight, right?"

"Usually, but the instructor is on vacation."

"Thanks for using your signal, dickhole!" she yells. "Sorry. Asswipe in a BMW just cut across three lanes of traffic and nearly caused a goddamn fucking pileup."

"Maybe you should pull over to have this conversation." Carmen's road rage is unparalleled.

"It's fine. He took the exit. Anyway, I need a favor."

"Do you need me to check on Barkley?" He's her Boxer dog. Sometimes her hours get messed up, so I stop by her place to feed him or take him for a walk. When I'm there, I'll do a little tidying or make sure she has something other than junk food in her cabinets and enough dog food for Barkley to make it through the week. She keeps telling me I don't need to do this stuff, but I can't help it.

"Please? I'll owe you big-time. Last time I was this late, he pooped on the throw rug in my bedroom."

"Yuck. I'll pick him up on the way to the dog park. Merk will love the company and we can avoid poop carpet bombs." Avery was allergic to dogs. Once I moved into my own place, I finally decided to get one, partly to feel protected and also to feel less alone. Merk isn't much of a guard dog, but he's a great companion.

"You're a lifesaver. Pineapple flavored."

"I prefer the green–apple ones."

"You always did." She laughs. "I have another favor, though, apart from walking Barkley."

"Do *not* ask me to pick up your dry cleaning." She's done

it before. And I picked it up, of course, but there was some guilting afterward. I'm happy to help, but picking up her dry-cleaned lingerie is where I draw the line.

"That was only one time and I didn't have time to pick it up before my date! I'm stuck in the city and there's wicked traffic. Even if I take all the back roads, my GPS is still putting me in Forest Lake after seven thirty, and I have a showing at seven."

"I'm not following." I have no idea what a showing has to do with me.

"It's for Ethan. It's the Hoffmans' house on Crescent Street. You know the one I'm talking about?"

"Carmen," I warn.

"Oh, come on, Lilah."

"Isn't it illegal or something for me to show a house when I'm not even a licensed agent?"

"I've cleared it with the owners. I've even emailed you the lock code and everything. Can you help me out on this? I could really use the commission, and it's a private showing. I don't want to miss out, and I don't know when, or if, I'll be able to reschedule." She's rambling now. It's how she guilts me into things. "Please? You know I wouldn't ask if it wasn't important. I know your history with Ethan hasn't always been easy, but he seems to want to mend his broken fences or whatever the saying is."

I'm annoyed at the way my stomach dips over this information. "What did he say to you?"

"Nothing, really; it's just the sense I get."

"When did you even talk to him about me?"

"When I was setting up the showing earlier today."

"I want specifics or I'm not doing this for you."

She huffs, realizing she's not getting out of this that easily. "He mentioned how grateful he is that you've been so helpful with his dad and that he's glad you're friends again."

"Friends?"

"Ha! Listen to how disappointed you sound." Her glee irritates me.

This feels like purposeful meddling, but I relent. "Fine. But only this one time. Don't ask again."

"Thank you!" Her voice is singsongy. "I'll take you out for drinks later this week."

"Sure. Whatever."

"I love you. I'll call when I'm back in town, and I'll meet you at the house around seven thirtyish." She ends the call before I can say anything else.

"Dammit."

I pull up the email with the listing. It's a big house, over four thousand square feet, retailing at three-quarters of a million dollars. I can see why Carmen would like the commission. If she gets it, she's taking me for more than a drink. I want a five-star meal for dealing with Ethan in a setting that doesn't have the buffer of his family before I'm ready. Not that I feel like I'll ever be ready.

It's already five thirty. I need to take the dogs for a quick run and get my ass in gear if I'm going to be at the house by seven. I change out of my scrubs and into running shorts and a tank. It's hot and humid as I run the short distance to my sister's house with Merk, pick up Barkley, and make the circuit around the block a couple of times. We don't have time to stop at the dog park, but I promise to take them tomorrow.

After I feed Barkley, I run Merk home and jump in the shower. My phone lights up as I'm sifting through the contents of my closet for something to wear. I check my messages—there are two from Carmen, one requesting that I not show up in my scrubs. The second is a series of emojis depicting a range of begging. I send her a middle finger back, throw on a sundress, then rush to do my makeup—which is two swipes of mascara and some lip gloss—and leave my house. I drive with the windows down so my hair will be mostly dry by the time I get there.

Ethan's truck is parked out front when I arrive. My stomach is doing that annoying flip thing already. I wish I felt less like the teenage version of myself when I'm near him. I park behind his truck, take a deep breath, glance at my face in the rearview mirror, peeved that I care what I look like, and cut the engine.

Ethan steps out of his truck as I exit my car. He's wearing dress pants and a polo that pulls tight across his broad chest and hugs his thick biceps. His wavy dark hair is styled neatly, he's freshly shaven, and he looks disgustingly delicious. Or just delicious. All my sensitive spots perk up in agreement. Stupid body, having stupid hormonal reactions. It's probably because I haven't had sex in more months than I'd like to admit. And because Ethan is even hotter than he was eight years ago. It would be great if I could stop noticing these things about him.

He tilts his head fractionally, a half smile quirking up the corner of his mouth. I know that smile well. It's his surprise face. The one he used to wear when I'd buy new clothes he liked, or when I'd suggest we skip second period and go back to one of our houses for an early lunch. We did that a lot. And now there are tingles between my legs. I knew this was a bad idea. My heart knows to keep some distance, but my hormones don't seem to be able to adhere to logic in the same way.

"Hi." His gaze drifts down, pausing briefly at the V-neck, skimming the tie at the waist and then lower, to where the hem grazes my knees, all the way to my shoes. I'm wearing wedge sandals since they work with this dress. And they might make my legs look good. Not that I care. Much. He repeats the circuit in reverse.

"You, uh"—he blows out a breath and rubs at his full bottom lip—"you look amazing in that dress."

"Oh. Uh, thanks." I don't expect the compliment. I run my hands nervously over my hips.

He jams his hands in his pockets and clears his throat. "Not that I'm not happy to see you, but uh, where's Carmen? Are you meeting her here, too?"

I sigh. "You mean she didn't tell you?"

"Tell me what?" He appears genuinely confused.

"That bitch." I'm going to kill my sister. The least she could've done was warn him that she would be late. "She's stuck in traffic and didn't want you to miss out on seeing the house, so she asked me to meet you."

"Oh." His smile widens. "Well, that's good news for me."

"I guess we should go in?"

"Sure. Lead the way." He motions toward the house and we walk up the driveway together.

I have to check my messages for the code Carmen left, and I'm suddenly nervous. I swear I can feel the heat of Ethan's body behind me. It takes me back to when we were halfway to becoming adults and the innocence of our youth was replaced with unexplored desire.

I remember very vividly the first time Ethan kissed me. The way his touch changed from soft and familiar to heat fueled and needy. How the peck on my cheek lingered and his lips brushed close to the corner of my mouth, the gentle caress of his fingertips on my skin, followed by his soft lips on mine.

We'd stayed like that for long seconds until the warm, wet press of his tongue shocked me. I'd gasped and clutched his shoulders and then he'd really kissed me. Tongue sweeping my mouth, fingers tangled in my hair, his moan vibrating through my entire body.

All of this flashes through my mind as I key in the lock code, and heat licks through me in a fiery wave. I need to get a handle on myself when I'm in Ethan's presence. Memories that I've worked to push down all these years keep breaking the surface, like the little bubbles in a glass of soda.

I push the door open and Ethan motions me forward, following me inside. The foyer is a grand, open space, with a curving staircase that leads to the second floor. An ornate chandelier hangs at least twenty feet above our heads, catching the sunlight as it streams through the windows, creating rainbows on the floor.

"So this is what an NHL salary gets you in the housing market, huh?" I cringe at my inappropriateness.

Ethan gives me a wry grin. "This is the top of my budget, and the house I have in Chicago has appreciated thirty percent in the past year thanks to the crazy market out there, but yeah, I guess this is what playing with sticks gets you."

I snort at the thinly veiled innuendo. "I can wait here while you look around."

"You don't want to come with me? See what kind of weird art the Hoffmans have hanging in their living room?"

The Hoffmans are eccentric. If anything, I'm curious about the decor. I suppose it doesn't hurt to have a look around. "I can tag along."

Ethan's smile grows a little wider, and he picks up the listing papers, flipping through them. The house has five bedrooms, a separate pool house to complement the Olympic-size pool, and access to the lake—because why not have a pool and the lake if you're going to live in a three-quarters-of-a-million-dollar home—all on one acre of property.

The kitchen is spectacular, and I'm immediately glad I didn't wait in the foyer. I grew up in an older four-bedroom house. Carmen and I shared a bedroom growing up, but with my mom working late shifts as I got older and Carmen's involvement in after-school sports I often ended up going to the Kases' after school and staying there. No one ever questioned my sleeping on an inflatable mattress on the floor in Ethan's bedroom, which was twice the size of the one I shared with my sister. When I was too old to stay in there with him, he'd sleep in the living room on the pullout sofa. I never considered the sacrifice in that until I had to spend a night on the uncomfortable, lumpy, thin mattress myself.

Our kitchen was small and felt crowded with more than two bodies in it. Dinner was always a race, especially with four older brothers and an older sister. If you weren't quick enough, you'd miss out on all the good things.

This kitchen is the opposite of that. The appliances are state-of-the-art, stainless steel without a single fingerprint marring the shiny metal and endless granite counters.

I spin around and motion to the wall of windows and the French doors leading to the backyard, which is hardly a "yard." Beyond the natural-stone patio is a huge swimming pool, and a path of stones marks the way to the lake, where a boathouse and a massive dock sprawl out into the water. "Look at this view."

"Let's save the backyard for last." Ethan nods toward the foyer and I follow him through a formal dining room with a table that seats twelve comfortably, and a living room that seems to be designed to hold the same. This is definitely a house meant for entertaining. Maybe that's why he wants it, so he can throw hockey parties here with his new teammates. I wonder if puck bunnies get invites to those kinds of parties. The possibility irks me.

The second floor has its own private sitting room and deck that boasts the same view of the lake as the kitchen, except from a higher vantage point.

Each bedroom has a private bathroom. They're a little outdated, as if the owners cared most about the kitchen and the dining room, which are the only parts of the house that seem to have been updated in the last twenty years. My skin grows hot when we step into the master suite, and the back of Ethan's hand skims my hip. The space is huge and lavish. I laugh at the painting on the wall opposite the bed.

Ethan's eyebrows lift along with the curve of his lips. "That's a little cliché, isn't it?"

The massive white-and-pink flower is far more vagina inspired than it is rose or daisies.

"Just a little."

I brush past him to stand in front of the French doors leading to a balcony with yet another stunning view of the lake. To the right of the pool is a second small house—and it's probably bigger than the one I live in.

"Are you really thinking about buying this place? Why such a big house? For parties?" I voice my earlier thought, frustrated by my bitter tone.

He opens the French doors and I follow him out onto the balcony. "It's the pool house I'm actually interested in. This place is undervalued because the owners haven't updated it, and I'm not sure what's going to happen with my dad, so I want to have space for them if I need it."

"You'd buy this house so your parents can move into the pool house?"

Ethan shrugs. "It's a thought. I want to have the space for Dylan and his family, and for my parents' friends if they came to visit."

"What if you get traded again? Won't you have to sell it?" My throat tightens at the possibility that Ethan's return will be brief. Part of the reason I'm so hesitant to allow this friendship is the fear that he'll come back into my life long enough for me to care about him again, and then he'll be off to another city in another state.

"I'll probably be here permanently if I can't up my game this year."

I note the tightness of his jaw and the frustration shadowing his eyes.

"Wouldn't that be a good thing? Not having to move from city to city, I mean?"

"They sent me home for a reason, Lilah."

"I don't understand."

His smile is rueful. "If I don't pick it up and play well, better than I have been, this could be my last season."

"So this is your 'in case I fail' house? That's a little fatalist of you, isn't it?" I'm pushing his buttons, something I used to do when he'd play street hockey, or any kind of hockey with his friends in lieu of studying for tests.

Back then we were both reasonable about his prospects with the NHL—how short most careers were. And here he is, telling me his might be over. He's not even twenty-eight yet. Life has hardly even started and he's looking at the end of his dream when I'm starting to pursue my own.

"I'm sorry—that was uncalled for."

His jaw works for a few seconds. "I'm trying to be realistic. I'm buying a house because I need a place to live that isn't my parents' basement. I'm looking at this one in particular because it's a sound investment, and because my parents could easily live here without us driving each other insane. Even if this season goes well, I have no idea what's coming next, so I want to be prepared for anything."

I don't ask any of the questions I want to, like what happens if he *does* do well this season? Will Minnesota extend his contract? Will he still be traded? Does he plan to come back here for good when his career in the NHL does eventually end?

"I guess that makes sense." I step away from the balcony and Ethan, suddenly aware of how close we're standing. "Why don't we check out the basement?"

chapter seven

CLOSED SPACES

Lilah

Ethan follows me down the hall to the stairs. The basement has high ceilings and a walkout to a patio in the backyard.

Ethan immediately checks out the home movie theater and bank of arcade games. The last door on the left seems to be a cold cellar at first glance. A closer look at the shelves reveals not food, but bottles upon bottles of wine.

The space is probably bigger than my bedroom, but the walls are concrete, and there don't seem to be any windows. It's not cold, but not the same temperature as the rest of the house, either. Along one wall are several tall fridges, which hold more bottles. I'm not a fan of closed spaces, especially ones without windows, but I'm curious, and I'm not alone, so I step inside despite the shiver that runs down my spine.

"These people are serious wine aficionados." I run my fingers along the bottles. I'm more of a margarita girl, but I'll drink wine if the occasion calls for it. I note another door at the far end of the wine cellar, but it doesn't have a handle. That's weird. I wonder if it's some kind of huge safe, and if so, what the hell is in it?

"Hey, Ethan, come look at this!" I call out as I spin around. I crash into his chest, grabbing hold of his forearms to steady myself. "Christ, when did you become so stealthy?"

"Back when I used to sneak up to my room to sleep with you after my parents fell asleep." His wide palms rest on my waist. He's always been so much bigger than me—it made me feel delicate when we were younger, strangely feminine when, in reality, I was more of an athletic tomboy.

I fight not to allow those memories to surface. His gaze is hot, warming my skin, starting with my cheeks. Pushing away, I step to the side so I'm a little closer to the exit and gesture to the handleless door behind me. "Is that a safe?"

He lifts a shoulder and moves around me to take a closer look. "Dunno. What's that?" He pushes a button I failed to notice, and the door slides open with a metallic click.

He peeks inside and I grab on to his arm. "Do you really think you should go in there?"

He looks down at me, clinging to him, the hint of a smile on his lips. "I'm sure it's fine. I'm going to check it out." I don't let go as he takes another step forward, and another. He's pretty much dragging me along with him, but my body has locked up, and no matter what I try to tell my brain, I can't seem to let go.

Over the past several years I thought I'd gotten past my fear of tight spaces—I still avoid elevators whenever possible, but I thought I had it managed. Guess not. The wine cellar on its own created a little anxiety, enough to make my palms damp, but I find myself frozen, unable to unlock my arms from around Ethan's.

A red light flares as we cross the threshold. My heels slide across the floor with every step he takes. Half of me appreciates the feel of his body close to mine, protective, safe; the other half is highly in tune with my uncontrollable rising panic over the small, windowless space we're in.

"Ethan." My voice is high, shrill.

"You okay, baby?"

"I can't—" I dig my nails into his skin, while simultaneously trying to force myself to release him so I can get back to a room with windows.

"I think there's a light switch right here." He slaps at the wall to the right, spinning us around so I'm fully inside the room.

A metallic grating follows as the door begins to slide shut. My arms finally obey the command to release him. I shove him out of the way, which is pretty incredible considering he easily must weigh more than two hundred pounds. I catch him off guard, so he stumbles back with a grunt. I can't see well enough in the dim lighting, so I trip over his foot, falling into the closing door. I try to grab the edge and keep it from sealing us in, but it seems to function like an elevator, and I nearly lose my fingers as the wine cellar disappears from view.

I'm already in full-on panic mode, and as much as I'd like to keep my cool, this is my single phobia. Tight, dark spaces send me from logical and levelheaded to complete freak-out mode.

I pound on the steel door with my fists. I'm not drawing full breaths. I might actually be at risk of passing out if I keep this up, but there's no room left for reason in my brain. In my head, we're stuck in the room together until we die.

Strong hands grip my forearms and pin them to my side. Then I find myself straitjacketed by his arms as Ethan pulls me away from the single point of escape. I thrash and scream, because the only way out is through that door, so that's where my attention needs to be.

"DJ, calm down. You're fine. You need to take a breath." Ethan's voice is soft in my ear. There's no panic or anger, just that calm, smooth voice I remember from when we were young.

"We need to get out!"

"We will, but you have to calm down first."

"Let me go!" It feels like I'm trying to breathe under-water.

"I'd like to, since you keep kicking my shins, but if you go apeshit on that door again, you're going to break your hands, and I will not be responsible for that, so take some deep breaths with me and calm down."

"I don't think I can." I suck in another raspy, high-pitched breath, aware the panic is something only I can control.

Ethan releases my arms slowly.

As soon as they're free I spin around and grab his shirt. "What is this? What if we can't get out? What if no one finds us?" I wish I could get it together, but I'm just not capable.

Ethan must realize this, because he takes my face in his hands. "Delilah, baby, relax."

His words are gentle, but the intimate contact is jarring. Intense. Familiar and not. He regards me with uncertainty and then resolve. I don't understand the emotion until he takes action.

I'm shocked out of my panic as Ethan's lips descend on mine. They're so soft and warm. I know them, and yet they're not quite the same as I remember. At first he's tentative where he was once certain. But his tongue peeks out to stroke the seam of my mouth, and resistance isn't even a whisper in my head.

When he slides his fingers into my hair and tugs, I automatically tilt my head back and part my lips. When his tongue pushes forward to stroke mine, I moan.

It takes several more seconds, in which I meet his tongue in a soft tangle with my own, before I fully process that Ethan is kissing me, and I'm kissing him back. It's been so long since I've been kissed like this, felt anything close to this level of overwhelming desire. When he steps in closer and his body comes flush with mine, I feel him hard against my stomach. It's too much. It's not enough. I'm terrified to want this.

I push on his chest, separating our mouths, and step back. "What're you doing?"

He drops his hands and blinks at me, and blinks again. That weird red light makes his expression difficult to read. His voice is full of gravel. "Trying to get you to calm down."

"By putting your tongue in my mouth?" I wish I sounded incredulous rather than breathless.

"You're not freaking out anymore, are you?" He rubs his lips.

I can't tell if he's trying to hide a smile or not. "It's not funny, Ethan. We're trapped in here!" I cringe at my reedy tone.

"I'm not laughing." His voice is smooth satin, stoking the fire he's awakened with one kiss.

"How can you be so calm?" The panic is already rising again, a siren in my head growing louder, drowning out desire.

"Your sister's meeting us here soon, right?" He puts his hands on my shoulders. "You should sit."

I brush them away, my palms clammy. "How is that going to help us get out of this weird fucking box?"

"You're panicking again, so unless you want my tongue in your mouth, I suggest you take a seat."

I huff out an irritated breath, not wanting to follow his directions but uncertain whether I can control my reaction if he follows through with that threat. I enjoyed his mouth a little too much. After only the briefest hesitation, I drop to the floor.

Ethan barks out a laugh. "Wow—I'm not sure whether to be insulted or not." He crouches in front of me, hands coming to rest on my knees. I allow the contact because it makes me feel safe. "I'm going to see if there's a light switch in here somewhere. Is that okay?"

"Yes."

"Put your head between your knees and take some deep breaths."

When I do as he says, he strokes my hair. Eventually he severs the connection, and then it's just me in the eerie red darkness. It only takes a moment before pale, bright light filters into my line of vision. I turn my head, focusing on deep breaths even though I'm light-headed. He uses the flashlight on his phone to scan the wall.

In my panic I didn't even consider that an option. I feel around on the floor for my purse but remember I left it on the counter in the kitchen. Fat lot of good that does me when I'm stuck in here.

Ethan bumps around in the dark until bright light suddenly fills the room. At least now I can see where we're trapped.

I frown as I take in the space. One wall is lined with shelves containing a variety of canned and packaged food. Everything is neatly organized, labels facing out. I count six cases of water, two cases of ginger ale, which I find odd, and an endless supply of crackers, dried fruit, nuts, and other snacks on top of all the canned food. Under the shelves are totes labeled BEDDING, CLOTHING, and TOILETRIES. "Is this a bunker?"

"I think it's a panic room," Ethan replies. "Look at this."

"Well, that's fitting," I mumble, and spin on my butt to check out the other side of the space. The sudden movement makes me dizzy, and I'm forced to put my head between my knees again.

Ethan crouches in front of me and his palms smooth down my shins. "Hey, you okay? You need me to distract you again?"

"Don't make fun of me." I blindly smack at him, connecting weakly with his arm. He shifts his hold on my legs, fingertips pressing into my calves, kneading gently. I'm pushed into the past—he was always like this with me, touchy, sweet. He took care of me when no one else did.

"I'm not. I'm sorry we're stuck in here. We'll be out soon, okay?"

He starts to remove his hands, but I press my palms to the back of them. "Just let me breathe for a few more seconds."

"There's an intercom system and cameras that seem to feed to the whole house. It's actually pretty weird, to be honest. I had no idea the Hoffmans were paranoid, or part of the mob, or whatever would cause someone to build something so elaborate inside a wine cellar," he says.

I keep breathing, reminding myself that I'm safe and Ethan is with me. "Was it even on the house layout?"

"I don't think so. I'm not sure a panic room is much of a

selling feature. How you doing?" He brushes my hair back, twisting it out of the way so it's not hanging in my face, then sweeps his knuckle from the bridge of my nose to the tip. I hum at the sensation. It's been so long since anyone other than me has done that. I missed the feeling.

"I'm okay. I'm sorry I freaked out."

He runs his palms up and down my arms. "You don't have to apologize. I know how confinement makes you feel. Can you look at me?" He touches his finger to my chin, and I lift my head slowly. "There we go. There's my girl. What time did Carmen say she'd be here?"

"Seven thirty, I think. My phone's in the kitchen."

"There isn't any reception in here."

"What?"

"It's a dead zone." Ethan cringes at his choice of words. "Take another breath. We can watch the cameras and use the intercom when she gets here."

"What if she's late?"

"Don't worry—I'm good at distracting you."

"You're not kissing me again."

He gives me one of his smirky grins. "That wasn't what I was referring to, but it's interesting that's where your head went."

I give him a look, but I'm still sitting on the floor with my knees pulled to my chest, so I'm unsure how effective it is.

"Why don't we check this place out while we wait?" He holds out a hand and I accept it, as much to help me to my feet as an excuse to maintain the physical connection.

I'm still a little unsteady, so I grab his shirt with one hand and his forearm with the other to keep upright. I loathe this weakness in me. I try not to think about our current confinement. Instead I focus on Ethan's palm making slow circles on my back, thumb brushing my skin when he passes under my hair to the V-cut back of my dress. His head drops, and I feel the warmth of his breath on my cheek and the soft brush of his nose in my hair.

"Just keep breathing."

"You're making it difficult." I put my hands on his chest to push away, but his palm is still on my back, keeping me close.

"I'm just trying to keep you calm."

"By kissing me."

"Can you honestly tell me you don't feel this?" He runs gentle fingers up the length of my arm.

My body betrays me, goose bumps rising on my skin. I step out of his reach. "It doesn't matter what I feel. You left me."

"I know and I'm sorry. We were kids, Lilah."

"I spent my whole life loving you and I got nothing for eight years. Now you want what? To see if things are still the same? They're not."

"Some things are." He moves in close again and brushes his thumb over my bottom lip.

I twist my head away. "You can't do this. You can't force me into this discussion when I'm already trapped."

"You keep dodging this, Lilah. How can I explain when you won't even give me the chance?"

"An apology won't make the past disappear." I pace the perimeter of the room, looking for something that will get me out of here, away from this attraction and all the conflicting emotions that come with being near this man. I hit the button on the wall, the one that closed the door initially. A keypad lights up, so obviously it requires a passcode, which we don't have.

"Who the fuck made up a stupid system that locks you in a goddamn room?" The panic is starting to set in again.

"Someone paranoid. Lilah—" He reaches out, but when I hold up a hand, he stops, arm dropping to his side. "Just give me a chance to explain why."

I spin around, anger finally overriding the panic, frustrated at his insistence that we talk about this now, that I'm stuck in here with him, that he's kissed me, and that despite the adrenaline and the fear, I liked it and want it to happen again.

"What part do you want to explain? Why you broke up with me like a coward over the phone and I never saw you again until you were forced to move back here? Why you stopped talking to me? Why all of a sudden you seem so interested in being my friend again, or whatever you want to call this?" I gesture wildly between us.

"I want to explain all of it. Just give me a chance."

"Nothing you say is going to change the past."

"It could change the future, though."

My chest tightens, so many possibilities unfolding with that one truth.

"One minute we were making plans for our future and the next you were out of my life completely," I say softly.

"I'm sorry for a lot of things, Lilah, but I'm the most sorry about how things ended."

"So am I." I pull out a storage bin and sit down, my legs still shaky.

He pulls one out too and settles beside me, close but not touching. "Remember how hard it was that first semester I was in college? How tough it was to get used to only seeing each other a couple of times a month instead of every day?"

His absence left a hole in my world. I'd been so bereft at first, missing the person who'd been my constant since I was in kindergarten. "We managed." Barely.

"I almost dropped out after the first semester."

"What? Why?" This is new information. We'd had nightly phone calls back then. Sometimes we fell asleep talking, and I'd wake up in the morning to the sound of his breathing, or his alarm through the phone, and vice versa.

"Because I hated being away from you. Between studying and hockey, I had no time. There weren't enough hours. I had trouble keeping up with classes. You weren't there to keep me on track. But more than that, I just missed *you*. I thought about you all the time, the way you used to tap your lip with your pen when you were annoyed, how you used to get all grossed out when I'd try to kiss you after practice and I hadn't showered yet, the way you'd unwrap the entire package of Life Savers so you could pick out the green-apple ones and save them for last. I missed being part of your life every day. I didn't feel like I could do it without you, and I didn't want to. I thought maybe I should put the scholarship on hold and take a year off, wait for you to graduate so we could do college together."

"But then you were drafted to the farm team."

"Yeah." His head is bowed, shoulders curved forward, elbows resting on his knees.

"So you broke up with me instead."

"I was fucking miserable, DJ."

"Why break up, then? And why eradicate yourself from my life?" It's a strange feeling, being here with him, but not really knowing him anymore—not the way I used to. All of our history still exists but with a wall built between then and now. I don't know if it's possible to break it down, or if I want to.

"It was only going to get harder. The being apart from you. Minnesota State was only a couple hours away and it was barely tolerable. I was going to move to the other end of the country. I didn't want to put that much pressure on you."

"What kind of pressure would you have put on me?" I don't understand his logic. He's also had eight years to rationalize this. Enough time to frame it in a way that makes sense to him.

"To make it work. To make *us* work. You can't tell me the long distance wasn't hard for you. I know it was. I heard the ache in your voice, Lilah, and I shared it. I kept watching all these relationships fail in my first year of college, and I kept thinking as long as we could get through the year we'd be fine, because then you'd be with me. But being drafted changed everything. Nothing about my career was certain, and I didn't want to drag you along for that fucked-up ride."

"You didn't even give me a choice, though. I had no voice." And maybe that's the part that had eaten at me the most. We'd planned our paths together. We'd depended on each other for years. We'd made decisions based on a future that contained each other, and then all of a sudden I had no say.

He shifts until his knee touches mine. I want to sever the contact, but it's as comforting as it is painful. "Would you have been okay with breaking up?"

"I didn't have an opportunity to be okay with it."

"I know you, Lilah. Or at least I did back then. You wouldn't have given up on us like that if I'd presented you with a choice. You would've been determined to make it work. To prove all the statistics wrong, because that's who you are—or were—and it's one of many reasons why I loved you so fucking much."

He runs his fingers over the back of my hand. Reflexively I flip it over and he twines them together, squeezing. "Training was intense. Far beyond anything else I'd ever experienced. Hours of practice almost every day, not a lot of downtime. And that was just the farm team. NHL training is even more consuming. Off-season is a few short months, and the rest of the time I would've been away. I didn't want your focus split, or mine. You were in your last semester of high school, and I was being moved out to LA. It wasn't logical to stay together, and I was trying to be logical, because God knows, nothing about the way I loved you was rational."

The emotions that swirl and swell between us are so much different from the ones I experienced when he broke my heart all those years ago. He'd been so assured, so calm in his ending of things, so certain it was the right thing to do. Or at least that's how I had perceived it. Now his voice is full of sharp regret. It's in this picture he paints for me, in his broken expression and the waver in his voice, that my hurt over this is echoed in him.

"The worst part was that you did it over the phone," I say.

He nods and lifts our clasped hands, brushing his lips over my knuckle. I shiver at the affection, at the shadow of memories. "I never could've followed through in person. I wouldn't have been able to see the hurt I heard in your voice and stay away from you. That was really selfish of me. I was selfish about you. I always have been."

"That doesn't explain eight years of nothing."

"I don't think there's a simple explanation that doesn't make me look like an asshole."

"Well, give it a try, and really, I don't think you could elevate your asshole status by much, all considering."

He laughs at this sliver of levity. "I tried after that to reach out. I called you, remember?"

"Yes." Of course I did. He'd called a couple of times late at night, when I was on the verge of sleep—the conversations had been brief, painful. In the mornings I'd wondered if they had been a bad dream.

"I didn't know how to be friends."

"It felt like you were calling out of obligation and you couldn't wait to get off the phone with me."

"That's because I couldn't."

When I try to yank my hand away, he holds it tighter. "I didn't want you to be fine without me. I didn't want to hear that you were moving on. I didn't want you to be okay, because I wasn't. I was a mess, and every time I called I made it worse for myself. I was playing like shit. It felt like I'd done it all for nothing, but as much as I didn't want to stay away from you, I knew it was the right thing to do. It was painful, the not having any ties to you. I missed knowing what was going on in your life, if you found a better part-time job, one you actually liked, if you bought a car, if you'd moved into an apartment like you wanted to, like we'd planned to, or if all of that had changed."

"If it was so hard, why stay out of my life altogether?"

He sighs. "For me it was all or nothing with you. I knew if I saw you, I'd want to get back together. Then I found out you were with Avery—I think it was a few months before you got engaged."

"Wouldn't that have been a safe time to make contact? When I was already with someone?"

Ethan's laugh is almost bitter. "My dad told me not to."

I'm shocked by this. Martin knew how hard losing Ethan

had been for me. He'd been a huge source of support the entire time. "Why would he do that?"

"Because he knew I would fuck it up for you."

"How?"

"Your happiness made me miserable, which is a horrible thing to say. I should've been glad that you'd found someone, but I wasn't. Not even a little bit. That it was Avery didn't help. He was always such a douche in high school, always talking about how awesome his car was and how awesome he was. He just seemed so shallow. And you had such light and so many dreams. You were going to get a full scholarship and go into medicine and be amazing. I just couldn't understand how someone like him could make you happy. Seeing you together, knowing I'd let you go . . . I couldn't be your friend."

I think about how I would've felt had it been me in his shoes. Would I have been able to handle seeing him happy with someone else? I don't know.

"I wanted you to live your life, go to school like you planned to, and become a doctor, and that would've been impossible if we'd stayed together. I didn't want you to have to give up your dream so I could have mine."

"Just so we're clear, I love my job, and I made a choice not to be a doctor because I realized nursing was a better fit for me. But you never even asked *me* what *I* wanted. Why didn't that matter?" This time Ethan lets me have my hand when I pull away.

He rubs the back of his neck. "I would've been all you had

in LA. At least with you here I knew you had my family. I didn't want you to be alone."

"Who were you protecting, me or you?"

"Both of us? I convinced myself that as long as you were managing, it was better that I stay out of your life. I thought it was better for me to be the asshole who wasn't in your life than one who would keep fucking things up."

chapter eight

SETUP

Lilah

Perception is such a strange, illusive concept. Especially when perception is steeped in youth, inexperience, and heartache. So learning the reasons behind Ethan's actions all those years ago creates a new ache in my chest.

In his own screwed-up way, he'd always been protecting me, even if it caused us both unnecessary pain.

"I'm so sorry I hurt you the way I did. I'm even more sorry that you felt abandoned and that I couldn't manage my own emotions enough to stay in your life, even if it wasn't the way I wanted."

The soft brush of his thumbs under my eyes startles me. My tears are silent grief for lost years. When he starts to pull away, I lean my cheek into one of his palms and just allow myself to feel. I've missed him. Our connection has always been unique. Consuming in a way that sometimes felt over-whelming. His touch could calm and excite simultaneously.

Like being given a sedative and a shot of caffeine at the same time.

It's been a long time since I've felt this kind of intense draw to another person.

The tenderness of the moment is broken by the sound of the front door opening and Carmen's voice booming through the intercom system. I jump up and rush over to see my sister on the little screen, calling our names as she drops her purse on the table in the entryway. I find the intercom button. "Carmen? Can you hear me?"

"Holy crap!" Her hand goes to her heart and she spins around. "Lilah? Where are you?"

I drop my head against the screen and exhale a relieved breath. "Thank God. We're in the wine cellar."

I can see her eyebrows raise and a smile quickly form, but it disappears when I continue. "We're trapped in the panic room. Do you have any idea how to get out of it?"

Her hand goes to her mouth. "Oh God. I'll be right down!" She disappears from one screen, passing through several on her way downstairs until she ends up on the other side of the door we're locked behind.

"Can you still hear me?" She knocks, making a muffled tinny sound.

I press the intercom button. "Yes."

"Okay, good. When you talk, you're broadcast all over the house, so I can hear you anywhere, and I think it should be the same for me. I'm so sorry—I forgot to tell you about the panic room." She's scrolling through her phone frantically while she speaks. "The Hoffmans gave me the code in an email before they left for France. I just need to find it."

"We need a code," I murmur, maybe to myself, or Ethan, or as reassurance that I won't be in this room much longer.

Carmen says something under her breath on the other side. "Found it! Okay, you have to punch in the code from the inside." She purses her lips. "But I guess you already knew that."

"Just give me the goddamn code so we can get the fuck out of here, Carm."

"Right. Okay. It's five-eight-six-seven-one."

With a shaky hand, I punch in the numbers. Ethan meets my gaze as we wait a few shockingly long seconds before a series of metallic clicks reverberate through the room and the door begins to move. As soon as there's enough space for my body, mashed boobs or not, I squeeze through and slam right into Carmen.

Her arms come around me. "I'm so sorry, DJ. I know how much you hate closed spaces."

If I continue to let her console me, I'll probably cry again, and that's the last thing I want to do. I push away and rush for the door, stepping out into the basement. The bright light and high ceilings are disorienting. "I'm fine." I beeline for the French doors leading to the backyard patio. Wrenching them open, I step outside, sucking in lungfuls of fresh air, working to regain some composure.

"How long were you stuck in there?" Carmen asks Ethan, her voice wavering.

"Awhile." He's quiet and reserved.

"I'm so sorry. They mentioned there being a glitch with the door sensors. I didn't realize they meant it locked people in there."

"Why the hell do they even have a panic room?" I yell from the patio.

I hear the jingle of her bracelets before I see her approaching. "Apparently George Hoffman was a bit eccentric and paranoid. He had it installed about a decade ago, before he passed away, and then his son moved in with his family and no one maintained it, because, well, no one needs a panic room in Forest Lake."

I glare at her when she chuckles.

"I'm so sorry, Lilah. I didn't even think to warn you about it. Do you want a few minutes? I can answer any questions Ethan has about the house."

I need time to get my emotions under control, and not just because I was locked in a dark, windowless room. I'm reeling from our conversation. "Please. I'll be up in a minute." She squeezes my arm and goes back into the house, leaving me to collect myself.

"Lilah?" Ethan's voice is full of worry.

"I'm fine. I need a minute." I'm sure he's aware I'm lying, but the kiss, the revelation, and the confined space are a lot to handle all at once.

"Okay. I'm sorry."

When the words aren't followed by the sound of his departure, I glance over my shoulder. It's the worst possible thing

I can do. He's standing with his hands shoved into his pockets, huge shoulders hunched in what looks like defeat. But it's the haunted regret that cuts through my heart. "Me, too. Carmen's waiting for you. I'll come up soon."

He sighs but heads upstairs. I take a few steps farther out onto the patio, staring past the pool to the lake beyond. I don't know what to do with everything he's told me. With one conversation, Ethan has reframed the last eight years. My heart aches from the phantom pain made real again.

I pause at a bathroom on my way upstairs. My lipstick is gone and my hair is a bit wild, maybe from Ethan's hands being in it when he kissed me.

I'm embarrassed my panic was the impetus. Still, it's probably one of the most passionate kisses I've experienced since . . . him. Past and present are merging, and I don't know how to separate them.

Now that I'm no longer locked inside a panic room, I'm mortified that I lost it in there like a kid throwing a temper tantrum. I kicked Ethan in the shin for Chrissake.

I consider slipping out and going home without telling them, but my purse is in the kitchen, along with my car keys, so I don't have a choice but to go get it. Just as I'm about to take the last step from the carpet runner to the marble floor, Carmen says, "If you want to think about it and come back later in the week, we can schedule another appointment. The Hoffmans are in France until next Friday."

I step into the kitchen, arms crossed over my chest. "I

thought you said this was urgent, that Ethan only had a short window to view the property."

Carmen looks up, eyes wide—the way I associate with being caught in a lie rather than innocence.

I point an accusatory finger at her. "Did you set me up?"

"Lilah—"

"You're unbelievable." I shift my anger, finger wagging to Ethan. "Were you in on this? Was the whole panic room thing part of the damn plan?"

"I don't even know what there is to be in on." His confusion seems genuine, but I'm too upset with my sister's meddling not to project my anger on him, too.

"Bullshit."

"And I would never lock you in a windowless space on purpose," he adds.

I prop a fist on my hip and narrow my eyes. "Are you sure about that? It seemed to give you opportunities you otherwise wouldn't have had."

"Come on, Lilah—it's really not what you think," Carmen says.

"You tricked me," I say to her. "You pushed me into this." I swing around and point at Ethan again. "And you—I don't know what you want from me. You say you want to be friends, but friends keep their damn lips to themselves!" I'm embarrassed and overwhelmed all over again. "I'm going home."

I need time to process. Alone.

chapter nine

WORDS AND DEEDS

Ethan

I admit I check out Lilah's ass as she stalks out of the kitchen. It's a great ass, even in a flowy, pretty sundress. Especially in a flowy, pretty sundress.

"Should we go after her?" I ask Carmen.

I'm at a loss here. Eight years ago I wouldn't have thought twice about chasing her down to find a way to fix whatever I'd done wrong, but now I'm not so sure. She's really damn angry. And I just unloaded a lot on her while she was trapped with me. Her anger might be justified. The slam of the front door echoes that thought.

Carmen grimaces. "Probably not? You know what she's like when she's upset."

"I used to know what she was like." I tap on the counter, memories of past arguments flooding back, when frustration and lust sometimes collided in the tornado of emotions exacerbated by hormones.

"For a long while there she was flat, but since you came back, well..."

"Since I came back what?"

Carmen shrugs. "There's some fire in her soul again."

I motion to the empty space she occupied seconds ago. "That's not the kind of fire I'd like to evoke." Now, that kiss in the panic room—I could totally handle more of that.

"She needs time to calm down. I'll go by her place when we're done here and explain."

"What exactly are you going to explain? Why does she think you tricked her?"

Carmen looks down at the counter and rearranges the papers. She and Lilah have very little in the way of sibling resemblance. From the color of their hair to body type, they're complete opposites, but they have a few of the same mannerisms, such as the way they fidget when they're nervous.

"Carm?"

"Well, I sort of did."

"I'm sorry, what?"

"I wasn't lying about being stuck in traffic, but I might've made it seem like this was the only opportunity for you to see the house and that there was a time constraint."

"Ah, fuck. Why would you do that?"

She blows out a breath that makes her bangs puff up and settle funkily. "I was trying to help."

"By pissing her off?"

"By getting you two together for reasons that don't directly involve Martin, or under the guise of her being helpful."

"What does that mean? 'Under the guise'?"

Carmen tilts her head and regards me with that expression women have, the one that implies I'm clueless.

"Come on, Ethan, she's not just helping with Martin because she loves your family. I mean, she does love your family. It's just...you two have so much history. It's been years, but she's never really gotten over you leaving." Her eyes go wide and she makes a hissing sound. "Shit. I should *not* have said that."

"She got married."

"And that didn't work out, did it?"

"Lots of people get divorced."

"I'm just saying, things happen for a reason, don't they? You're here and clearly there's still something between you."

"I'm not sure that's true—not on her side, anyway."

"But on your side there is?"

I sigh. Seeing her again after all this time has brought back a lot of memories and all the feelings that go with them. And if I'm completely honest, I don't think I ever really allowed myself to get over leaving her, either. The kiss in the panic room reminded me of how intense things always were between us, and as amazing as it was to finally have that again, I pushed her too hard today, and now I'm paying the price for that. "I was aiming for friendship first."

Carmen gives me a sly grin. "Oh, really? So the keep-your-lips-to-yourself-next-time comment pertained to a friendly kiss?"

"She was having a panic attack in the panic room."

"So you laid one on her?" She arches a brow.

"It was a good distraction," I mumble.

"Oh, I bet. Did she kiss you back?" Carmen is all over this.

I rub the back of my neck, uncomfortable with the kiss-and-tell and Carmen's apparent enjoyment over it. "She might've."

Carmen laughs. "No wonder she's so pissed."

"Well, that and I forced her to finally talk to me about what happened when I was drafted. So yeah, she feels set up."

"Well, the whole point was to get you to talk, so mission accomplished."

"I wanted to make it better, not worse, though."

"Just let me talk to her, and it'll be okay."

"Will it? I don't know, Carmen. It feels like every time I get a little closer, she's off running again. It's like she has this brick wall around her heart and I'm the reason it's there."

"You can't blame yourself, Ethan. It's a lot more complicated than that."

"I'm not so sure it is. She was always such an easy person to love when we were young, her heart open—at least for me. It makes me sad that she's so untrusting now."

"You have to earn it from her, and that's going to take time. You're not the only person who left her, Ethan."

I don't want to do that to her again. And I don't know

where I'll be next year with a one-year contract and no certainty of renewal.

℮

Once we leave the Hoffman estate, I drive to the local florist,
but it's late, so everything is closed downtown apart from the
bars. I stand in front of the shop's darkened window and consider my options. I'm not planning on pushing Lilah any more
than I already have tonight. I want to leave something for her
so tomorrow morning my apology is the first thing she gets
when she walks out her door.

There's a convenience store down the street, one we used
to ride our bikes to when we were kids. With my allowance,
I used to splurge on bags of bulk candies for me and DJ—
something she couldn't afford.

I'm pleased to see the store still has them available, although
the boxes I remember, with their tiny plastic tongs, have been
replaced by a bank of clear plastic bins with lids and little
scoops. I grab a bag and browse the selection of gummies and
candies. I layer it with all of Lilah's favorites; Hot Lips seem
rather appropriate, all things considered. I add Watermelon
Slices, Fuzzy Peaches, a gummy snake, bears, Wine Gums,
black licorice—she was the only kid I knew who ate it and
liked it—jawbreakers, and top it off with more Hot Lips. It's
an apology rainbow of sugar.

A teen sits behind the cash register, tapping away on his

phone, probably updating the world on his boredom. I drop the bag on the counter and slide my wallet out of my back pocket.

He glances up and his eyes go wide, his phone clattering to the floor. "Oh, man!" He fumbles in his chair, almost tipping it over as he tries to retrieve his phone and still keep his eyes on me. He pops back up, slapping the device on the counter. "You're Ethan Kase!"

I can't say the recognition or the excitement is bad for my ego these days. "That's me."

He shakes his head. "I can't believe you're here."

"Well, I live here, so it kind of makes sense, right?" I'm grinning. I'm not at the top of the league, so normally I go under the radar, unlike Alex Waters or Randy Ballistic back in Chicago. They couldn't go to a bar without at least half a dozen selfie shots. Although, I think all the endorsements Waters has scored along the way—particularly the ones for prophylactics—have made him that much more recognizable outside of the hockey world.

But here, in a place like Forest Lake, I'm more likely to get this kind of reaction. It's novel for now because it's so new. But I don't ever want to take it for granted.

"My dad was talking about you at dinner, saying you were a good trade for Minnesota. You used to go to my high school. Your pictures are in the gym hallway. You won the most valuable player award all four years. Man, the guys aren't gonna believe this. Can I get a picture? Can I take a selfie?

Will you sign something for me? I wish I had my Minnesota jersey."

I laugh at his enthusiasm, and his face goes red. "Come on out and we can get a picture; then I'll sign whatever you want."

He's so bouncy it's hard to take a decent picture. When he does, he posts immediately to every social media platform he's intravenously hooked into.

"Got what you need?" I ask, after I sign a Minnesota team flag the store sells.

"Yeah. For sure. Thanks so much."

"No problem. You wanna ring me through?" I tap the bag of candy.

"Oh, right!" He drops it on the weigh scale. "You're allowed to eat all this stuff when you're training?"

I laugh. "Not a chance. It's for a friend."

"Right. Yeah. Exhibition games start soon, too. Me and my dad have tickets for when you play against Colorado."

"That'll be a good game."

"Yeah. It's super cool. Do you know if you'll be starting yet? Or is it, like, too soon to know that?"

"Depends on how preseason training goes."

"It's good so far, though, right? I saw somewhere that you're, like, kicking ass." He's still bouncing with excitement.

I smile at his enthusiasm. My performance at practices so far has been on point, so it's nice to know other people are seeing it, too. "Well, that's good to hear."

"I can't wait to see you play."

"You bring a jersey and I'll sign it for you—sound good?"

"Cool. Awesome." He keeps nodding and grinning, his face still red.

The candy ends up costing twenty-five bucks, which my new friend Matt seems to think is totally crazy. I add a card so I can write a note to go with the candy. Once I'm back in my truck, I put the address Carmen gave me into my GPS. Lilah's house is in a small subdivision away from the water, where homes are more affordable.

Carmen's car is parked in the driveway behind Lilah's. It's a quaint little row house. The front garden is neatly tended, as I'd expect from Lilah.

I park my truck on the street and search for a pen in the glove box. All I come up with is a blue colored pencil. I can't erase anything I put down, so I chew on the end, debating what I want to write. I decide the best way to go is direct with a bit of tongue-in-cheek, so to speak. I sign the card, slip it into the envelope, and leave the engine running because I don't plan to stick around. I finger the dog tags hanging from the rearview mirror for a second before I open the door and hop out of the cab.

My hands are stupidly sweaty for dropping off a bag of peace-apology candies. I can see inside the house since the door is open, and the screen provides a clear view through to the backyard. To the left is a living room, simply furnished, to the right a staircase. Beyond that is the kitchen, and straight ahead is a set of sliding glass doors that lead to an outdoor patio. A pair of bare feet are visible, as is the edge of an Adirondack chair.

What I don't account for is the presence of Lilah's dog, lying beside her outside. She's brought him by my parents' house a couple of times. He's too friendly to be an actual guard dog, but he's far more effective than a doorbell. I cringe as his ears perk and his head pops up. He jumps to his feet and barks a couple of times, then presses his nose against the screen, tail wagging.

"What's up, Merk?" Lilah leans forward.

She can see through to where I'm standing under the porch light. I lift a hand and wave.

"Give me a minute." I can hear the wryness in her voice.

If I wasn't holding a bag of candy and a card, I'd shove my hands in my pockets, but that's not an option, so I rock back on my heels and wait as she opens the sliding glass door. Merk tears across the kitchen and through the living room, running in a circle and stopping at the door with a single bark. He likes me. Possibly more than Lilah currently does. Probably is more like it.

"Merk, sit," Lilah orders before flicking the lock and opening the door just enough that her body fits in the opening. When Merk makes a move to stand, she snaps her fingers. "Stay." He whines but obeys. She turns her attention to me, eyes shifting to where my hands are clasped behind my back.

"How'd you get my address?"

"My parents have it in their address book because they're old-school." It's a lie, but I don't want to get Carmen in more trouble with Lilah than she already is. Although I'm sure it is in the book my parents keep by the phone.

Her lips are pursed and her cheeks are flushed. I bet she's been drinking.

"Are you here for a reason, or were you planning to stand on my front porch and stare at my mouth?"

I fight a grin, glad she hasn't lost the sass I always loved. I meet her hazel glare. "It wasn't part of my plan, or my reason for stopping by."

"My sister's here, so . . ." She trails off, not opening the door any farther. Clearly I'm not getting an invitation to come inside.

"Right. Of course. I wanted to drop this off. You can share or keep them to yourself—whatever you prefer." I hold out the bag of candy and the card.

Lilah regards the offering before she reaches out slowly and takes it from me. "You brought me candy?"

"The flower shop wasn't open; candy was the next best thing."

"But why buy me candy at all?"

"To apologize for kissing you when I shouldn't have."

She lifts the bag, inspecting it. "Where in the world did you find honey licorice beehives, and God . . . There are a ton of Hot Lips in here." She graces me with a small smile. "These were all my favorites."

"Except for Sour Keys, because they were out. I don't know if you like any of that stuff anymore or if you hate it like you seem to want to hate me, but I'd like another chance to find out, Lilah. I know I put a lot on you tonight and that you probably need some time, but I just want to know you again. I promise I'll keep my tongue to myself from now on, unless otherwise requested."

I'd apologize again, but I'm actually not all that sorry I kissed her. It confirmed what I already suspected, that the chemistry between us is still there. It gives me hope that if I'm careful, this friendship could eventually become more.

Lilah rolls her eyes, and her cheeks flush pink, but that small smile grows a little.

Instead of pushing my luck, I take a step back. "I'm going to go now."

It takes an extraordinary amount of restraint not to say anything else, to turn around and walk back to my truck with my hands jammed into my pockets and the tip of my tongue caught between my teeth.

"Ethan?" Lilah's voice is barely audible.

I turn but stay where I am, halfway between my truck and her door.

"Thank you for this." She clutches the bag close to her chest.

It's progress, like a quarter of a second shaved off my skating sprints—little gains that individually don't seem like much but over time add up to something significant.

chapter ten

HOT LIPS

Lilah

Everything okay?" Carmen calls from the patio.

"Everything's fine." I watch Ethan get into his truck—which is already running—and drive away before I head back outside, still holding the bag of candies and the card.

I flop into the chair and toss the candies on the side table, trading it for my margarita on the rocks. I have a rare late shift tomorrow, so I don't have to be up early. Still, it's my second drink, so I should switch to water after this, since Merk gets up at five thirty no matter what.

Carmen's smile grows as she nabs the bag. "What's this?"

"A bag of candy." I state the obvious, flipping the card between my fingers. My name is written in Ethan's rushed scrawl in what appears to be blue colored pencil.

"He bought you a bag of Hot Lips?"

"Among other things." I fight a smile as I slide my finger

along the edge of the envelope, careful not to tear it. Inside is a card with a sunset on the water. I flip it open.

The same messy scrawl in blue colored pencil covers the inside. This is exactly the kind of note I'd expect from Ethan.

Lilah,

I promise to keep my tongue to myself in the future. For now, these are the only hot lips I'll force on you.

Yours,
Ethan

PS. Your lips are still my favorite part of you.

"What does it say?" Carmen grabs for the card, but I hold it out of her reach. "I will eat every single one of these Hot Lips unless you show me what he wrote."

I hug the card to my chest. "You would not."

"Would, too."

"You hate Hot Lips," I argue.

"I'll still eat them." She scoops a handful of candy from the bag, as if to demonstrate her seriousness.

"And then barf."

"Just show me the damn card, or I'll dump the whole bag on the ground." She holds it up threateningly.

"Okay, okay!" I toss the card at her. "Now, gimme the candy."

She laughs and passes it to me. I covetously cradle it in my lap. I may be conflicted about Ethan, but I won't waste a bag of my favorite candies over it.

"Is this written in colored pencil?"

"Yup." I hide behind my glass so she can't see my scowl turn into a smile.

She's quiet as she reads the card. When she's done, she sets it on her lap and gives me an arched eyebrow. "Are you going to give him a chance?"

"I already said yes to being friends."

"And you want it to stay platonic?" She motions to the Hot Lips.

"I don't know that it can be more than that. He'll be traveling in a few weeks, so he won't even be in town half the time." I drop my head and give Carmen the truth I don't want to face with Ethan. "When his contract is up in a year, he'll be off to some other city, in some other state, unless Minnesota renews. I'm scared if I let him back into my world, he'll walk right out of it all over again." I have a life here, people I care about, a job I love, and a plan for my future. I was willing to follow him anywhere once, but now there's so much more to lose than just my heart.

"Or maybe he doesn't get traded and he stays. It kind of seems like that's what he's planning for, doesn't it?"

"Maybe." My worry is what he's planning for me. Us. I might not want to admit it, but as much as we've changed, the connection between us is still very much the same.

Two days later I find myself folding my hands around a travel coffee mug. "Come down to the water with me." Ethan's lips are at my ear, his voice soft.

While it's phrased as a statement, it comes out more like a question.

Martin is sitting in his lounger watching TV, and Jeannie is on the couch folding laundry. Progress is slow with Martin, but every step forward is a positive.

Ever since the kiss and our conversation, Ethan has given me space and time to process. Both things I needed. "Okay."

Ethan's smile is nervous and pleasantly surprised. "We're going down to the lake for a bit, Mom."

Jeannie looks up from the towel in her lap and smiles. "You kids have fun."

I follow Ethan down the path to the dock and we sit on the edge, dangling our feet in the cool water. Summer is fading quickly; the heat and humidity will disappear soon, replaced with fall's frosty fingers.

"I put in an offer on the Hoffman estate today." Ethan's arm brushes my shoulder as he settles beside me on the end of the dock.

"Oh! That's great! Why didn't you say anything until now?"

"I haven't told my parents yet. I want to see if the Hoffmans counteroffer first."

"Do you think they will?"

"Dunno. I lowballed, so we'll see if I offend them with my offer." His dimple appears below his eye, maybe pleased at the idea that he could offend the Hoffmans. We went to school with the kids—they drove expensive cars and acted like they were better than everyone else.

Ethan settling in Forest Lake when he could be in Saint Paul, closer to his teammates, seems significant, but I'm aware his father's health is a big part of this. It's not about me. "How long until you find out?"

"They have forty-eight hours, so it's a wait-and-see."

"I bet you'll be happy to have your own place again."

"Yeah. All I wanted as a kid was to have that basement to myself, and now that I do, I can't wait to get out of it."

"Funny how the things we want change, isn't it?"

"Not everything, though."

I'm not sure I'm quite ready to dive into what happened in the panic room yet, so I shift away from that topic. "How was practice today?"

"Good. Great even. The routine is kind of a relief, you know? It gives me a place to put my energy that isn't my dad or finding a house. The team has been really welcoming and it helps that I played with Josh Cooper when I was in LA. And this is familiar." He motions to the water and then me. "So that makes it easier, too."

I focus on the coffee cup clutched in my hands. Our unfinished conversation from two days ago hangs heavy between us.

Once this door opens, I can't close it, and I'm not even sure I want to anymore, which is terrifying.

"I'm sorry about the other day. I shouldn't have pushed you like that, especially not under the circumstances," he says softly.

"I get why you did."

"It doesn't make it okay. I just...want your forgiveness, even if I'm not sure I deserve it."

I make circles in the water with my toe, watching it ripple out. The water breaks against Ethan's ankle. "I shouldn't be holding something over your head that happened eight years ago. We've both had a life since then. It's unfair to keep harboring this anger. Like you said, we were kids."

"Don't diminish what I did to you, Lilah. It wasn't fair. The way I managed the end of us was shitty. You can be angry about that. You should be."

I set my cup beside me on the dock. "For a long time I was, but holding on to that anger doesn't do either of us any good."

His expression turns imploring and hopeful. "You have every right to guard your heart against me. I've earned your mistrust, and I'm under no illusion that my apologizing or explaining absolves me of the pain I've caused us both."

"But?" I prompt when his two deep breaths are followed by silence.

He trails his fingers down my cheek. It's like a blanket in winter, catching static. "Do you feel this the way I do anymore? Still? It seemed like maybe you did when I kissed you."

"Ethan—" Emotionally, I don't know if I'm prepared to

cross this line again, but physically, my body responds to his touch, warming me from the inside.

"What we had, I think it's rare. I didn't understand it back then. I wish I had—maybe it would've changed things. I don't know..." He trails off, fingertips tracing the contour of my bottom lip. "I know so much has changed and that it won't ever be the same as it was, but maybe we could try—maybe you could let me try."

I watch the bob of his throat, the way his tongue sweeps across his lip, and he cups my cheek in his palm. Anticipation makes my breathing shallow as he leans in and I mirror the movement to meet him. My heart might want to fight, but the rest of me wants to give in.

His warm breath washes over my lips, and he stills as the end of his nose brushes against mine. "Can I kiss you?" The words barely carry.

I tip my chin up in response, and then his mouth is on mine, softly, sweetly—at least at first. I taste penance in his gentleness. I feel his regret in the tender way his palm curves along my jaw, and I sense his need for forgiveness in the tentative stroke of his tongue.

As I absorb all of his emotions, I let them tangle and swirl with my own, until need and desire overthrow years of unmanaged anguish. Ethan's hand skims my side, grazing the swell of my breast before dropping lower to rest on my hip. It's been years since I've felt this kind of rush, the heat of desire detonating, sending a backdraft of want crashing into me.

Ethan must sense it, feel it in the same way I do, because we're suddenly both scrambling and frenzied. He drags me into his lap, positioning my legs on either side of his hips, hands roaming, skimming the spot on my ribs that always makes me jerk and giggle.

He bites my lip through a smile that fades as soon as I settle over his straining erection. We both groan and he cups my ass, pulling me tight against him. Fire rockets through my veins as I roll my hips, lust quickly spiraling out of control.

The sound of a porch door slamming reminds me that despite dusk having crept in, we're not alone.

"Ethan, you have a call from Josh."

I cringe and attempt to scramble out of his lap while he grips my hips to keep me where I am.

"Your mom can see us," I hiss.

"It's almost dark. We're just a blob," he replies, then calls out, "Can you tell him I'll call him back?"

"He'll be right up to take it!" I shout after him. It's better we stop before it gets out of hand. I don't know that I'll have the willpower to say no to him, not when the draw between us is so consuming.

"Okay. I'll tell him you'll just be a minute, then?" Jeannie calls back. I can hear the smile in her voice.

"No!" Ethan yells at the same time I say, "Yes."

"I'll tell him you'll call back," she says with a chuckle. The porch door slams again.

When I try to use his shoulders to push to a stand, Ethan

slides his hands under my skirt, fingers dragging over bare skin. "Stay right here with me, Lilah."

"Isn't Josh your team captain? Don't you need to call him back?"

"What I need is to kiss you again."

"What you need to do is tell me what exactly is happening here."

"Well, we were making out until we were cockblocked by Josh."

I'm not sure if he can see my arched brow in the waning sunlight. He slips his hands out from under my dress and cups my face in his palms, caressing my cheeks. His touch is all sweetness, sending a shiver down my spine. "Spend some time with me."

"Time?"

He nods. "I have a hard time believing I've been brought home and all of this"—he gestures to the house—"my dad's stroke, your divorce, my trade, doesn't mean something. I don't expect this to be what it was before, but if you can give me some time to get to know you, then maybe we can be something again." He looks so hopeful.

"Okay."

"I promise you won't regret it." His smile pops his dimple. "I'm still super fun to hang out with."

I laugh. I don't doubt that in the least, and if I'm honest with myself, I want to know the man in front of me just as much as he seems to want to know me, no matter how much it scares me.

My phone rings as I finish up with the cashier at the grocery store on Thursday afternoon. It's likely one of two people, my sister or Ethan—I'm betting on the latter. I answer on the second ring.

"Hey, beautiful, what're you doing?"

"Currently I'm leaving the grocery store."

"I mean tonight. Did you stock up on snack food? We should have a movie marathon. And FYI, carrot sticks and hummus don't qualify."

I laugh, but there are nerves under the humor. A movie marathon with Ethan would be both fun and dangerous—hours snuggling in the dark is something I'm not sure I'm quite prepared for. "It's a weeknight. I can't do a movie marathon."

It's been two weeks since I agreed to spend time with Ethan. While we haven't gone a day without speaking, we've only been out a few times beyond my stopping by his parents' place. Last week we went on a walk-through of the Hoffman house. They accepted his offer and he'll take possession next month. This time I stayed far away from the wine cellar, but we spent quite a while in the master bedroom, Ethan making jokes about wanting them to include the art hanging opposite the bed in the sale.

A few days ago Ethan showed up at my house unannounced, with flowers, to suggest going for a run with me and

Merk, likely because he knows I've been reluctant to be alone with him unless there's some activity that takes us out of the house.

Coffee dates are safe because other people are around. Ethan in my house is another story. Any kind of cuddling opportunities will most definitely lead to other activities, the kind that might result in missing clothes. Every time he touches me, an arc of electric need passes between us. It's becoming more difficult to resist the pull. I'm afraid I'm not strong enough to keep my emotions locked down if I give in to that need. So my super mature strategy so far has been avoidance.

"Okay. No midweek movie marathon. What about dinner?"

"The professor just posted the syllabus for my stats course that starts on Monday. I want to get started on the first assignment."

"That's almost as bad as telling me you're washing your hair."

"It's been a long time since I took stats and it was never my favorite. I want to stay on top of things."

"Feeding your body feeds your brain, Lilah. You can't learn effectively on an empty stomach. There are studies to support that."

"I just bought all these groceries. I have loads of food."

"Please? I won't keep you long. Have dinner with me. Spend some time with me. Exhibition games start soon and I want to get in as much time as I can with you between then and now."

I sigh. I want to bend for him. I want the time, as well, and that worries me. Exhibition games signal the beginning of the regular season, and that will mean more travel and less time.

"I know that sigh, Lilah." I can hear his smile.

"It'll be casual? I don't need to dress up?"

"Not unless you want to. Maybe I can help you study after dinner."

"I'm not taking human anatomy, FYI." Back when we were young, half the time *studying* was a euphemism.

"I'll pick you up in an hour." He ends the call before I can come up with a sassy retort.

I slip my phone in my purse and head toward my car, both excited and nervous about this date with Ethan. As I'm loading groceries into my trunk, I note movement in my peripheral vision. I adjust the cart so it's not in the way but freeze when I look up to find my ex-husband standing in front of me, holding hands with a girl—I'm not sure she's old enough to actually be classified as a woman.

"Delilah." He looks me over while my gaze bounces between him and his new girlfriend, or maybe he's become a Big Brother recently.

"Hi." The word draws out, the *i* extending so long it becomes awkward.

A pang makes my chest ache momentarily, sadness over the failure of our relationship, maybe a hint of jealousy over being traded in for a coed. I'm pretty sure she's not wearing a bra. Her bright yellow tank top screams YOLO across her chest.

It's paired with cutoffs so short the pockets hang out of the bottom.

"Angelica, this is Delilah, my ex-wife. Delilah, this is my girlfriend, Angelica." Avery gives me a tight, questioning smile.

I can be pleasant. Civil in the face of this awkwardness. Conversation between Avery and me had been limited to ironing out the legal aspects of the divorce and nothing else. Papers have been signed, assets were long ago divided. It's not this girl's fault that any of this has happened.

I drop the final bag into my trunk and extend a hand. Angelica takes it, smiling uncertainly. "It's uh... I've heard lots about you."

"I'm sure you have." I smile wryly. I wonder what awful things Avery has said about me.

"Why don't you go on inside. I'll be in in a minute." Avery gives her hand a reassuring squeeze and presses his lips to her temple, whispering something that dissolves the worry on Angelica's face.

"Okay. It was nice meeting you." She still sounds a little uncertain as to whether that's true or not, but she lifts her hand in a wave and flounces to the entrance.

I glance over my shoulder, noting that her shorts barely cover her butt, before I turn back to Avery with one brow raised. "Can she vote?"

"Be nice, Delilah." Avery's smile is dry, though.

"It's a legitimate question. How old is she?"

"She's of legal drinking age."

"So you can do body shots at the night club—that's fun."

His lips flatten in a thin line. "She's sweet and uncomplicated, which is what I need right now."

I feel the sharpness of that statement cut across my heart. Our relationship was a huge, difficult complication in both of our lives near the end—and maybe before that. "I'm sorry— that was petty and uncalled for."

"It is, especially considering." He looks away, maybe to hide his own hurt.

"Considering what?"

"Come on, Delilah—it's all over the local papers." Avery's exasperation is something I'm all too familiar with.

"What're you talking about?"

"You and Ethan Kase. It's not like there's any real news in this town for people to focus on. There've been all kinds of pictures of the two of you together since he moved back."

"I've been helping him with his father. Martin had a stroke." I'd forgotten how little there is to pay attention to in this town.

Avery gives me a sad smile. "I don't know why you think you need to lie to me about this, but I hope whatever is going on between you works out this time, because Christ knows no matter what I did, I couldn't ever compete with him."

I shake my head. "Compete? It wasn't—"

"I thought with time you'd get over him, that I could

love you enough to make up for him leaving, but that never happened."

"That's not why we didn't work." As I say it, I have to question if it's true.

He sighs. "You never let him go, Delilah. Not him, not his family."

"They were my family, too. They were there for me when mine fell apart."

"I would've been there, if you would've let me." Avery rubs his chin on a sigh. "You don't need to defend your relationship with Jeannie and Martin, who I'm very sorry about, by the way. I know how important they are to you and that they always have been. But they took precedence over me. It was hard not to be jealous of that. And it was impossible to compete with a memory. So for now I need something simple. Angelica doesn't have the baggage we do. She's happy to make me the center of her world, and that's what I want to be. I hope this time around you won't hold back with Ethan the way you always held back with me."

"Avery, I—"

"I'm not saying this to be hurtful. Just try to allow yourself to be loved the way I wanted to love you."

I see so clearly, as I look at this man I spent all those years with, how I broke his heart. Maybe the same way Ethan broke mine. "I'm so sorry."

"I'm not blaming you. I just wanted you to be happy. I wanted to be able to give that to you, and I was caught up in trying to find a way to hold on to your heart, even though it was never going to be mine. It took me longer than it should've to figure that out." He swallows thickly and blows out a breath. "Anyway. I shouldn't keep Angelica waiting. Take care of yourself."

"You, too, Avery."

He gives my arm a gentle squeeze, and I grip his forearm, giving him pause.

"I'm sorry."

"Me, too."

I release his arm, watching him walk away. My knees feel weak as I sink into the driver's seat. I take several deep breaths, still reeling from his frankness and his honesty. More than that, I'm saddened by the clarity of his truths.

He's right, though, about everything. When we first started dating, I was so taken by how enamored he was with me. I'd been validated by his need for me and it had given me purpose again. But I still held back. I never gave him my heart, because it wasn't free to give. It was tied up in someone else, in a love I'd lost and couldn't let go of.

I have another chance. I can allow Ethan to dance around the periphery of my heart—the one he left a hole in all those years ago, or I can let him in and give him a chance to fill that void.

It's terrifying, the thought of opening myself to his love again. But I'll regret it if I don't.

chapter eleven

TRY

Ethan

I show up at Lilah's doorstep five minutes early with treats
for Merk and a bag from the local bakery containing
breakfast for tomorrow. Before I can lift my hand to knock,
Merk comes rushing to the door, tail wagging, barking
happily.

"Come on in!" Lilah shouts from somewhere in the house.

As soon as I let myself in Merk runs around in a circle, then
drops his butt on my foot and nudges my hand with his nose,
looking for pets. "You need help getting dressed?" I call out
and open my palm so Merk can get his treat. He takes it gently
and runs off to his bed in the living room to enjoy it.

I've been well behaved since our talk, not pushing for anything physical even though it's damn well killing me. I don't
think I've gone through so much lotion and so many boxes of
tissues since I was in high school. It's almost embarrassing.

"I'll be down in a minute!" Lilah calls back.

I haven't been up to her bedroom yet. In fact, most of the time when I come by her place we don't stick around long. I think being alone with me makes her nervous. When it's just us, it's hard to ignore the sexual tension, and it's becoming increasingly difficult for me to resist doing something to alleviate it. But I'm determined to be patient. I don't want to ruin this new start with her, not when I've been without her for so many years.

I look up at the sound of heels on the stairs. I let out a low whistle when Lilah comes into view, taking in the strappy sandals, skimming my gaze over her tanned, toned calves to where the hem of her sundress stops a few inches above her knees. It's pale yellow, buttery and warm like sunshine, with thin straps that tie behind her neck.

"You look delicious." A flash of gold catches my attention. A thin bangle with a hockey charm circles her wrist—I gave it to her a month after we started dating. I'd used all the money I'd saved to buy it for her. "You still have th—" My smile drops and my question dies when I meet her gaze, though, because as gorgeous as she may be, something's wrong. It's in the slight waver of her smile, the barely noticeable quiver in her chin, the way she clutches the banister, and the soft glassiness in her eyes.

"Baby? What's wrong?"

She lifts a shaky hand to her lips and turns her head to the side. A tiny laugh turns into what sounds a lot like a stifled sob. I set the bag of baked goods on the side table and take the stairs three at a time to reach her. Even on the step below her I'm half a head taller, but at least we're close to eye level.

I cup her face in my palms. "What happened?"

She covers my hands with hers, lids lowered as she takes a few deep breaths. "He was right."

"Who was? What're you talking about?" My stomach knots at the mention of another guy.

Her lids drift open. "How did you know something was wrong?"

"Seriously, Lilah? I spent more time with you than anyone else for over a decade. No amount of time changes the fact that I know you. Who is *he*? What was he right about?"

She searches my face for a few moments before she finally answers. "I saw Avery."

"What? When?" She's already signed the divorce papers—he can't have her now. I take a step back and almost lose my footing, having forgotten we're standing on the stairs.

I grab the banister to prevent us both from taking a header.

"When I was leaving the grocery store. He was with his new girlfriend."

I watch her face carefully. I'm familiar with the subtle nuances of her emotions—changes in breathing, the way she bites her lip, touches her face, shifts her weight, fiddles with her hair—but I'm uncertain how to gauge her sadness and whether it's in direct relation to her ex having someone new in his life. "And how did that go?"

"It was fine." She pauses, maybe reconsidering her answer,

because it's not quite the truth based on the threat of tears. "Awkward. He introduced me as his ex-wife. I felt bad for her. She's young."

"Was that hard for you?"

"To see him with someone who's barely able to vote?"

I'd like to think the sarcasm means she's not that upset, but I'm aware that sometimes it's a defense mechanism. "To see him with someone else period. Was that hard?"

Lilah sinks down, smoothing the skirt of her dress.

"I felt...sad. Not because we're not together anymore, but because I couldn't love him the way I should've. He's not a bad man. Sometimes he was difficult, but it makes sense now why. I can see things clearly where I couldn't before."

I nod, as if I understand, but I don't. None of my relationships since Lilah have had any real depth, and the few that shifted from strictly casual into real-feelings territory never had the opportunity to grow into something substantial, because I'd moved to another team before they ever could.

Lilah is my relationship baggage and likely the reason why I've never gotten as far as she did with anyone else. "You said he was right. Can you tell me what about?"

Lilah blows out a slow breath. "That I never really got over you. That I didn't move on and I didn't let him in. That he couldn't compete with the memory of you."

"He said this to you in front of his new girlfriend?" That's one way to end a new relationship fast.

Lilah shakes her head. "No. She went into the grocery store

and he stayed to talk for a minute. He wasn't trying to be mean or hurtful. He mentioned seeing pictures of us together in the local paper. He said he hoped I wouldn't hold back with you the way I did with him." She looks up at the ceiling, chin trembling as she fights against tears that want to fall.

I kneel in front of her and clasp her hands in mine. "Listen, baby, he's probably just having a hard time——"

Lilah gives her head a quick shake. "He's right. I am holding back, like I did with him. And if I'm honest with myself, I probably never should've married him in the first place."

"Then why did you?"

"Because I thought maybe at some point I could love him back the way he seemed to love me. I wanted to be able to. I thought I tried, but now, looking back . . . I don't know. I think I locked my heart away because I was scared to have it broken again, so instead I ended up breaking his." Tears track down her cheeks and drop to her dress.

"Don't do that to yourself, Lilah. You can't own all the blame."

She pulls her hands from mine to brush away the tears. "But I am to blame. I took what he gave and I never gave back the way he needed me to. I don't want to do that again. I don't want to jeopardize this, not when you're right here and wanting to try with me again."

This is why I've been so patient with her. No matter how valid my reason for walking out of her life all those years ago, it doesn't erase my absence or the pain I caused. I have to earn my place in her life and her heart. "I know you're afraid. I understand why."

"The season starts soon. You'll be away a lot. This whole thing scares me." She curves her palm along my jaw, and I see the shift in her, the sudden resolve. "But I won't risk losing you again because I can't handle my own feelings. I'm going to try my hardest not to safeguard my heart anymore. I know you're being patient. I know it's not easy."

"You say it like you think I'm not tenacious enough to persevere."

She gives me a real smile. "You've always been astoundingly tenacious."

"I don't know about that. But for you I'll be whatever you need me to." I run my finger from the bridge of her nose to the tip.

She closes her eyes, dragging in an unsteady breath. I give in to the desire to trace the contour of her perfect, pouty bottom lip.

When her eyes open again, the sadness has disappeared, replaced by uncertain longing. Her eyes drop to my mouth, lips parting as I repeat the action.

"Ethan." It comes out on a breathless sigh. The shift from serious to needy is palpable. "I think you deserve some kind of merit badge for patience. A reward even."

I tilt my head, returning the smile. "What kinda reward we talkin' 'bout?"

As intense as the attraction is between us, there's a playfulness there, too. I missed this about her—the sweet sexiness, the sometimes brazen way she'd taunt me. "The kind we'll both like."

I slide my palms along the outside of her thighs until my fingertips reach the hem of her dress. Lilah pulls me closer, until our noses brush. I savor this moment, the short seconds in which the anticipation becomes heady intoxication, where sensation is heightened, and need and desire envelop us.

The press of her fingernails against the back of my neck becomes a sharp sting as I skim the sensitive skin at the back of her knees. A shiver runs through her and she arches, lips barely touching mine. I part her knees, making room for myself between her thighs.

Lilah's breath comes faster and she drags her palm from my shoulder to my elbow, encouraging me to move my hand higher. The whole time I'm working to process and memorize every single sensation, because this is what I've been waiting for.

When our lips meet again, it's soft and unsure. I taste the faint vanilla of her lip balm and the sweetness of cinnamint toothpaste when her tongue sweeps out. I meet the gentle stroke, that warm, wet tangle tentatively at first. But that tender reconnection quickly unravels as the lightning bolt of lust hits us.

Lilah moans, the hum across my lips shooting straight through to the base of my spine to my cock. She hooks a leg around my hip, seeking to unite more than just our mouths.

Our chests meet, too many layers of fabric preventing the kind of contact both of us are looking for. Lilah tilts her head to the side, angling back, opening wider as I stroke inside her mouth, drowning in the taste of her, the feel of her body melding to mine. I run my hand up her thigh, fingertips grazing lacy fabric, sliding under to grip the swell of her ass and drag her forward so my erection can provide the friction we seek.

I know why she's been holding back—because this is how we've always been together, this frantic desperation, need, and want that overpower, steamrolling logic and reality until it's about being connected in the most primal, visceral way.

Lilah breaks the kiss long enough to pull my shirt over my head, and then her mouth is fused to mine again, nails raking down my chest, hips pushing hard into mine and dropping just as quickly so she can work my belt buckle free.

I groan into her mouth when she palms me through the fabric. I consider that it might be a good idea to relocate to a bed, but then she pops the button and drags the zipper down, slipping her hand inside.

I pull at the tie behind her neck, and the top of her dress falls to expose a strapless bra. Reaching behind her, I flick the clasp and free her breasts. I want to put my mouth everywhere, touch every part of her, savor her, but we're both beyond desperate. Lilah shoves her panties over her hips and I sit back on my knees so I can help yank them off. And then I'm right where I want to be again, my erection sliding along soft, smooth skin, wet and hot and so achingly familiar.

"Condom?" I ask between kisses. I fumble for my wallet, stuck in the back pocket of my dress pants—which I'm still wearing.

"Pill."

I lean back enough so I can focus on her face. "You want me to go without?"

"Can you?" Those two words hold a million questions.

I haven't gone in bare since Lilah. I've always been safe. Always taken care of myself and my partners in the years between then and now. "Yes."

"Then please."

I slide low and enter her on a slow stroke. This feeling, being with her, surrounded by her, enveloped by her—it's fucking bliss. I keep my eyes on hers, watch the way her mouth drops open, relish the soft moan that passes as warm breath across my lips.

After a few seconds of stillness, in which we both adjust to newness fusing with familiarity, Lilah pulls my mouth back to hers and circles her hips. I move with her, reclaiming her body, more aware than I've ever been that she was mine first before anyone else.

Lilah's moans turn into guttural pleas not to stop, to *please, please, please, Ethan* as I pump into her. And then she's coming, eyes locked on mine, soul swimming to the surface as she shudders and clamps tight around me.

And I know now why I never found anyone else who compared to her, why she never let me go, because she's meant to be mine just as I'm meant to be hers. She's still pulsing around me when I come viciously, violently, kissing her hard, pushing as deep as I can, getting as far inside as her body will allow.

When the white-hot heat in my spine dissipates, I push up on one arm, taking in Lilah's flushed cheeks and kiss-swollen lips. "You okay?"

She blinks and glances around, so I do the same, taking stock of our surroundings. We're sprawled out on the stairs like a couple of drunk teenagers who couldn't be bothered to make it to a bedroom or a flat surface.

Lilah laughs and I echo the sound.

I give her a wry smile. "Well, that sure as hell lacked finesse."

"I haven't come like that in forever, so don't worry about finesse."

Her legs slide off my hips, one of her heels tumbling down the stairs. I can't believe they managed to stay on this entire time.

"I owe you foreplay." I grab the banister and sit back on my knees, taking in the vision of woman before me. Her pale dress is pooled around her waist, soft, round breasts still heaving with panted breaths, legs spread wide, my cock still inside her.

"I'll take that in a bed. After dinner."

I run my hands up her bare thighs. "Are you inviting me to spend the night?"

"I don't know if that's a good idea. I have to work in the morning, and I'm a little worried that if you stay, I won't be allowed to sleep."

"You think I'll keep you up all night?"

She laughs and then groans when I graze the junction of her thighs with my thumbs. I slide them back and forth, along the slick skin, edging closer to her clit with each pass. I'm still keyed up. Going another round won't be a problem. Relocating might be a good idea. But I'm too enthralled by the way she's stretched around me, pretty clit all swollen.

I pull out until I can see the ridge at the head. I glance up to find her eyes trained on the same place. They flip to mine when I don't move to either pull all the way out or push back in.

"Maybe you should show me your bedroom now, and we can do dinner later," I suggest.

"That might be a good idea."

I push back in, smiling at her gasp. "Wrap your legs around my waist, baby, and hold on."

Lilah's arms circle my neck as I grip two handfuls of ass and pick her up. I quickly adjust my pants so they don't trip me on the way to her bed.

"Second door on your right," Lilah says while kissing a path from my shoulder to my neck.

It's a modest room, the bed only a double, the headboard one I recognize from her room as a teenager. The comforter is feminine, different from what she used to like when she was younger and a tomboy.

I shove the throw pillows out of the way and pull back the covers. "I hope you have some clean sheets. You're gonna need to change these by the time we're done."

"Planning to get dirty on me, are you?" Lilah bites her lip through a smile of giddy anticipation.

"Fuck yes, I am."

I climb up on the bed with Lilah still wrapped around me, moving us to the center. I push the pillows into a pile behind her and take a moment to pull her dress over her head so she's naked. A bikini tan line frames her breasts and the triangle between her legs, the rest of her skin sun kissed.

I dip my head and capture a nipple, tonguing it. Lilah gasps and arches. Unhooking her legs from my hips, she spreads them as I sit back on my heels. "I know what you're going to do." Her grin is devious, tongue peeking out to wet her bottom lip.

"Do you, now?" I run my hand up the inside of her thighs, spreading them even wider.

She nods. Trailing a single finger down her stomach, she circles her clit and goes lower, until she skims the place where we're connected.

"Why don't you tell me, then?"

"You're going to pull almost all the way out."

I keep my hands on the inside of her thighs, holding her open as I shift my hips back until just the head is inside her. "Like this?"

"Exactly like that."

"And then what am I going to do?"

"You're gonna tease me, like you do."

"Is that right?" I push in a couple of inches, eyes still fixed where we're connected. "I used to love watching my cock disappear inside you."

"I'm not sure that's changed much." Her eyes move over my body in a hot sweep, one that I can almost feel as if it were her hands.

This time when I pull out all the way, she bucks up, chasing what I'm taking away. I keep her spread wide, and she props herself on an elbow so we have the same view. I nudge at the opening with the tip, teasing like she expects me to. My cock is coated in both of us, and the next time I give her a couple of inches and pull out, the hand resting near her hip slides down and she pushes two fingers inside. Her eyes flutter closed, head falling back as her mouth drops open.

She pushes deeper until the remnants of our desperate fuck drips down her sex.

"Fucking Christ, Lilah."

She laughs and then gasps as I move in closer, edging one knee against her inner thigh so I can free a hand. Turning it palm up, I ease a single finger in alongside hers, following the slow steady pump, curling my finger against hers so we can apply more pressure to that place inside that makes her gasp and arch.

"I want you to come like this, with both of us finger

fucking you, and then I'm going to make you come with my mouth before I get inside you again."

Lilah moans and her next finger curl is fast and hard. "God, I missed your dirty mouth."

She withdraws her fingers, making room for more of mine while she circles her clit. Her movements grow less fluid and more aggressive as the edge of bliss closes in. Her elbow gives out and her back bows, her high-pitched moan the most delicious sound.

She's barely over the crest of the orgasm as I adjust my position, stretching out on the bed, shouldering my way between her thighs. I brush her fingers away and latch on to her still-throbbing clit, sucking hard. "Oh fuck, oh fuck, *oh fuck*," she chants on a scream.

I lick and suck, fuck her with my tongue, lost in the taste of her, the feel of her against my mouth, and the sound of her need, memories becoming a new present.

Her thighs try to close, body writhing under me as I draw the orgasm out, building it back up, pushing her higher and higher, until she's crashing down again, fingers tight in my hair as she bucks against my mouth.

The rigid arc of her body becomes a languid puddle, and I place a soft kiss on her clit, then trail a path up her stomach, pausing at her nipples before I reach her mouth.

I drop my hips, the head of my cock sliding over her sensitive skin, and then I'm pushing inside her again, feeling the still-present pulse from the waning orgasm.

Lilah gasps and those fingers of hers tighten in my hair. When my lips touch hers, she moans, licking at my mouth, the slide of her tongue aggressive and searching.

I pull back, cupping her face. "Can you taste yourself?"

"Yes." Her legs tighten around my waist.

"Are you getting off on it?"

"Didn't I always?" Her smile is full of heated mischief. "I want to ride you this time."

"Anything for you." I flip us over and she takes my mouth again, long hair shadowing her face. Eventually she sits back, palms flat on my chest as she grinds over me. The lean lines of youth have turned into lush curves.

"You're so beautiful." I hold her hips, helping her rock.

"So are you." She bends to kiss me.

When we come, it's within seconds of each other, but I'm privileged to watch her fall first.

chapter twelve

DATES

Lilah

If there was any question as to whether the chemistry between us had faded over the years, it's certainly been put to rest over the weeks leading up to the exhibition games.

I honestly have no idea how Ethan and I ever got anything accomplished back when we were in high school and hormonal impulses dominated any kind of rationality. I'm currently using lunch breaks and the nights he has practice or team meetings to keep up with course work.

Tomorrow morning Ethan gets on a plane for his first exhibition game away from home, which will give me much-needed study time, but it comes with a price: Ethan's anxiety. He's very much a creature of habit when it comes to prepractice and game rituals—even exhibition games. He doesn't like that he can't follow the ones he's already set in place—which usually include a good luck kiss from me. There's a lot riding on this game for him, and Ethan stresses most about his away-game performances because he doesn't have the comfort and familiarity of home ice. I worry he's going to give in to the superstitions he sometimes gets hung up on.

Tonight Ethan has something special planned—maybe as a distraction from his anxiety. I figured we'd stay in, I'd wear a pair of his favorite boxers for good luck, and we'd order takeout and have one of our marathon sex nights. But he's excited about whatever he has set up, so instead of luring him inside, I step out onto the front porch as soon as I hear him pull into the driveway.

As I walk toward the truck, he jumps out, hands behind his back. "I have something for you."

"Oh?" I pause and grin.

He produces a bouquet of flowers in one hand and a bag of candy in the other.

"What are you apologizing for now?"

He gives me a look. "I'm not apologizing for anything. I'm taking you out on a date and I thought you might be out of Hot Lips, so I got you more, but if you don't want them..." He makes a move to throw them back in the truck.

"No, no! I want them."

"I knew you would." He hides them behind his back again when I reach for them. "A kiss first."

I wrap my arms around his neck and give him a soft peck on the cheek.

"Not good enough. I need your hot lips on mine."

I laugh, but he wraps his arms around me, and our mouths

meet, the kiss soft at first and then needy. It goes on long enough that I think maybe we won't be going out after all, but he disengages and presents me with my gifts. "Why don't you run those inside and I'll stay here."

"You sure you don't want to come in for a few minutes?"

"I'm sure."

He waits while I put the flowers and candy in the house and out of Merk's reach. I grab a few Hot Lips on the way out the door. Ethan meets me around the passenger side, pausing to kiss me again, much more chastely, before he helps me into the truck. Once I'm buckled in, he rounds the hood and hops behind the wheel. He's wearing dark-wash jeans and a green shirt, the sleeves of which hug his biceps in the most delectable way.

"You look nice." He gives me a lingering once-over, gaze traveling from my sandals up my bare calf to the hem of my dress. Summer is fading, the nights growing steadily cooler, so I've brought along a wrap to cover my bare shoulders.

"So do you." I fiddle with the bangle on my wrist, playing with the charm as I glance at him. I only take it off for work these days. Ethan thinks it's a talisman of luck when I wear it. Much like the dual set of dog tags hanging from the rearview mirror, boasting his jersey number—I had them made for him back in high school, and I recently had a new set made prior to the first exhibition game this season. "You're sure you want to go out tonight?"

Ethan stretches his arm across the seat, fingertips brushing along my collarbone as he reverses out of the driveway. "Yes, and don't worry—we'll still have lots of time to get naked later. I promise."

"I'm not worried. I'm just wondering how difficult dinner is going to be with you sporting that." I point at the very obvious erection pushing at the fly of his jeans.

"It'll go away."

I shrug and cross my legs, smoothing out my skirt when it rides up, drawing attention to my legs. Ethan is an ass man, but he loves legs almost as much. They get him all riled up, especially when the only thing covering them is a flippy skirt. And panties that can be just as easily pulled down. Those might be in my purse at the moment—he's not the only one who can be a tease.

"How are you feeling about tomorrow?"

He taps on the steering wheel and bites his lip. "Excited but nervous."

"Because it's away from home?"

He nods. "I know my dad is doing a lot better, but I worry about my mom managing on her own."

"I'm here to help, and Jeannie knows that."

"I know. And I appreciate it. I just don't want anything to happen while I'm gone."

"He'll be fine. You focus on the game, exactly like you have been. I know it's daunting, but you're going to be amazing. Just remember that everyone is already talking about how well you're playing."

"Yeah, that's the thing, though. I'm worried I'm going to get out there and mess up. I just want to prove I can play off home ice."

"You will."

He nods but doesn't say anything else. He needs to see for himself that he can do it. He makes a left onto a back road that takes us out of town.

"Where're we going?"

He gives me a secretive smile. "You'll see. It's a surprise."

Ethan has been big on surprises lately. Particularly since the night I finally stopped fighting my feelings.

Simplicity has always been the best way to get my attention, such as the bouquet of wild daisies that appeared in my locker at work, exactly like the ones he picked for me when we were kids, a bag of Hot Lips tucked into my purse, one of his old high school shirts that still fits me but was hilariously small on him folded neatly in my pajama drawer. Every gift is a reminder of what we've been through together and how well he still knows me.

Earlier this week, he picked me up after work and took me to Cosmo's for sandwiches. We sat at our table in the corner, my foot hooked behind his calf as we ate, and for once he actually made an attempt to help me study. Mostly it was me explaining things, but the effort was sweet on his part. Ethan loathed statistics in high school, and the only ones he enjoys now pertain to hockey.

I'm curious as to where exactly he's decided to take me

tonight. On our way out of town, we pass a few familiar farms. We used to come this way to go to the drive-in or the theater in Minneapolis. It took a little longer, but then there was a reason behind the scenic route.

"Remember the first time I gave you road head?"

Ethan glances at me, then shifts his attention back to the road, a smile tugging at the corner of his mouth. "That's quite the conversation starter."

"You were so excited. It seemed like such a good idea at the time. Get you off before we got home so we could have more sex." I ponder that for a moment. "Or maybe that was some excuse you fed me because you really wanted road head. It wasn't like you couldn't go forever back then."

"I can still go forever," Ethan says defensively.

"You've got stamina, maybe not eighteen-year-old jack-rabbit stamina, but the professional-hockey-playing kind, and that's almost the same."

"I have way more finesse than I did back then—that has to count for something."

"Oh? You think you have finesse now?" I'm playing with him, obviously.

Ethan arches a brow. "You can't tell me if I'd come inside your place tonight that we wouldn't have been naked on the closest available surface within five minutes."

I give him the same brow back. "Wow, you either overestimate your irresistibility factor, or you underestimate my self-control."

"You're the one who mentioned road head, not me."

"Any hints on where we're going?" I inspect my nails.

"Subtle, Lilah."

"I hope it's nowhere windy." I bite the inside of my cheek to stop from smiling as I wait for him to take the bait.

His brow furrows. "Why would you be worried about wind?"

"Oh, I don't know." I lift a shoulder and let it fall. "Maybe because I'm not wearing underwear."

"Bullshit." He glances at my lap, and his eyes stay there long enough that he starts to veer over the yellow line.

"Steady there." I nod at the windshield.

Ethan pulls back into his lane. "I want to see."

"It's not a good idea for you to take your eyes off the road. It's dangerous, don't you think? Besides"—I poke at the lump still jacking up the front of his pants—"you already seem to have an embarrassing problem that doesn't want to go away. If I confirm my pantilessness, I'm potentially setting you up for an indecent-exposure charge."

Ethan hits the brakes and makes a hard right. At first I think we're taking a detour through a field, but then I realize he's taken one of the dirt tracks we sometimes made use of pre- or postmovie date. How the hell he managed to see it, I'll never know. He pulls in about twenty feet and shifts into park.

Before I can react, Ethan punches the button to release my seat belt. "Show me." He's right in my face, almost on top of me.

I push on his chest. "Sit back."

It's only seven, and while the sun is starting to tuck itself below the horizon earlier these days, it's still light out, which means there are no shadows to obscure his view yet. Shifting so my back is to the door, I set my left foot on the seat. Opening my legs wide, I lift my skirt so Ethan can see I'm very much telling him the truth.

"Fucking Christ, Lilah."

I shriek when he grabs behind my knees and drags me across the seat, my head bumping the window and the armrest on the way.

His focus shifts from between my legs. "You okay?"

I nod. "Fine."

He smiles. "You're about to be a whole lot better than fine."

Ethan's hands slide up the inside of my thighs, holding them wide as he dips down, tonguing a path from my entrance to my clit, where he latches on and sucks.

The hot press and suction send a welcome shock of pleasure through my body. I brace one hand on the dash and grab the headrest with the other, slinging my leg over the seat to give Ethan more room. He's so tall and broad, shoulders taking up all the space between the seat and the dash.

I come hard and fast, my foot slipping and my heel hooking the steering wheel. I'm barely over the crest of my orgasm when Ethan lifts his head, licking his lips as one corner of his mouth turns up a smirk.

"Fuck. Just look at you. Still so fucking naughty, aren't

you? Getting in my truck with no panties on." Ethan slips a hand behind my neck, stroking softly along my throat with his thumb. At the same time he mirrors the movement between my legs, fingertips skimming my clit, sliding lower. And then he's pushing two fingers inside, curling up and in, hitting that sweet spot.

"Kiss me," I moan, wanting the taste of me on his tongue while he finger fucks me.

He shakes his head. "Not yet."

"Ethan." It's whiny and embarrassing.

His eyes lift from where his fingers slide in and out. He leans in until his mouth is a few inches from mine. He tightens his grip on the back of my neck so I can't crane to reach him. "Such a greedy girl. Aren't you already getting what you want?"

"Almost." It's hard to concentrate on any one thing with the way he's touching me, how intense his eyes are, and how close, but out of reach, his mouth is. I feel lost in the ocean of blue, in the burst of amber, a late summer sunrise cresting his iris.

"Almost? This isn't enough for you? I was trying to be good tonight, take you out, make you feel special, appreciated. I'm trying to date you here, Lilah, and then you have to pull this no-panties trick and shred my self-control." His mouth is closer now, less than an inch away. "You like to do that, don't you? To see how much you can push until I break."

"Yes." My admission is more moan than word.

The scent of his cologne fills my lungs. His fingers move faster, harder, more insistent inside me, until I'm on the precipice, teetering on the edge. And then I'm free-falling, nerve endings lit up, intense pleasure dominating, Ethan's name a worship tumbling from my lips.

His eyes are dark, hot with need. He slips his fingers into my mouth and our gazes stay locked as I sweep my tongue along the length. His guttural groan sends another wave of desire through me, and I suck hard, then bite his fingers. He withdraws them, crushing his mouth to mine, biting my lip and then my tongue in punishment when I push past his.

I've never wanted like this. Never felt this level of desperation with anyone but him. Ethan hits the button on the glove compartment and fumbles around while I fight with the button on his pants.

He bangs his head on the roof when he folds back on his knees, tearing open a condom.

"Why do we need that?"

"Too much of a mess otherwise."

I stop him before he can position it over the tip and roll it on. "Come in my mouth."

"I don't want a blow job. I want you to ride me." He's gripping his erection in his fist; the bead of wetness pooling at the tip spills over, trailing down the head.

"Oh, I plan to. You tell me when it's time, and I'll manage the mess." I straddle his thighs, wrap my hand around his, and guide him to me.

His head falls back, mouth dropping open, eyes fluttering shut as he sheaths himself in me. "Fuck, fuck, *fuck*, so good." His lids flip open, eyes finding mine in the shadows cast by the field and the trees now blocking the slowly setting sun. "It's always only been you—you know that, right? Nothing compares to this feeling. I should never have let you go in the first place."

With a roll of my hips I lean in and brush my lips over his. "You have me now. We'll make up for all that lost time."

We kiss slow and fuck slower at first, but the tenderness fades, desire its usurper. I brace one palm on his shoulder and the other on the roof above me to prevent my head from hitting it, thanks to the vigorous thrusting.

The skirt of my dress is an obstruction to Ethan's view, something he isn't particularly fond of. Pulling the tie at my neck, he shoves the top down, along with my bra, then tucks the skirt into the fabric. Holding my hips, he pumps into me, helping me ride him.

"I'm close, are you?"

"Yes." I drop a hand between my thighs and rub my clit, voracious in my quest for yet another orgasm when I've already had my fair share. I'm aware that he won't be here to provide any for the next two days, but having this many in a row won't ease the need for him in the slightest.

I'm still pulsing when he tells me it's time. I keep grinding, ignoring his warning.

A flash of headlights through the back window draws my

attention. I note another vehicle pulling up behind us on the dirt track. It takes a moment for me to realize it's a police vehicle—cherries unflashing and siren silent.

"Shit." I rise up as the vehicle comes to a stop and the driver's side door swings open.

"It's too late." Ethan grips my hips and tries to get back inside me before he comes.

"We have company."

Ethan swears, body no longer under his control as the orgasm steals his coordination and makes his mind a blank space capable of only one sensation.

A hot burst of wetness soaks the inside of my thighs. So much for not making a mess.

chapter thirteen

CATCH

Ethan

"There's an officer, Ethan."

Her words are slow to compute through the orgasm buzz. "What?"

Lilah's eyes are wide, her hands covering mine on her hips. I realize she's trying to pry them off. "Police car!"

I glance down to where she's barely hovering over my still-pulsing cock. Fuuuck. Well, that's a right mess. It'd be a hot one if we weren't about to get caught. I release Lilah and she flops down on the passenger seat. She quickly fixes her bra, pulls her dress back into place, and fans her hair across her shoulders.

I have no choice but to tuck myself into my boxers, which are just as much a mess as the inside of Lilah's thighs. That image is going to be coming with me on my away game tomorrow, and probably until the end of time.

I glance at Lilah as I zip my fly, noting the heat in her cheeks and the wet spots appearing on her skirt. "Oh my

God," she mutters, running her fingers through her tousled strands in an attempt to put herself back in order. She grabs her purse and sets it in her lap to cover the mess.

"Don't worry. I got this," I tell her, just as the officer knocks on my window.

I roll it down and smile with relief when I recognize him as a member of Lilah's class in high school. I rack my brain for his name and manage to siphon it out of my memory.

"Hey, Luke." I try my best to come off as nonchalant, but the fogged-up windows aren't much help. Neither is the smell of sex wafting out, I'm sure.

Luke's bored, slightly put-out expression changes to surprised amusement. "Ethan Kase? Well, shit, man! Congrats on the trade. Nice to have you playing on the right team for once."

"It's nice to be home," I reply, meaning it.

He holds out his hand and I reach to take it but make a fist instead. "Props might be a better idea. I, uh…need to wash my hands."

Lilah slaps me on the arm closest to her and mutters my name. Her eyes are comically wide, face turning an incredible shade of red. Lilah makes a choking sound and goes back to sitting all prim-like, legs crossed over each other, purse clutched in her lap.

"DJ?" Luke's smile falters as his eyes flare and understanding dawns.

She lifts her hand in a wave, voice cracking a little. "Hi, Luke. How're you?"

"Good. Yeah. You're looking...well." He scratches at the edge of his collar, seeming a little uncomfortable now.

"Thanks; you're looking well, too." She lifts a hand as if she's going to tuck her hair behind her ear but then thinks better of it. It's a nervous habit. I'm sure getting caught is part of the reason, but I suspect there's more, particularly considering the way he's looking at her—with a mixture of something like possessiveness and disappointment.

"Job at Fairview going well, then?" he asks tightly. It's at this moment I remember why I'm not fond of Luke. He had a thing for Lilah in high school. I'm pretty sure he was going to ask her out, but then I made it clear we were a thing, and he had no choice but to back off.

"Really good. Your sister and I work the same shift sometimes. She's a real sweetie, great with the patients."

He grins. "Yeah, she's real good at taking care of people, just like you."

Okay. I'm about done with the high school–crush, let's-catch-up chitchat. "What can we do for you, Luke?"

His attention returns to me, eyes narrowed, lips pressed into a line. "Got a call a little while ago about a truck out here in McFarlane's field. Said it'd been here a long time, more than half an hour. It's a popular place for teenagers looking for some privacy. Course you don't need that, since DJ's house isn't far. Guessing you decided to take a trip down memory lane." His derision makes me bristle.

"Remember when we all came out here in senior year with

those bottles of peach schnapps?" Lilah cuts in, her attempt to calm the testosterone storm raging between us obvious.

"Got us outta here without getting caught, didn't I?" He winks.

Lilah laughs, high, nervous. "Saved me from getting grounded all of second semester! My mom would've killed me if she'd known what we were getting up to."

Luke's grin is wide and knowing. "Glad I could rescue you. Otherwise you would've missed out on all the best parties."

Yeah, this is turning into bullshit. He's way too familiar with her, and I don't like that she's pacifying him. "I guess we should probably get off McFarlane's property. Don't want to make the old man angry."

"Yeah. Probably wouldn't look good on you getting a trespassing charge, being a hometown NHL player and all." He's smiling, but it's more of a sneer than anything. He slaps the side panel. "Anyway. Good to see you again, DJ. You know where to find me if you ever need anything." He throws another wink her way. "See you around, Ethan."

"Later, Luke." I wait until he backs out of the narrow lane and do the same, heading toward town instead of away from it.

"Wanna tell me what that was all about?" I try to keep my voice even, but I don't think I'm particularly successful with the way her head snaps up.

"Excuse me?"

"Seems like you two have some history."

"Is that your indirect way of asking me a specific question, Ethan?"

I don't know where the spike of anger comes from, or why I can't seem to manage it. "Did you date him?"

I can feel her glare as if it were lasering its way through my cheek. "We hung out in high school during senior year a bit. Mostly in second semester, after you dumped me."

"So that's a yes."

"He asked me out before I was ready to date. We went to a few parties as friends, but he wasn't interested in anything platonic. He gave up and moved on, started dating Stephanie Murphy until she went away to college. By that time I was already with Avery. And then I got married. A few months after Avery and I separated, Luke asked if I wanted to go for coffee, just to talk. I said yes because he's a nice guy, and I was lonely and needed a friend. We went for coffee a few times, but I just wanted to keep it platonic because I didn't feel that way about him."

"He sure seems to feel that way about you."

"He does, and he's made that very clear, but I couldn't manufacture feelings for him and I wasn't in any kind of headspace to start dating. Any more questions?" Her hard tone implies she expects the inquisition to continue, and she's definitely gearing up for a fight—one I don't want to have right before I leave for two days. It's a bad omen, and I don't want that hanging over my head while I'm away from her, so I back down. "Sorry. No. No more questions."

I pull into her driveway, and before I can even shift into park she's out of the truck and heading up the front walk. I cut the engine and follow after her. Her movements are jerky as she shoves the key in the lock, throwing the door open.

Merk comes running, tongue lolling and tail wagging. He stuffs his nose right in her crotch. "Stop, Merk." She gives his head a pat but pushes him away, turning for the stairs.

"Hey." I reach out, clasping her wrist to keep her from running away.

She yanks her arm free and crosses them over her chest. "I need a shower. I'm a mess. Maybe you should go home and do the same."

"I'm not going anywhere. I'll wait until you've cleaned up, but I'm not leaving with you mad at me."

"I had a life, Ethan. My world kept turning just like yours."

"I know you did. I get that." I run a hand down my face. "I know I'm the one who left and that I ended things. But I won't lie and tell you it didn't kill me to know that there was a mile-long line of guys waiting for a chance to ask you out as soon as you were available."

"So you figured you'd have a pissing contest with one of them? Luke is a police officer."

"That you dated and who's still interested in you." That was definitely the wrong thing to say.

Lilah gives me a hard glare, her teeth clamped together. She runs her finger down the bridge of her nose. Shit. She's really mad. To the point of tears.

"That's not the point, Ethan. We were fucking in the middle of a field, in your truck, like goddamn teenagers!"

"Are you embarrassed that we got caught, or upset that I acted like an asshole?"

She throws her hands up in the air. "Both! You acted like a jealous boyfriend."

I blow out a breath, trying to figure out how to smooth things over. Truth is probably the best option. "That's because I am a jealous boyfriend."

"There's nothing to be jealous of."

"You can't tell me he didn't make a point of rubbing in the fact that there's history between you, or that he didn't make it seem like it was recent, or maybe even current."

Lilah grits her teeth. "I can't help how he reacts, but you can certainly help the way you do. I stayed here, and you left for almost a decade. I dated. That's what people do. Or at least I did. I have no idea what the last eight years looked like for you because you've never talked about it. I don't know whether you worked through an endless stream of puck bunnies, or if there was someone you cared about, but I can't and won't apologize for any of the relationships I've been in while you were off living your life without me."

"I'm not asking you to apologize."

She crosses her arms over her chest, her frustration gathering steam instead of losing it. "Then what are you asking? You already know I never got over you. Shouldn't that be enough for you? I'm not interested in Luke. I never really was, not back in high school, and not last year, and definitely not now."

I step closer, lift my hand and drag my index finger along the bridge of her nose.

She bats it away. "What're you doing? Don't do that."

"I'm trying to calm you down so I can explain myself, and so you'll actually listen to the words instead of that angry white noise up in your head."

"I don't want you to calm me down! I want to be angry! I have a right to be mad at you."

"I totally agree." I clasp both of her hands in one of mine and bring them to my lips. They smell a whole lot like sex. This fire, her refusal to back down, is something I'm glad she never lost. "Do you remember the first time I kissed you?"

"Of course I remember. What does this have to do with anything?"

"I'm getting to that. Do you remember what precipitated that kiss?"

Lilah shrugs. "I don't know. You were in a bad mood. We were walking home from school through the forest, and you just laid one on me. I hadn't been expecting it."

It's amazing how memories shift and change with time, or how one person's recollection of events varies so greatly from another.

"You were wearing jeans and a button-down shirt that was a purple, green, and black plaid. The first three buttons were undone and the black camisole underneath came down a little low, so you had to constantly adjust it to avoid flashing cleavage."

"Is there a point to this?"

"Yes."

"Wanna get to it, then?"

I smile at her irritation. Before she can go off on me for continuing to be a jerk, I press on. "You were standing in front of the school, waiting for me. I remember thinking how beautiful you were and how unaware you seemed to be about all the attention that outfit was getting you, how many guys I'd had to stare down between classes, how freaked out I was because all the stupid posters for the Halloween dance had gone up that day, and you were so damn excited to go to your first high school dance."

I can see the moment when the memories start to click into place for her. "I was talking to Luke."

I nod. "I interrupted right when he was asking if you were going to the dance."

"You came up behind me and scared the crap out of me."

"That's right." I did a lot more than that. I'd staked a claim when I'd come up behind her, wrapped an arm around her waist, and lifted her off the ground while I stared Luke down. My expression had said everything. *She's mine. Don't even think about it.* "When we were walking home, all I could think about was how some guy was going to get the balls to ask you to go to that dance and how I'd have to kill him. And that was the moment I realized I was in love with you, and there was no way I was letting anyone come between us."

She'd been chattering about the dance and costumes, hands flailing wildly, eyes alight with excitement. She'd asked if I was going to go, and when I shrugged, I'd wiped the joy right off her face. I wanted to put it back, so I suggested we go together. She'd stopped, hope quickly overshadowed by uncertainty. And I saw, for the first time, that this love I'd had for her all these years had morphed into something deeper for both of us. So I'd kissed her.

It changed everything.

"I'm going to be traveling a lot starting tomorrow. Luke brought back a lot of memories, and with them, insecurities. I want this with you, Lilah. I want this feeling, your fire; I want us to work this time, and I'm worried that not being here as often is going to make that difficult. So I acted like a jealous jerk, because I am one."

Lilah drops her head, but a smile and a soft laugh follow. "Your apologies are always so elaborate."

"I think my behavior required an elaborate apology. I don't want to leave tomorrow with you misunderstanding my reaction. I won't make the same mistakes I did last time, Lilah—I promise."

I pull her closer and wrap my arm around her waist. She comes willingly at first, but she puts a hand on my chest and pushes away, wearing a grimace. "Oh my God. My dress is crunchy. I really need to get out of these clothes."

"I would be more than willing to help with that."

She laughs, her anger having abated. "Of course you would."

"We could consider it penance."

She rolls her eyes but takes my hand, tugging me toward the stairs.

chapter fourteen

GAMBLE

Ethan

I feel like I'm standing in a minefield, when what I should be doing is celebrating. With Lilah. Naked. We won our exhibition game against Colorado.

Unfortunately, when I arrived in Minneapolis, I had a message from Lilah that she was at my parents' house babysitting my dad while my mom went out for dinner with a friend.

He's in a shit mood and he's watching a recording of the exhibition game. I'm on edge. I don't want him to pick apart my performance. I scored a goal. I should be happy about that, but now all I can do is brace for some snide comment I'm sure is coming.

I jam a pair of jeans, boxers, and a T-shirt into my duffel, throw in my toiletries bag—I have duplicates of most things at Lilah's, but I like to have it just in case—and toss the duffel over my shoulder. We won't leave until my mom gets back, so I figure I can get in a quick swim before we go, since the summer weather seems to be holding for a while longer. I'm sure Lilah would be more than happy to escape Eeyore moping in the lounger.

I climb the stairs, dressed in a pair of board shorts, pausing at the top when the game goes to a commercial and my dad looks to Lilah, who's stretched out on the couch, a pen tucked behind her ear, tapping her lip with a yellow highlighter. She's wearing a gauzy skirt and a pale tank with wide straps.

"What're you doing?" my dad asks in his slow, garbled speech. He has to work on fine motor control to fast-forward through commercials, or wait for the show to come back on. Apparently he's not in the mood for TV remote physio.

It takes her a second or two before she looks up and smiles. "Statistics homework. Remember I told you I'm taking a course?"

My dad nods, then taps on the arm of his chair as he clears his throat. "You should've been a doctor."

I step into the living room, the floorboard under my foot creaking. "Dad!"

He glances over his shoulder at me, face ticking as his mouth tries to catch up with his brain. "'S true." He motions from Lilah to me. "Botha you."

This has been the hardest part to get used to since the stroke. My dad has always felt free to speak his mind, but now, in addition to his lack of censor, he's also tactless, and sometimes the things he says are unnecessarily hurtful.

"I enjoy nursing. I like that I get time with the patients and their families," Lilah replies, an edge in her otherwise serene tone.

My dad taps his temple, then points at me, while still focused on Lilah. "This one wasted his brain."

"That's enough, Martin," Lilah snaps. "That's not even remotely true. Just because Ethan didn't follow in your footsteps doesn't mean he wasted anything. You're being cruel for no other reason than you're in a bad mood. If you can't say anything nice, don't say anything at all."

"He should've stayed." My dad jabs at the couch with a finger, still focused on Lilah, mouth moving as he fights to string the syllables together. "Stay. For you."

I bark out a laugh. "Well, that's rich, considering you're the one who told me to break up with Lilah in the first place, or don't you remember that conversation?"

"So you stay!" he shouts.

"What? You're not even making sense, Dad. You're the one who pushed me to end things. You said it would be selfish for me to leave her here and keep her tied to me."

He slaps the arm of his lounger, more agitated than I've seen him in a long time. "No! I-I-I..." He blinks furiously, struggling harder because he's so upset. "Th-thought you would stay. For DJ. Not go."

The shock of this revelation is a punch in the chest. "You told me to do one thing and expected me to do the opposite?"

"You ne'er listened to me!"

My father and I had always been at odds with each other, especially when I was a teenager. I spent all my time at the hockey rink, and he pushed me toward a career in medicine. When I made the NHL, instead of sharing my excitement, he wanted to know what I was going to do afterward, since I'd likely be retired by my midthirties. We're very much alike, and because of that we argued a lot. But this is . . . more than I can handle, especially with how good things have been with me and Lilah recently. "Well, that was a pretty shitty fucking gamble, wasn't it?"

"It cost you eight years." It's the clearest sentence my dad has spoken in the weeks since his stroke.

I glance at Lilah's wide eyes and pale face. I feel the weight of this admission in my bones. All the time I lost with her because I listened to my father the one time I shouldn't have, and then I did it again when I had the chance to come back for her. I don't understand why he would chance something like that.

"Time wasn't the only thing it cost me." If I stay in here, I'm going to go off on him, say things I can't take back, so I look to Lilah. "It's been a long day. I'm going down to the lake for a quick swim. When my mom gets back, we can go." I punch through the screen door. It slams roughly behind me, the hinges rattling. The porch boards shake beneath my feet, and guilt at leaving Lilah in there to deal with him makes me pause when I reach the grass.

"Why, Martin? Why say that to him with me here? We're

trying to figure things out. He just got home from an away game where he scored a goal. The least you could do is be supportive instead of tearing him down with your black mood."

When he replies, his tone is broken, distressed, apologetic even. "You get one soul mate. I don't want him to lose his again."

The damage is long done, though. An apology can't give me back what he took from me. From Lilah. I drop my bag on the porch and walk across the grass, gaining speed as I go, desperate for an escape from what's in my head now.

I take the dock at a run, pushing off the edge, arcing in a dive. The cold water is a welcome shock as I go under. I stroke hard and kick fast, propelling myself forward, breaking the surface only when my lungs are screaming for air. I keep pushing, swimming out, creating distance between me and the words that feel like a knife still buried in my chest.

We could've been building a future together. Instead, we have years of separation from a history so thick with emotion, so full of love, it's almost painful to have it back after being without it for so long. And even though my career seems to be on an upswing, I have no idea if I'll be able to carry this through the season. And if I don't, what then?

I don't know when the hourglass on my career is going to run out, but I know I don't want this to be the end. And if this contract isn't renewed, what the hell am I going to do? What if I have to move to another city, or worse, back to a farm team—what then? Am I going to up and leave her again? Uproot her life and take her with me? What if she doesn't want that? We're still so new again, and I don't feel like I have the right yet to ask her these questions, to put that kind of pressure on her when she's just started on a new path for her own life.

When my muscles are aching and my legs feel like rubber, I stop and roll onto my back, staring up at the darkening blue sky. The sun is cresting low on the horizon, and with the fading light, the cold settles beneath my skin, seeping into my bones.

I flip over on my stomach and orient myself, catching Lilah's silhouette standing on the dock in the distance. I raise a hand to show her I'm okay, and she mirrors the movement, dropping down on the edge of the dock. It takes me a while to get back to her, my adrenaline having waned.

She makes small circles in the water with her feet, the ripples colliding with mine on my approach. "You okay?"

"I don't like this version of him. I don't want this to be the one who stays." It's not an answer to her question, but it's an answer all the same.

Lilah sighs. "He's frustrated. He doesn't have control. His filter is missing, so he words things in ways that aren't kind."

"He's a mean fucking bastard without it." I tread water looking up at the sky as pink threads through the clouds. A shiver runs through me, my skin pebbling as the air cools with the loss of the sun.

"You have a right to be angry about what he said, Ethan,

but it's not how he meant it. He's just worried, about himself, about you, about us." She pats the dock. "I can go get you a towel. Come on out and sit with me so we can talk."

I swim to the end of the dock and grab the edge, resting my forehead against her shin. The skin-to-skin contact feels good. I've missed her in the short time I was away. It reminded me a lot of when I first left for college, that dull ache in my chest that never seemed to go away, aware it would be weeks before I could touch her again. At least it's only days now.

"I never listened to him, and the only time I did I made the biggest mistake of my life," I say to her knees.

She traces the shell of my ear. "You did what you thought was best, Ethan."

"I did what he told me would be best. I didn't want to, but I didn't want to be selfish with you anymore. I thought it was the right thing, and now I find out that all this time we lost could've been avoided if I'd just done what I usually do and ignored him."

"If it makes you feel any better, I think he's just as angry at himself over it as you are." Gentle fingers thread through my hair, pushing it back. She keeps doing it, over and over. The sensation is calming, warming.

"I damn well fucking doubt it." I slide my free hand up the back of her calf and she stills. "Are you okay?" I can't be the only one shocked by this.

"Yes. I think so. I'm just sad."

"Why sad?" I lift my head and fit myself between her legs,

wrapping my palms around her calves and pulling myself up so I can rest a cheek on her knee. God, I need her in ways I'm not sure she understands.

She regards me with soft affection. I've missed being this close to someone, having this kind of effortless connection to another human being. "Because you're both so intent on either holding or placing blame. Yes, it was a lot of time to lose, but we're here now, aren't we?"

"I don't think I can forgive so easily."

"I can do that for both of us until you're ready." She runs her fingers through my hair again.

"Don't stop, please." A wave of goose bumps covers my body.

"You're cold."

"It's warm in the water." I hoist myself up higher so there's more contact, wetting her skirt, turning it transparent, making it stick to her skin. She doesn't stop me when I slide my wet hands under the hem. Instead, she traces the edge of my jaw before returning to my hair.

"I used to love when you did this," I murmur. "I still do."

"I know." This time she runs her nails over my scalp and I shudder. "Why don't you get out of the water? I'm sure Jeannie will be home soon. You can grab a quick shower and we can go back to my place. Spend some quality time together."

Instead of using the ladder, I pull myself up into the space between her legs. Lilah leans back on her elbows with a laugh. I lean in and kiss the end of her nose. "Hi."

"You do realize you're getting me all wet, right?"

"I love it when you're wet."

She snorts and rolls her eyes.

"I'm glad I'm home." This time I kiss her warm mouth.

"Me, too," she says against my lips.

"Remember when we used to do this all the time?" She shivers as I kiss along her throat. "Late-night swims. You on the ladder, me between your legs."

"I remember how many times we almost got caught."

"That was part of the fun, wasn't it?" She whimpers when I stretch out on top of her on the dock, my hard-on pressed against her through layers of wet fabric.

"Ethan." It's a warning, but she hooks a knee around the back of my leg and arches under me.

"I missed you." I kiss her again, stroking inside her mouth as I roll my hips.

"I missed us." A violent shiver rips through her as a cool breeze blows up from the lake, and I realize this probably isn't the greatest idea.

"Come on—let's get you out of these wet clothes." I jump to my feet and extend a hand, pulling her up. We rush back to the house, teeth chattering as the sun sinks below the tree line.

My dad has his tablet with the external keyboard in his lap, brow pulled low as he types with one finger, apparently concentrating so hard he doesn't notice us until the screen door swings closed with a slam.

He looks from me to Lilah, the front of her outfit soaked,

thanks to me. She hugs herself as her teeth clack against each other. His brows pop up. "Happened?"

"Your son tried to use me as a towel."

My dad's expression is difficult to read as he turns to watch Lilah scamper up the stairs.

"Are you gonna grab me a towel?" I call after her.

"Sure." A washcloth lands at the bottom of the stairs, too far away for me to reach, not that it'd be much help, anyway.

My dad's cheek tics as if he's fighting a smile.

"Come on, Lilah."

"It'll cover the important parts!" The sound of a door closing on the floor above means she's not going to help me out more than she already has. I suppose it serves me right.

"You're not gonna rat me out to Mom if I walk across the house like this, are you?" I ask my dad, gesturing to my wet suit.

He shakes his head, subdued.

I bust my ass across the living room, trying to stay off the hardwood, and skid across the floor, rushing down the stairs to my bedroom. I'm quick about changing into jeans, a tee, and a sweatshirt. Now that I'm not as angry and the adrenaline has worn off, I have a chill. I grab a couple of towels from the basement, mop up any water on the living room floor, and throw everything in the laundry before my mom returns from her dinner. It's after eight already, and I have no idea what time she left, but I have to assume she'll be back soon. She's not big on leaving my dad for any length of time, even less when he's without a chaperone, which he loathes. Unless it's Lilah, of course. Although tonight even her presence didn't seem to temper his bad mood.

I put the kettle on and return to the living room. If I'm cold, Lilah must be, too.

"Ethan."

I look over at my dad, who's sitting on the couch with the tablet still in his lap.

"You want tea, too?" I ask, not quite ready to forgive him, but I don't think staying angry does me any good, either.

He nods, then pats the cushion beside him.

"You want me to sit?"

I get another head bob.

I cross my arms over my chest and stay where I am. "You planning to say more shitty things to me?"

He has the decency to look guilty as he shakes his head.

I flop down on the couch beside him. If he wants something from me, he's going to have to ask.

He passes me the tablet and taps the screen. "Read, please?"

I glance down, expecting a question or a couple of lines asking me to do something for him—that's not what I get, though.

Ethan,

I've been stuck inside my own head for a while now, and it hasn't been a great place to be. I've had time to reflect, encumbered by my body's unwillingness to do what I want it to. I've also had time to watch this relationship between you and Delilah blossom again.

It's my fault that you were apart all this time.

I wish I'd said this years ago. Maybe I could've saved you both a lot of hurt and myself a lot of regret, because I forced you to make a choice without weighing the consequences. I wanted you to stay, and I thought I could push you to decide between the two things you loved the most. I didn't realize the damage I would do to Delilah, to you, to our relationship.

Your mother was angry for a long time. It took me until now to understand why. She knew what I had been blind to.

You only get one soul mate.

You just found yours before you understood what it meant, and I interfered when I shouldn't have.

I'm so sorry for keeping you two apart for as long as I have.

Right now I'm trapped inside this body that doesn't work properly, and half the time I can't even find the words I want to use, and then I use them in ways that hurt instead of help.

I love you. I'm proud of you.

Dad

I read the letter twice, hearing his voice the entire time. I can't imagine the weight of living with this. Watching Lilah marry someone else, seeing that relationship fail, watching my career decline over the past eight years. When I meet his gaze, it's full of sad regret, and I finally understand where the wall that's been between us came from.

He pats my leg with a heavy, clunky hand. "I'm sorry."

I could be angry, but it serves no purpose. Life is full of what-ifs and uncertainties. "If it makes you feel any better, I probably would've fucked it up along the way if we'd stayed together. She missed my worst years."

The kettle whistles, and the front door swings open, announcing my mother's arrival home. My father's face lights up, and I suddenly understand what he means about soul mates.

Those two belong together. My mother is the pepper to his salt.

I don't recall a time when they've been apart. Not for more than a day or two when my dad would go on one of his fishing trips.

My father reaches for the walker he detests and struggles to get it open on his own, but he manages after two tries. My mother takes slow steps toward him, and when they're within reach of each other, he finds the strength to let go of the walker, cup her face in his unsteady palms, and kiss her.

chapter fifteen

THE WOODS

Lilah

A few days later Ethan shows up at my door dressed in sports gear and hiking shoes, holding a bag from my favorite bakery. I've been home for all of five minutes and I'm still dressed in my scrubs.

"What's this?" I nod to the bag.

"So you don't have to stop for breakfast on your way to work in the morning."

"That was thoughtful."

He grins. "No stopping for breakfast means more spooning time for me."

"Ah, ulterior motives to go with your sweetness. I see." I step back, smiling, as he invites himself inside and drops his duffel on the floor. I barely give it a glance—if he comes for a visit now, it's typically overnight. He's about three hours earlier than I expected, though. "I thought you were coming over around eight."

"Sorry. I got a little antsy. I thought we could go for a walk." He wraps his arms around me and gives me a warm kiss.

I cringe as Merk runs a circle around us, nudges up with his nose, then rushes to where his leash is hanging by the door and barks. "You said the *w* word." There's no way we're getting into any kind of make-out session now.

He kisses the end of my nose and grins. "Looks like I have a taker."

"Awesome. Why don't you take him for a nice long one? I have some reading to do for class." I give him a cheeky grin.

"You'd rather read a book than spend quality time with me and Merk?"

I hesitate, weighing the things I have to do against this opportunity to spend time with Ethan. Despite it being early in the course, the load is already pretty heavy. "I have homework when we get back, though." I suppose I could put it off for an hour or so.

His hands go lower, cupping my ass. "You're sexy when you study."

"I mean it, Ethan. If you're a distraction, I'm sending you packing. I have an assignment due in two days that I haven't started."

"That's not like you."

"No. It's not. There's a six-foot-two hockey player who keeps interfering with my study time." While I very much enjoy having Ethan around, I don't want to lose sight of my goal—which is only two stats courses away from being possible.

"I promise not to interfere—just don't make me go home."

"Martin in a mood?"

"Nah. He's good. Moving around so much better these days, and he needs a lot less help, but you know how it is. I'm on family overdose. I need my space."

"So you're planning to invade mine—is that it?"

"Your bed is nicer."

"You take up ninety percent of it." I poke him in the chest.

He grins. "You love it."

"Don't kid yourself. I tolerate it." He knows I don't mean that. I love it when he curls himself around me. Ethan's love of spooning hasn't changed at all.

"It won't be long before I take possession of the Hoffman estate. Then we'll have a king-size bed to make good use of."

"Things to look forward to this fall, huh?" I push his wandering hands away so as not to disappoint Merk. He needs fresh air, and I'll be more focused if I get some, too. Maybe it'll help Ethan be less of a study distraction. "Just let me get changed, then."

I leave Ethan standing in the foyer and rush upstairs to throw on a pair of yoga pants and a light tank. It's still warm, but it's cooling faster in the evening, so I grab a hoodie as well. When I come back downstairs, I find Ethan waiting on the front porch, Merk leashed and ready to go.

He looks me over, cocking his head to the side. "All set?"

"Yup." I lock the door and follow behind Ethan and Merk.

His truck beeps and he heads toward it instead of the sidewalk.

"What're you doing?"

He opens the passenger door. "I thought it would be nice to head out to the path that runs along the lake. I haven't been down there in years."

I eye him suspiciously. "You mean the one we used to take in high school?"

He blinks innocently at me. "Is that okay? We don't have to."

"No, no. It's fine." I climb into the cab and shift to the center of the bench seat when Merk jumps up beside me, tail batting me in the arm with his enthusiasm for the trip. Nothing beats a ride in Ethan's truck *and* a walk.

Ethan rolls the window down as he pulls out of the driveway, and Merk sticks his head out, tongue lolling and ears flapping in the breeze. He's a big dog and takes up a lot of room, forcing me close to Ethan. Every time we turn a corner, his arm brushes mine. I expect him to put a hand on my thigh, or one around my shoulders, but he keeps it surprisingly PG.

It only takes about ten minutes to get to the high school from my place. Ethan parks in the corner of the lot closest to the forest. Merk prances with excitement once we're out of the truck, and I have to encourage him to sit while Ethan lifts the dog tags from the rearview mirror and slips them into his pocket. He takes them with him everywhere and apparently always has. Even when I wasn't part of his life, he kept me close. It makes my heart ache as much as swell. He slings a backpack over his shoulder and locks up the truck.

"What's in there?" I ask as he meets me around the hood.

"Just some snacks and bottles of water." He laces his fingers with mine. "Come on. Merk is going to lose his mind if we don't get moving."

He's right. Merk is trotting in place, whining his frustration with not being able to tear through the open field. I unclip the leash and let him loose to chase poor, helpless butterflies and roll around in the grass. He's probably going to need a bath when we get home, which isn't necessarily a bad thing. I can have Ethan take care of that while I study.

We pass the football field, where a group of teenagers toss a ball around. A few girls sit on the sidelines watching them play, shouting and laughing.

"So carefree," I observe.

He squeezes my hand. "We were like that once."

I can feel his eyes on me, and I look up, seeing the shadows there. Trying again with him means sometimes we get bogged down with the past instead of staying in the present. "Well, you had your moments, but I was always pretty zeroed in on the goal. If it wasn't for you, I probably never would've had any fun."

"Totally untrue, we had fun all the time. You had big plans. You knew exactly what you were doing and how you were going to get there, you just figured out how to prioritize it all better than I did."

I laugh a little at that. "I thought I knew what I was doing; half the time I had my head in the clouds." I whistle for Merk as we approach the tree line, and he changes course, running circles around us.

I clip the leash back on, giving Merk slack so he can sniff around on the path. Under the cover of the trees it's cooler, and beams of sunlight filter through gaps in the branches.

We continue down the path, away from the sound of the kids playing ball in the field. Eventually we have to unlink our hands when the path narrows, and we're forced into single file.

"Can I ask you a question?"

I glance over my shoulder at him. "Sure."

"What made you decide not to become a doctor?"

I can read between the lines. He wants to know if he's the reason, or maybe Avery. Neither is true, although I suppose in some way, both were factors in the ultimate decision. "For the first two years of college, premed was my goal, but then I started to realize I didn't love the idea of setting up my own practice, and I didn't want to be a surgeon. It's the people part of the job I love the most, being able to help and being involved in the treatment plan beyond signing off on papers and interpreting test results, so I switched gears and went into nursing instead."

Ethan chews his bottom lip, regarding me thoughtfully. "So it had nothing to do with finances?"

"Not for me, no," I reply, tugging on Merk's leash when he tries to go after a squirrel.

"That seems like a loaded answer."

I debate how to frame this. There's so much he doesn't know about my life in the time he was gone from it. And yet, as much as I've changed, much remains the same. "Well, Avery was all for the switch because it was less expensive, and I wouldn't be in school as long."

"Doctors make a lot more than nurses, though," Ethan says.

I glance at him. "It was never about the paycheck. Doctors also work insane hours. I wanted some balance between my job and my life, and Avery wanted a family."

"So that's why you went into nursing? So you could start a family?"

There's discomfort in this conversation. I'm glad I have to focus on navigating the uneven terrain rather than seeing his reaction. "I didn't make the decision for him; I made it for me. He wanted to start a family, but I... didn't."

"You always wanted a family, though."

"Eventually yes, with the right person." I sigh, considering the year leading up to my separation from Avery. It had been coming for a long time; the end of us had been inevitable from the beginning, for exactly the reasons Avery cited in the grocery store parking lot. "And that wasn't him. It took me a while to recognize that. I wanted to go back to school; he wanted to focus on starting a family. We were moving in different directions, and at some point, we both realized it wasn't going to work, for a lot of reasons." At first I loved the way he seemed to need me, constantly bringing me to work events, meeting me for lunch during the week as often as he could, calling during the day just to check in. After a while it felt suffocating, and the more he tried to pull me closer, the more I pulled away.

Ethan's quiet for a few seconds. "So now you're free to do what you want."

I'm glad for the shift away from Avery. "It was always my choice, but for a while it wasn't practical. I want to be a nurse practitioner, but I'm missing a couple of courses, which is why I'm taking stats, and then a second stats course in the winter, so hopefully I'll gain admission into the master's program next fall."

"At the University of Minnesota?"

"That's the plan."

He nods but doesn't comment on it further. I wonder if we're both thinking the same thing—about whether he'll be here next fall or somewhere else. This plan of mine has gotten me through the most difficult part of the separation with Avery. I needed a sense of purpose so walking away from our failed marriage didn't feel like a mistake. A goal, even a long-term one, helped ease the transition from partner to individual again. I'd been so used to being Avery's everything, and then I was just... on my own. And I used that time to figure out what I needed. What I wanted. I don't want to lose sight of that now. But with Ethan back in my life, it's harder to focus. I know I don't want to lose him again. But I can't let him consume me, either.

"I'm glad you're doing what you love," he says finally.

"Me, too. How was practice today?"

"It's been good." He cringes. "I almost hate to say that out loud. I don't want to jinx myself this close to the beginning of the season."

"Still so superstitious."

Ethan has always had crazy routines when it comes to his games, from what he wears to how he prepares. I figured it would change over the years, but based on the preseason practice and exhibition game rituals I've witnessed so far, it hasn't. Personally, I think it's a little ridiculous, but I know Ethan takes it seriously, so I try to not make light of it too much.

He gives me a lopsided smile. "It's tough not to be, sometimes. The first year I played was probably my best, but then I started to slide. Now things seem to be going a lot better again."

"Why do you think that is?" I ask.

"I dunno. That first year I pushed hard, maybe to prove I'd made the right decision. Then I had that chance to play for Minnesota, but I was already too late to come back for you. After that everything started going to shit. I kept getting further and further from where I wanted to be, and it felt like I'd given up all the things that made me who I was, apart from hockey, and it had all been for nothing. Maybe it became a self-fulfilling prophecy. Anyway, preseason is going well. I might even get ice time right away. We'll see how it goes." I falter when we approach a fallen tree covering the path, and Ethan nearly collides with me. "I don't remember this being here."

"Me, neither." Although, it's been years since I've gone for a walk down here, and this tree looks like it's been here for a while.

Merk goes under, pulling me against the fallen tree. It's too tight for me to follow him so I have to awkwardly grab for the leash while I hoist myself over. I overestimate my agility and the slipperiness of the moss and land on my knee. My palm skids across the rough ground and I roll to my hip with an *oomph*. Merk barks his surprise while I shout mine.

"Shit! You okay?" Ethan plants a palm on the moss-covered tree and hops over it effortlessly. "I should've gone first so I could help you."

I sit up and brush my palms off on my yoga pants with a hiss. I'm definitely going to need a shower after this. I'm covered in dirt and pine needles.

Ethan crouches beside me. "Let me have a look." He takes my palm between his hands, inspecting the damage while Merk tries to fit himself between us so he can help, too. He barks when Ethan nudges him out of the way.

"I'm fine. It's just a few scratches."

"What about your knee?" He rolls my pant leg gently over my knee. It's in worse condition than my palm, but it's by no means terrible.

"It's not life-threatening. I'll survive."

He shrugs the backpack off and unzips the front compartment, pulling out a small first-aid kit. His brow furrows in concentration as he carefully cleans the wound. As embarrassed as I am, I can definitely appreciate the care he's taking in fixing me up. I also find it rather ironic that the hockey player is taking care of the nurse.

I glance over at Merk when he barks, probably at another squirrel. He rubs himself on a tree next to the fallen one. I squint a little, sure it can't be . . . but it is.

"Oh my God. Look." Ethan finishes bandaging my knee and follows my finger. "I thought you were so romantic for doing that. I didn't even consider the poor tree." Inside a knot on the side of the tree, DS + EK is carved for all eternity.

"We were such environmental heathens." Ethan shifts to run his fingers over the carved letters. "I hoped we would find this today. I kissed you for the first time right here." He smiles, and then frowns at the downed tree resting against the side of the one with our initials carved in it. "This one almost took our tree down when it fell."

Ethan's superstitions are mostly related to hockey. But he was a big believer in fate and things not just being coincidental. In high school he always wore the same type of boxers to practice. Home games had a different pair, away games yet another. If they made it into playoffs, he had a pair of socks he refused to wash until they lost. It was vile at the best of times, deadly at the worst.

"Even if it had, it wouldn't have been an omen," I say softly.

A small grin appears and he moves in close again, running a gentle finger from the bridge of my nose to the tip. "Stop reading my mind."

He's always been sentimental, holding on to ideas and grounding them in something tangible, like initials carved into a tree.

"I know how that mind of yours works, Ethan Kase." I slip a hand behind his neck. "This would be a good time to kiss me, since I'm pretty sure that was the whole point of bringing me all the way out here."

His smile is soft, warm. "Mind reading again, huh?"

I laugh a little, but then his lips are on mine, a whisper of touch. The rush of heat is instantaneous. Every part of our relationship has always been steeped in inescapable intensity. He sucks my bottom lip, then dips inside my mouth, tongue stroking velvet smooth against my own. His groan is low and needy, fingers twining in my hair as he angles my head to the side so he can go deeper.

I part my legs as his knee comes between mine, and I have to use a hand for balance as he leans over me, tilting my head back so he can take control of the kiss. As teenagers, there were many occasions when we'd used the forest as our bedroom, but I'm not so sure I'm inclined to re-create those particular memories.

A tickle along my arm distracts me. I assume it's Merk, annoyed that he's not getting enough attention, until a sharp sting on my side makes me gasp. And then another on my leg.

"God, I love your mouth," Ethan rasps against my lips, misreading my sounds.

Several more sharp stings have me pushing on his chest. "Ow! Dammit, something keeps biting me!" I glance at the ground and realize it's moving. "Holy fuck!" I crab crawl backward and jump up. Swearing a blue streak, I pull my tank over my head, swiping at the ants crawling all over me. The sheer number leads me to believe I disturbed a nest.

"Get them off!" I scream like an idiot. They're crawling up my legs, and now it feels like my entire body is covered in them. I kick off my shoes and yank my yoga pants down. "How the fuck did they get in there?" I'm still yelling because they're literally everywhere and it's gross.

Ethan is doing the ant dance just like me, pulling his shirt over his head and dropping his shorts around his ankles.

It feels like there might be a few in my bra, and I'm suddenly paranoid that they've found their way into my underwear. I stick a hand down the front—there is no back since it's a thong—and check to make sure I'm in the clear. Ethan—who's ant-free, apparently—has stopped his search to watch me.

"Do you want me to check inside your bra?" His cheek tics.

I pick my shoe up off the ground and throw it at him. "You jerk! Don't laugh at me!"

"Trust me—I'm not laughing."

His eyes roam over me in a slow sweep. I'm dancing around in a forest, wearing only a bra and a thong, and a pair of white ankle socks. Well, the soles are no longer white. "I can't believe you're checking me out! Stop drooling and start helping!"

"Is that a thong?" He peeks around behind me. "Ah, fuck, it is."

He licks his bottom lip and takes a step closer.

I point a shaking finger at him. "Oh no. No way. Don't even think about it."

His grin is wicked. "Too late for that."

Even as miffed as I am, my nipples perk up, especially when I note the way he's straining against his boxers. The sound of voices not too far off in the distance freezes us both.

"Oh my God." I rush to shake out my tank, making sure it's ant-free. Then I quickly do the same with my yoga pants, yanking them up my thighs and over my butt. Ethan checks his own shirt and shorts—although he makes a point of watching me the entire time I dress. I've just slipped my feet back into my shoes when a couple of teens approach the fallen log. The girl who's hanging off the arm of the boy she's with shrieks when she sees us, apparently startled. She laughs and apologizes, then shrieks again when she notices the swarm of ants.

"Careful, those bite," Ethan says as they skirt the hazard, rushing off.

Dusk is creeping in and the temperature drops as we make our way back to the truck. I can't shake the creepy-crawly feeling or the shivers that run up and down my spine as I get in the cab.

"You all right?" Ethan asks, cranking the heat when I run my hands up and down my thighs. Merk sits beside me, tongue hanging out, happy and oblivious.

"I still feel like there are ants on me."

"Me, too." He puts the truck in reverse. Pinks and oranges color the clouds in a pastel rainbow as the sun dips below the tree line. I can't appreciate it the way I'd like since my focus is on the phantom tickle and sting of ants on my skin.

"That didn't go quite the way I'd planned." Ethan squeezes my hand. "When we get back to your place, I'll make sure you're ant-free—sound good?"

"You just want to get me naked."

"I'm pretty transparent, huh?"

"Just a little, but I don't mind." I wink and settle back in my seat. I know I should focus on course work when I get home, but I want this time with Ethan. I don't know how long I get to have him in my life again, or if he's going to end up leaving, like everyone seems to.

chapter sixteen

FALLING BACK IN

Lilah

Dips in the lake become a memory of another summer past, and hot days give way to the frosty mornings of fall. The official hockey season begins and leaves turn yellow, then sunrise orange before vibrant red flutters to the ground.

Tonight we're getting in as much one-on-one time as we can before he leaves in the morning for a five-day stretch. I have an assignment that needs my attention, but I'm wrapped up in Ethan, and with him gone starting tomorrow, I'll have more time to focus on school.

I shift away from his side and he makes a grab for me. "Where you going?"

"I want to take a look at your ankle." He rolled it last week during a game but powered through anyway, as men full of adrenaline tend to do. For a couple of days after, it was stiff and achy.

"It's fine, baby."

"Great. I still want to look, though."

"You don't trust the team doctors are doing their job?"

"I'm sure they're doing a fantastic job. I just want to make sure you're not playing it off as nothing when it's really something." I roll his sock off and check for any kind of residual swelling. It looks good, but I make him do range-of-motion tests and watch his face for signs of discomfort.

"See, Nurse Delilah? Nothing to worry about."

"Someone has to make sure you're not pushing when you should be resting." I roll his sock back on.

"I do have another spot you might want to check, though," Ethan says before I settle back into his side.

I sit back up, alert. "Did you pull something during practice?"

He purses his lips and nods. "Maybe. It might be good for you to look at it."

"Where does it hurt?"

"It's more of an ache, really."

"Okay." I nod. "A muscle ache? Maybe I can rub it for you."

"Oh yeah, that'll definitely help. It might be swollen."

"Why didn't you say something before?" I'm irritated that his doctors haven't been more thorough.

Ethan shrugs, chewing the inside of his lip. "It wasn't a problem before."

"Well, let's have a look. You might need heat or ice therapy."

"Heat therapy is probably the best." He reaches down and pulls at the elastic waist of his sweats, where an erection makes itself known against the gray fabric.

"Oh my God!" I shove his shoulder. "You jerk. I thought there was really something wrong."

"But there's swelling, see?" He's laughing now.

"Don't make fun of me!" I try to push away from him, but he wraps me up in his arms so I can't get away.

"I'm not. I love that you want to take care of me. It's too bad you can't be my personal nurse when I'm at away games. You could give me sponge baths after games."

"Wouldn't you love that."

"So much." He flips me over, edging his way between my thighs. "But I do think I need some heat therapy."

I snort a laugh that quickly turns into a groan as he rolls his hips.

◦

Half an hour later, we're stretched out on the couch again, mostly undressed and covered in a blanket, watching a replay of Ethan's last game against New York, which they lost.

Ethan rewinds a play for the third time so he can pick apart where he went wrong.

"You don't have to be perfect, Ethan. It's okay to make mistakes."

He kisses my forehead. "I know. I prefer when I learn from them and don't make them again. I don't like that my game isn't as good when we don't have home ice advantage."

He plays best in Minnesota, and it gets to him when he

makes what he considers rookie mistakes. "What do you think the difference is?"

He fiddles with the charm on my bracelet. "I don't know. Comfort maybe? Confidence?"

I push up off his chest so I can look at him. "Don't take this the wrong way, but do you think maybe you expect not to do as well, so you don't?"

He sighs. "I've considered that, yeah."

I pull the blanket around my shoulders, shivering at the loss of direct body heat. "And what are your thoughts?"

"That there has to be some truth to it."

"And you think picking apart your mistakes will make you play better?"

"Probably not." He nabs the remote from the coffee table and shuts the TV off. "I need this to be a good season."

"It's turning out to be your best since you played for LA," I remind him.

"So far."

I poke him in the chest. "Stop doing that to yourself."

He grabs my hand and threads his fingers through mine. "Christ. I'm exactly like my dad, aren't I? Always looking for a black cloud to stand under."

I laugh. "Hardly. I think you get nervous about away games and then you get all up inside your head and start picking things apart."

"It'd be great if you could come with me." He lifts my knuckles to his lips.

"I have this thing called a job." I try to make light of it, worried about the heaviness seeping into this conversation and weighing down his mood.

"I know, but you make everything so much easier."

"It's not like I can be out there on the ice with you."

"But you'd be with me. You could come to the practice, the game, and then you'd be there after."

"When would I get studying in?"

"You could do it during practice. Or whenever you need the time. It'd just be nice to know I'm starting and ending my day with you."

"Don't you have a roommate? How awkward would that be?"

Ethan's eyes darken. "I'd get us our own room."

"That would probably be for the best. You're not great at quiet sex." I'm teasing now, mostly to lighten up his somber mood.

His eyebrows rise. "Me? You give Merk an anxiety attack every time I go down on you."

I grin. "You love the praise."

"Damn right I do." He shifts around, until he can move me to straddle his lap.

"It's only five days—you can handle it."

"Five days is nothing." Ethan wraps his arms around me and pulls me into a tight hug, lips against my temple. I sink into the embrace, aware this simple affection is soon going to grow heated again.

Away series mess with Ethan's pregame routines, which

have come to very much include me. When he's home, he stays over the night before his games. If he has a chance before he leaves for the pregame skate, he'll stop by my work and steal a few good luck kisses and a butt squeeze. At times I wonder if I'm contributing to his anxiety by encouraging this, but it's nice to feel so necessary and needed.

When he's on the road, we're forced to communicate through text messages and occasional video chats, but those are rare since a roommate is often around.

His away games allow me to balance the demands of work and school. I do the bulk of my course work when he's out of town, and as much as I miss him, I need the time. Even still, my marks aren't where I'd like them to be, since I'm also trying to catch up on missed sleep in his absence. But when he's home, it's hard to say no to him. It often feels like we're making up for not only the time he's away, but the past eight years, too.

Regardless of his apparent devotion to me, the shadows of past insecurities breed anxiety, especially with how relentless the puck bunnies are now that he's getting so much more ice time and drawing media attention. It doesn't matter that I'm very clearly his girlfriend. Even when he plays in Minnesota and I'm with him, they're always on him, looking to take selfies and fawn.

I see now, in a way I never would've been able to back when he was first drafted, how difficult this would've been for us. Especially with him being in LA that first year.

Martin was right, even if inadvertently. Breaking up was the only logical answer. So I try not to think about the end of this season and the uncertainty that brings.

Eventually Ethan murmurs, "Let's go to bed, baby."

I don't argue. It's late. He has to be up early. More than that, bed means more closeness and connection—the kind he needs from me to get him through the coming days. The kind I need, too.

At five in the morning I'm woken by Ethan hovering over me, dragging my boxers down my legs—well, they're actually his boxers, and his plan is to take them with him. It's an odd quirk leftover from his high school days. I writhe as his fingers tickle my ribs while pushing up the shirt. "I'm taking this with me, too."

"Figured," I mumble, still half-asleep—at least until his head disappears under the shirt and his lips cover a bare nipple. He kisses his way across my chest, pushing the shirt over my head so he can continue the path up my neck, his body stretched out over mine.

"I want to love you before I go." He fits himself between my legs.

"I like it when you love me."

So he does, with soft reverence that fills my heart. I wish that feeling wouldn't disappear as soon as he walks out the door.

e∿

We survive the next five days and the five after that. Days bleed into each other and turn into weeks. Finals for my first course come and go. The holidays sneak up on us, and I spend Christmas Eve with Ethan's family and volunteer at a women's shelter with my sister on Christmas Day, something we've done for years. Ethan leaves early the following day for an away series and doesn't come back until New Year's Day. Not that it matters—I work New Year's Eve in the pediatric unit.

My final grade for my course comes in early January. I pass, but not with the kind of marks I'm accustomed to, or what I used to receive during nursing school. It's been four years since I've taken college classes, and stats aren't exactly my best subject. I have a full-time job and a life. But I know those are not excuses. I didn't put the time in the way I should have; I was too focused on Ethan and our relationship. We feel stable, so I promise myself I'll do better in second semester.

But as January dissolves into February and my second stats course is well under way, I'm not so sure I'm keeping that promise, considering the grades on my last two assignments have been mediocre at best. I'm currently lying on Ethan's couch when I probably should be studying.

"Come with me this weekend," he says suddenly.

I laugh and push my fingers through his hair, trying to keep it from tickling my chest and neck.

He lifts his head. "I'm serious. Fly out to Chicago with me. Just two days. It'll make the time pass quicker. Ten days is too long to go without you."

"I have a midterm on Tuesday that I need to study for."

"You can study on the plane. And in the hotel room when I'm at practice. Come on, Lilah, please?" He rests his chin between my breasts and blinks his wide, sad eyes. His hair is a mess, lips dark and full from so much kissing.

I cover his face with my spread fingers so I can't see his puppy dog eyes. "Don't look at me like that."

"I want you with me. It's one weekend. You've never been to an away game. We hardly had any time together over the holidays. Finals will be coming up before long and we're playing well. My dad is way better. Mom will be okay on her own with him for a couple of days."

He's right. In the past few months, Martin's speech has improved significantly, the words coming faster and smoother, although never as smooth as they were. And he's walking with the assistance of a cane, rather than a walker.

I don't want to say no to Ethan. I want to be there with him, because I love being able to support him, and I miss him when he's gone. But on the other hand, I can't just drop everything. I have a job and I'm legitimately concerned about this course. The midterm is worth 30 percent of the final grade. If I don't do well on this, it could hurt my chances at making it into the master's program, and then it would be another year before I could apply again. Ethan's already succeeded at his dream—he's living it. This is mine and it's what I'm good at. I don't want to lose that.

When my silence drags on, no commitment either way, his

eyes go soft and pleading. "This game is important. Please."
He plays with my bracelet, fingering the hockey stick charm,
symbolic of so much more than just his love of the game. He's
almost obsessive about me wearing it.

"If I come, you have to respect that I'll need time to study.
This course is important to me like hockey is important to
you."

"I know that. I want you to do well. I promise I'll give you
whatever time you need—just come with me."

The look on his face and his pleading break me down and
make me give in to him, even though I know I shouldn't.
"Okay. But only for the weekend. I can't take time off
work."

The smile that lights up his face is so stunningly beautiful,
I'm convinced this is the best idea in the world.

~

Two nights later I'm standing in the middle of the crowded
hotel bar among Ethan and his teammates, celebrating their
win against Chicago.

"Shots!" his teammate Josh yells and passes one over his
shoulder to Ethan. "You, too, princess." He hands me one as
well.

Ethan throws a glare his way and I laugh. "What is this?" I
sniff the amber liquid.

"Just drink it." Josh clinks his shot glass against mine and then Ethan's before tipping his head back and draining it in a single gulp. He follows it up with wide eyes and a violent shake of his head. "I need another one of those!"

Josh turns back to the bar and Ethan's slightly glassy gaze finds mine, a small smirk pulling up the corner of his mouth. "You want me to do it for you?"

"I don't know if that's such a good idea if you're planning on scoring goals off the ice tonight."

His grin widens. He scored twice tonight—on the ice. It's his best away-game performance so far, and against his former teammates, at that, so he's riding a serious high, and people keep feeding him shots. He tips back his glass and drains the liquid, then wraps an arm around my waist. He's wearing a suit and a tie with his team logo on it. He looks incredibly sexy and he's cocky as hell tonight. He dips his head, nose skimming along the edge of my jaw, lips following until they're at my ear. "Oh, I plan to score, all right."

He flattens his palm against my low back, bringing me flush against him so I can feel what his suit jacket is hiding. "I can't wait to get you back to the room."

"You think you'll be able to perform by then?"

His hand eases lower, giving my bottom a squeeze. "You questioning my stamina, baby? I think we both know I'm more than capable of taking care of you."

"Stop manhandling your girl, Kase." Josh elbows him in the side and hands him another shot. "Drink up, princess." He passes me another, too, and gives me a conspiratorial wink with a head nod to Ethan. "Pisses him off when I call you that, doesn't it?"

"Seems that way." I down one shot and then the other, coughing on the back end. Those were definitely not broken-down golf carts. "What the hell was that?"

"Liquid cocaine."

"What?" My panic over the nonsense idea that they legitimately serve cocaine in liquid form at a bar is short-lived.

"Jägermeister, Goldschläger, and peppermint schnapps—heavy on the Jäger, though." Josh laughs and slaps Ethan on the back. "You're gonna be a mess tomorrow morning, my man."

He pulls me into his side. "I plan to work it off later."

"Oh my God." I duck out from under his arm, my cheeks flushing. "I need to use the bathroom. Please give him some water before you feed him more shots," I say to Josh.

"Wait." Ethan grabs my hand and yanks me back into him. Taking my face between his palms, he tips my head back and covers my mouth with his. He tastes like cinnamon as his tongue sweeps my mouth. He's on such a high from the win. I can only imagine how voracious he's going to be when we get back to the room. I can hardly wait. He breaks the kiss, eyes hot. "Don't be gone long."

"I'll just be a minute." I'm actually several minutes because there's a line for the bathroom.

Women in tight dresses and team gear primp in front of the mirror, talking players and who they want to hook up with. Someone mentions Ethan's name and another woman says something about him having his girlfriend with him while I'm hidden in the stall. They make a joke I miss because of a flushing toilet, but their bitchy laughter fades as they leave.

I check out my own appearance. I'm in a pair of jeans and a Minnesota T-shirt. I'm not particularly sexy. I didn't have Carmen to help me with my hair or makeup. And I'm definitely a little drunk. Or maybe more than a little. Those shots are hitting me and so is the insecurity, all of a sudden. Ethan has eight more days on the road after this. Without me.

I leave the bathroom and make my way through the crowd, back to the bar and Ethan. I finally spot him, talking to some dark-haired exotic-looking woman. She's wearing a slinky black dress and sky-high heels that accentuate her ample curves and long, toned legs. She looks like a goddamn swimsuit model.

I mutter excuse me and push through the crowd, slipping my arm around his waist and tucking myself into his side. "Hey, baby, sorry I took so long."

Tall and Exotic glances at me, a small smirk curving her very-full lips. One of her perfectly plucked and shaped eyebrows lifts and her nose crinkles. "Is this a fan of yours, Ethan?"

I mirror the raised brow and the condescending smirk. "His biggest." I look up at Ethan, whose expression is slightly panicked. Oh, this should be interesting. "Aren't you going to introduce us, Ethan?" I ask sweetly.

He wraps an arm around my shoulder and squeezes—maybe a warning, maybe a reassurance; I have no idea—but I don't like the way she's looking at him or how awkward this has become. "Lilah, this is Selene. She's, uh, a friend." His throat bobs with a nervous swallow. "Selene, this is my girlfriend, Lilah."

Selene's smug smile drops and she blinks, eyes darting from Ethan to me and back again. "Oh. I didn't realize." She smooths a hand over her hip. "I thought..." She shakes her head and offers me a palm. "It's so nice to meet you—Lisa, is it?"

"Lilah." I grip her hand firmly.

"So sorry. It's so loud in here." She motions to the noisy crowd. "Well, Ethan, it was so nice to see you again. Congratulations again on the win." She turns her fake smile on me. "It was nice to meet you, Lilah." She seems to want to hug Ethan, but since I have no intention of letting him go, she's forced to wave and walk away.

As soon as she's gone I turn to Ethan. "Who the fuck was that?"

"She's just a friend." He runs his palms down my arms.

"She looks like a damn swimsuit model."

Ethan makes a face.

"Oh my God. *Is* she a swimsuit model?"

"She did a few shoots for *Sports Illustrated*," he mumbles as if he doesn't want me to hear.

I prop a fist on my hip and ask, probably louder than I should, "Have you slept with her?"

He glances around. "Maybe we should go up to the room."

I snap my jaw shut and my nostrils flare. He's definitely slept with her. I've never considered myself a jealous person, but dear God, that woman is the epitome of physical perfection. And Ethan has seen her naked. Probably more than once based on the look on his face. I spin around and start making my way through the thick crowd lining the bar.

"Princess, where ya goin'?" Josh yells after me.

"Lilah." Ethan's fingers wrap around my wrist and he drops his head so it's close to my ear. "Calm down, baby. I'll explain when we're upstairs. There are too many people taking pictures and shit here."

I clench my teeth, wanting to defy him, but seeing his point. I allow him to lace our fingers and lead me through the crowd. It's simultaneously easier and more difficult since people move out of his way, but he's stopped several times to chat.

When we finally make it to the elevators, we have to wait, and several people get in with us, a few of whom recognize Ethan and want autographs. I back into the corner and keep a placid smile on my face while I watch the numbers on the elevator. I step out around Ethan, who quickly says goodbye and follows after me. Neither of us says a thing while he opens the door and motions me in ahead of him.

I stalk across the lavish penthouse suite he booked for the weekend—definitely not covered by the team—and drop my purse on the couch. I spin around and cross my arms over my chest. "You fucked a swimsuit model." I don't even want to think about him being with her the way he is with me. Two physically perfect people having sex with each other. It makes me want to claw her eyes out. Or chop off her perfect, silky hair.

Ethan unbuttons his suit and blows out a breath. "Lilah—"

"Was it just a hookup? Did you date her?"

"We went out a few times at the end of last season." He shrugs out of his jacket as he crosses the room, tossing it over the arm of the couch.

"So you slept with her more than once?"

"Do you really want me to answer that?"

No. I don't. "Has she been to other games this season?"

Ethan's voice turns steely. "Excuse me?"

"Why was she here tonight?"

He crosses his arms over his chest. "Are you accusing me of something here?"

"No. I don't— There were all these women in the bathroom, talking about who they were going to try to hook up with. Someone mentioned your name and then this fucking supermodel shows up who you've slept with before. Just...fuck!" I'm not sure if I'm on the verge of tears or not. I scrub a hand over my face.

Ethan sighs and drops his arms. Crossing the short distance, he runs a single finger from the bridge of my nose to the tip. "I haven't talked to her or seen her since I moved to Minnesota. It wasn't anything serious. We went out a few times. That's it."

"She's gorgeous."

He tips my chin up. "*You're* gorgeous."

"Hardly."

"Don't you dare diminish how I see you. If I say you're gorgeous, I mean it. She's got nothing on you. Selene was someone to pass time with. You're the one I want. Why else would I have flown you out here?" He runs his thumb along the contour of my bottom lip. "This mouth——" He dips down and brushes his lips over mine, then cups my cheeks in his palms. "This face." He runs his hands down my sides. "This body is mine. You're the only one I want, Lilah."

I let him tip my head back, our lips meeting with gentle penance. I don't want soft and slow, though. Tender and sweet isn't going to cut it tonight.

I'm aggressive and demanding, and Ethan bends to my whim, meeting my fervor with his own. Postwin makeup sex ends up being the most intense we've ever had. He pushes my body's limit, taking satisfaction in the scratches and bite marks I leave behind in a bid to contain my screams as he coaxes orgasm after orgasm out of me, until I have to beg him to stop.

The next morning I'm mortified by the state of his back and chest, marked by my nails and a number of hickeys. Ethan, on the other hand, seems to wear them like a badge of honor, strutting around shirtless until it's time to take me to the airport.

And the hangover. Dear God. Liquid cocaine shots are the worst.

I sleep the entire flight home. I pick up Merk from my

sister's on the way to my house, take both dogs for a quick walk, and make the short drive home. I find fresh flowers in the front entryway from Ethan and my fridge stocked with premade meals he had delivered in my absence, something either Carmen or Jeannie had a hand in, I'm sure. I'm too hungover to enjoy any of the food, so I go straight to bed.

Monday morning I'm still hungover, and it's punctuated by a killer headache and some unfortunate stomach issues. It's the first time I've ever called in sick to work, and I feel horribly guilty, but there's no way I'd be functional. I'm exhausted and jet-lagged, but I try to study. I end up falling asleep on my textbook.

Tuesday evening, I'm staring at a midterm paper with questions on it that I can't answer.

I have to guess at half of the multiple-choice questions and do the same with a good chunk of the short answers, as well. By the end of the eighty-minute class, I'm at risk of tears, out of time, and unable to answer the remaining questions with anything but wild guesses.

I pack my bag and hand in my paper, angry at myself for making such careless choices over the weekend. As much as I love seeing Ethan's career on the rise, I dislike immensely that I seem to be getting further from my goal instead of closer. I don't know how to balance this, and it's starting to become a real problem. One I don't quite know how to address with him.

I wake up to the sound of my phone ringing. I've fallen asleep in front of the muted TV, having put the game on for background noise while I worked on an assignment due later in the week, determined to stay ahead rather than fall behind. Again. An infomercial for high-absorbency sheets flashes on the screen, so it must be pretty late.

"Hey." My voice is raspy with sleep.

"I'm sorry. I forgot the time difference. I didn't mean to wake you." Ethan is slurring and difficult to hear.

I rub my eyes. "Where are you?"

"In my room. D'you see the game t'night?"

"You scored a goal in the second period." I move the papers from my lap, which haven't fared well, since it appears I tried to snuggle with them.

"D'you see the assist in the third?"

"I might've fallen asleep. I recorded it, though, so I can watch it later. Did you do a little celebrating?" I try not to think about all the bunnies hanging around after the games, or women like Selene who know exactly how proficient Ethan is in the bedroom. I looked up the puck bunny wannabe once I got home—she's been in more than a few magazines.

"Just a few beers with the guys. I wish you were here. Home in five days, though. Then I get you back in my bed. I miss you."

He's a little scattered. Still amped up from the win and the alcohol, I'm guessing. I want to ask about the bunnies, but I bite my tongue, aware it will only make me look insecure and dampen his good mood. The bunny stuff never bothered me when we were younger. But then, there weren't any Selenes back then, either. It doesn't matter that he's always asking me to come to his games, at home and out of town, or the constant little gifts that show up at my door in his absence. I still can't shake the worry. "I miss you, too."

"You have a rough day, baby? You sound a little down. Oh, shit—you had the midterm, didn't you? You killed it, right?"

"I think it went well, considering." My still-hungover state and my complete lack of preparation being the parts to consider. I can't tell him the truth, not when he's riding this high.

He's not responsible for my inability to say no to him, or my poor study habits. When he's home, I'll set some boundaries for him and myself.

"You've got this. I should probably let you sleep, yeah? You've gotta work in the morning and I need to do something about my hard-on."

I bark out a laugh. "Nice, Ethan."

"Unless you wanna help me out."

"Kind of hard to do from two time zones away." It's a joke, but there's a tightness in my throat that has everything to do with having met his former swimsuit model fling this past weekend.

His voice goes low. "You could talk me through it, be my cheerleader."

"You and I both know I never would've made the squad."

"My personal cheerleader. No fucking way would I have wanted you bouncing around in one of those little skirts in front of anyone but me."

"The sundresses you liked so much back then didn't cover much more than those cheer skirts."

"I wish I still had a locker for you to leave your panties in. Tuesdays were my favorite in sophomore year."

Leaving my panties in his locker during second period used to be my code for "Let's have lunch at home." Obviously any eating that happened didn't involve food.

He groans and I have to wonder what's happening on the other end of the line. "Hey, I have a fantastic idea. I should call you back on video chat."

I need sleep desperately. "Don't you have a roommate?"

"He's off to some club. Won't be back for a few hours at the very least. Whaddya say?"

I should tell him he can wait to see me in five days. But I don't. Because I miss him. Because he wants me. Because I want him, too, and I don't want him to end up at some club with someone who isn't me.

Less than one minute later I'm staring at Ethan naked on my phone screen. "Fuck this. Hold on. I'm getting my iPad. Get naked, baby."

He hangs up and calls back while I'm in the middle of taking off my shirt.

He's sprawled out on the hotel bed, pillows propped behind

him. His fist is wrapped around his erection, stroking slowly, eyes on the screen. "Fuck, I wanna touch you."

I bite my lip and get up on my knees and adjust the position of the phone so my head isn't cut off.

Ethan's lip curls up into a sexy smirk. "You gonna strip for me?"

I slip my fingers into the waist of my sleep shorts and push them over my hips, pausing at the crest of my pelvis.

Ethan's thumb slips over the head of his erection. "Don't stop now. I wanna see all of you."

I turn around so my ass is facing the phone and peek over my shoulder as I lower my shorts.

"Fuuuuck, Lilah. So sexy."

I shimmy the shorts lower and hold the headboard so I can take them off the rest of the way. Once I'm naked, I move so I'm angled to the side.

"Where would you want me to touch you if I were there with you?" Ethan asks, chest rising and falling faster, muscles in his arms flexing as he continues to stroke himself.

"I'd want you to kiss me." I touch my fingers to my lips. "Here first." I circle a nipple. "Then here." Then walk my fingers down my stomach. I shift so I'm facing him and part my legs, dragging a single finger along my slit with a soft moan. "And here. You'd make me come with your mouth before you fucked me."

Ethan nods. "I sure as fuck would."

"But since you're not here..." I pout a little and reverse

the circuit. Dragging my finger all the way back up my body, I slip it into my mouth. "I'll just have to do it myself, won't I?"

Ethan's eyes are locked on my mouth as I run my tongue over my index and middle fingers. "You're gonna make yourself come for me, now?"

"Is that what you want? You want me to finger fuck myself while you fuck your fist?"

"Listen to that dirty mouth." Ethan's lip curls in a sneer.

"If you were here, you could fill it with your cock." I grin as his mouth drops open and I slide two fingers inside me on a groan.

It's a heady feeling, this power I suddenly wield. I can keep him happy. Give him what he needs even when I can't be with him. I can be whatever he wants.

His fist moves at a punishing pace, much faster and harder than I ever stroke him. I come right after he does, his name a scream on my lips.

⁓

Four days later I'm still exhausted and lacking sleep. It turns out Ethan is a big fan of video chat conversations and feels like he's been missing out on the benefits all these months. I'm actually grateful this discovery didn't happen until now, because Ethan's time away gave my poor body a break from all the intense friction. Now I'm hopeful the Epsom salt baths will be enough to prepare me for his return tomorrow.

Minnesota won the last two games, and last night Ethan scored another goal and added two assists to his stats. His performance on the ice is garnering positive attention in the media. The sportscasters are referencing his time with LA, when he'd been one of the most promising new players in the league. While it's exciting to see him rise to his potential, I worry about what this means for the future. On one hand, Minnesota may want to keep him, but there's also a possibility—and a good one—that other teams will be looking to pick him up. It's unnerving to feel so wrapped up in him, not knowing what the future will look like.

Since tomorrow night will be dedicated to Ethan, and likely a high level of nudity and physical activity, I'm spending my lunch break working on yet another assignment. I don't want it to be on my mind when I'm with him. I also don't want to think about the midterm results I expect back next week.

Finishing this current assignment shouldn't be difficult tonight, as long as I can stay awake, which is why I'm getting a head start now.

As I flip through the textbook, searching for the Post-it note I used to mark my page, someone slips into the chair across from me. I hold back the annoyed sigh. I don't want to be rude, but clearly I'm in the middle of something.

"Are you ignoring me?"

I look up, shocked to see Carmen. "Hey! I didn't know you were coming by for lunch."

"I've hardly seen you in the past two weeks. I figured this

would be a good place to find you, maybe get more than a couple of short text messages from you, especially since the last three have gone unanswered."

I check my phone, then roll my eyes when I see she sent them three minutes ago. "Seriously?"

"Ethan's been away for over a week, and I've only seen you for yoga. Are you suddenly too good for me now that you're dating some huge NHL player?"

I motion to the textbook in front of me. "You know I have this course I'm working on. It's keeping me busy."

She pops a grape from my Tupperware into her mouth. "What're you doing tonight?" she asks midchew.

"More of this." I gesture to the pile of books and papers in front of me.

She taps her nails on the table and frowns. "I get that you're busy being in love and stuff, but you must have a couple of spare hours."

I haven't been a very good sister, not in the past couple of weeks, probably not in the past couple of months. "We could do dinner."

Her face lights up. "Really? How about Mexican?"

"Um, I'm going to say probably not. Ethan's coming home tomorrow, so . . ."

"Right. No bean bloats. What about Italian?"

"Sure. That works. Can you come to my place, though? We can order takeout."

"And watch the game?" Carmen asks.

"Is that okay? I also have to finish this assignment. It's due before the end of the week, and with Ethan coming home..."

"Are things okay there?"

"They're good. He's good." I don't want to be unsociable, particularly with my sister, whom I have admittedly seen little of lately, but with my current workload and Ethan's impending return, I need to squeeze in every second of study time I can. Ethan is only in town for four days, two of which he has games, so sleep will be at a premium until he leaves again. Now that video chats are a thing, I'm on the fence as to whether his away games are a help anymore, or if they've become a hindrance.

"Good, as in you're happy and things are awesome and the sex is better than it was when you were teenagers and he could screw until the sun came up, or good as in you're stressed and juggling all of this is super difficult?"

"Um... both?" I reply honestly.

"Hence the reason I hardly see you these days." Carmen spins my Tupperware container of grapes between her palms. "He seems pretty invested."

I shrug. "I hope so. There's so much history and nostalgia between us. Sometimes I worry I'm... kitschy? It's like flipping through an old photo album. Remembering all the best things is easy when you can pretend the rest never happened, you know? We have so much of our pasts tied up in each other."

"I get what you're saying, but you and Ethan are different. He's not going to walk away from you again."

"You can't know that."

She gives me a wry grin. "I saw him a couple of times when he came home, just at a bar or a restaurant, and the first thing he always asked about was you. I could tell it hurt him that you were married, that you'd moved on, but he never came out and said it."

"Why didn't you ever say anything?"

"What purpose would it have served? As far as he knew you were happily married. He didn't want to interrupt your life, Lilah. And that's exactly what would've happened."

I consider this for a moment. Ethan and I don't do gray areas very well—that much is clear.

"Leaving you broke him. Maybe coming home to you healed him," Carmen offers.

"I'm not the reason he's playing so well."

"Directly, no. But indirectly, maybe. You were the most important person in his life for more than a decade, and then you were gone. He may have initiated the breakup, but that doesn't mean he didn't grieve the loss just like you did."

In all of my selfish suffering, I hadn't fully considered the way it affected Ethan. I'd assumed because he broke it off with me that it was somehow easier, that his pain, his loss were in some way diminished as a result. But I can see now that maybe that's not quite true.

Or maybe I didn't want it to be.

Loving Ethan was only painful when I lost him.

Loving him now is only painful because of the threat of losing him again.

chapter seventeen

BREAKS

Lilah

I pick up the stack of files at the nurses' station and flip through them. The first is a patient with a broken ankle. Scratch that. *Broken* doesn't exactly cover it. Her ankle is shattered. At least she has age on her side. Emery Dove-Smith is an eighteen-year-old college student studying at the University of Minnesota.

Her chart indicates that once she's released, she'll require weekly checkups to monitor progress on her ankle until the cast comes off. Mercy General is much closer to where she lives, but we have the best orthopedic surgeon in the area, which is probably how she ended up here in the first place. An intensive physiotherapy regime will follow. Before I check on her, I take a quick look at the X-ray. Dear lord, the before and after pictures of that ankle are enough to make my stomach turn. Several pins are holding those bones together.

I knock on the door and peek my head in. "Hi, Emery."

She looks away from the TV in the corner of the room and gives me a small smile. "Hi."

"I'm Lilah. I'm your nurse, and I'll be checking in on you this afternoon while you're in recovery."

"Okay." Her eyes have that postsurgery glassiness about them.

"How's your pain?"

She lifts a shoulder. "I don't know. Okay? I feel high. Like I'm floating."

I laugh. "That's the morphine. If it makes you feel queasy, let me know and I can speak with the doctor about adjusting the dose."

"I think I'm good for now." She nods a little, as if she needs to convince herself.

"Your file indicated this happened during a soccer game. Do you play for the college team?" I make small talk as I take her blood pressure and monitor her vitals, giving her something to focus on other than my poking and prodding.

She nods. "Yeah. I'm on a soccer scholarship at the University of Minnesota."

"That's great. I went there for my undergrad. It's a good school. Where's home?"

"I grew up in Texas."

"Minnesota is a bit of a change, then, isn't it?"

"Oh yeah! There's so much snow in the winter. I'm used to playing outside all year, and here we're stuck inside for half of it. And now that we're getting close to the end of all the crappy weather, this happens." She gestures to her casted leg. "I don't even know if I'm going to be able to play again after this."

"You're young and Dr. Lovely is a fantastic surgeon. The best, really."

"Oh my God! He's gorgeous. I can't even function around him. How do you deal?"

I chuckle. Dr. Lovely certainly isn't difficult to look at, but he's a drill sergeant in the operating room and highly professional. "Often he's wearing a surgical mask when we're around each other, so I don't get the full force of those dimples."

"I think my heart rate went through the roof when he was in here. It was so freaking embarrassing. How old is he?"

"Um, midthirties, I think?"

She gives me a saucy grin. "Hmm. I don't suppose he'd be interested in a freshman college girl, huh?"

"I can always ask him for you." I wink. I have no idea what kind of women Dr. Lovely is interested in, but I don't think barely legal college students fit the bill. Regardless, I like this girl. She's got sass, especially for someone who came out of surgery less than two hours ago.

She waves me off. "Nah, he's too old for me. I think twenty-five should be my cap for now. But I'm definitely not into college boys. All they want to do is get drunk and hook up."

"I'm sure they're not all like that."

She lifts one shoulder and lets it fall. "I had a boyfriend for, like, three years, but I got accepted to college out here and he got a scholarship in Texas. We thought we would try to make it work long distance, but my schedule is so busy and it was hard being so far away. So we broke up."

"I'm sorry. That's so tough."

"Thanks, and yeah, it is. Or was. Maybe it still is. He said maybe we could try in the summer when we're both back home. Like, this was just going to be a temporary break, but, like, less than a week later he started posting all these drunk party pictures where he's hanging off other girls."

I feel for her and how difficult that would be to see. "That must've hurt."

She blinks a few times, eyes dropping. "My mom said it was for the best, but yeah, that really sucked, ya know? Like, we were together for all that time, and he couldn't even wait a week before he was hooking up all over the place and posting it where he had to have known I'd see it." She presses her fingertips together, studying them. "I wasn't planning to move back home this summer. I had a lifeguard job lined up here, but now"—she motions to her leg—"I don't even know how long this is going to be on and whether I'll be able to keep that job or not."

"It's only the beginning of March, so pool weather is still a long ways off. You have lots of time, and there are lots of other jobs if that one doesn't work out."

"Yeah. I just don't want to go home and see him and have

to deal with all of it. Relationships suck. I spent this whole year focused on sports and keeping my grades up so I don't lose my scholarship, and I've done well, but, like, sometimes it'd be nice to have, like, a person." She looks up at me and cringes. "I don't know why I'm telling you all of this. You don't even know me and I'm, like, barfing out my life story on you."

My smile is genuine. "I don't mind." We call it "morphine motor mouth," and it can be quite entertaining, but I don't tell her that.

"Do you have a boyfriend? Wait. Can I even ask you that? It's kinda personal, isn't it?"

"That's okay. Yes, I have a boyfriend."

"I figured. You're too pretty not to have one."

I laugh at that. "Thank you. And my current boyfriend was actually my high school boyfriend."

"You've been with him since high school? That's, like, forever!"

"We broke up when he got drafted."

"To, like, the army?"

"No; the NHL."

"Oh my God! No way! So wait—you broke up for, like, how long?"

"Eight years."

"Holy shit. That's a long time."

I laugh again. "You're right—it is. But last year he moved back to Minnesota, so . . ."

"You got back together." Her smile is wide, hopeful.

I keep the part to myself where I don't know if he's going to stay here with me this time, or whether he'll have to take another contract somewhere else. She's young; she has lots of time to learn about the highs and lows of relationships. "I'm going to test the sensation in your toes, okay?"

"Sure."

I check for discomfort, sensation, and mobility. I'm grateful all of her responses are in the normal range.

"Will I make the metal detectors go off in airports now that I'm bionic?" Emery asks.

"Everything is titanium, but there's still a chance."

"I was hoping for the extra-thorough search the next time I go home. When I flew back at Christmas, there was a super-cute TSA agent I wouldn't have minded getting a pat down from." She wags her eyebrows. "I think I have a thing for men in uniforms."

"And scrubs count as a uniform?"

She grins. "Maybe not the hottest uniform, but still a uniform."

When I finish reviewing Emery's chart, I let her know the doctor will be back to check on her in a while and that there's a good possibility they'll keep her at least overnight. "Are your parents on their way here?"

"Uh, no. They're in Europe on some big monthlong trip."

"Do they know you've had surgery?"

"Oh yeah. I called them as soon as the accident happened so I could get the insurance information and stuff. I told them it wasn't that big of a deal. This is, like, the first time they've ever gone on a vacation for this long. I don't want them to fly back because I broke a few bones."

That's an unusually mature way to handle having a bunch of pins and metal rods put in your leg. "Do you need someone to arrange for a ride back to your dorm later?"

"I have a place off campus with a roommate, and I have a car. I guess I'm lucky it's my left leg and not my right, otherwise I'd have to take public transit for the next couple of months."

"You didn't drive yourself here, did you?" I can't imagine that would've been safe.

"Oh no. The ambulance brought me straight from the soccer game. Someone will pick me up."

"Okay, that's good. Well, I'll be around in a couple of hours to check on you. You'll receive a follow-up appointment for next week before you leave."

"Will you be around the next time I'm here?"

I smile. "It's very possible."

"Okay. Out of all the nurses, you've been the nicest, so it'd be cool if it was you doing all the poking business."

"I'll be back to check on you before my shift is over. It's been a pleasure meeting you, Emery. I hope that ankle heals up fast."

What a sweet girl. I don't like that she's downplayed the injury to her parents, but she's eighteen and legally an adult. By that age I was pretty much taking care of myself.

She's asleep when I check on her before I leave for the night. She'll be staying until morning. Dr. Lovely is being cautious, possibly because I mentioned that she has no family in Minnesota and she's relying on her college roommate to help her.

e⁓

The following evening I'm sitting in class, only half paying attention because Ethan keeps sending me messages, asking when I'm going to be at his house. And the messages keep coming. Have I eaten? Should he get Merk? Can I call in sick tomorrow? Can I walk around his house naked for the next twenty-four hours?

Eventually I stuff my phone in my bag, which is the exact moment we're given a pop quiz on the information that's just been shared by the professor. The information I haven't been paying attention to because I've been fielding messages from Ethan. Whom I haven't seen in a week.

I fumble my way through the quiz, angry at myself for being so distracted, certain there's no way I've passed. To top off an already crappy class, we get our midterms back, and I've failed. Not by much—I have 63 percent and I need a 65 to pass—but I've never failed anything, so this mark is a kick in the pants.

The barely passing last semester and late assignments are bad enough, but failure is inexcusable, and I'm totally to blame for this. I allowed this to happen. I ignored the things that required my attention in lieu of time with Ethan, and that's on me. By doing that I've put my own dream at risk, compromised my potential future.

I'd been so certain I'd have a place in the master's program next year, but it's highly competitive and these marks are going to pull my average down. I'm terrified that I might have screwed my future because I'm putting video chats with Ethan in front of my own goals.

I already put my dreams and goals aside for Avery, and now there's a chance I'm going to lose out on the opportunity again because I'm compromising my own needs to meet someone else's. I can't lose myself like this. Not again. Not for someone who's already made it clear once that I wasn't as important as his dream.

"Delilah." My professor stops me as the class files out of the room, ready for tonight's pub crawl. "I'd like a word with you, please."

"Of course." *Please don't let this be a lecture.*

Students file quickly out of the room, and she taps her pen on the desk a few times. "You work at Fairview, is that correct?"

"Yes." We filled out a survey at the beginning of the semester with basic information. I'm astounded that she can recall this.

She nods. "I went back and reviewed your transcript. You were at the top of your graduating class."

I nod. My humiliation grows with her scrutiny. "I was."

"I recognize that working full-time and the responsibilities you must have in addition to this course may impact your grades, but I don't believe your midterm mark is reflective of your abilities." Before I can speak, she holds up a hand. "In fact, I know that mark doesn't reflect your abilities, because on the occasions you've contributed to class discussions you've been insightful and articulate."

It's a significant compliment, but the unspoken part, asking what the hell happened to make me bomb the midterm, dampens it. "Thank you. I promise my next assignments will be reflective of that."

She regards me for seconds that feel like an eternity. "The next two assignments are essay based. I'm hopeful that will help bolster your mark. I'd also like to see you participate more in class discussions. Your in-field experience is valuable to the rest of the students."

"Of course, professor."

She smiles. "I'm sure you have things to do with the rest of your night that likely don't include pints at the student pub."

I return her smile, thank her for her time, and head for the parking lot. The "you can do better" speech is somehow worse than a disappointment lecture. It only serves to exacerbate the self-flagellating. I toss the papers on the passenger seat and check my phone for new messages.

There are several from Ethan, asking for an ETA. I message back that I should be there in less than an hour. It's already eight thirty. I have to be up early for work and tomorrow night Ethan has a game, so the hours we have are limited.

I shelve the failed midterm and the assignments that need my attention. I won't be effective tonight anyway in my current mood. Which I need to put a pin in. I don't want to bog down tonight with negativity, especially since I'm going to have to bail on the game tomorrow night. It's exactly what has to happen so I can bring my mark up before the final exam, which is only weeks away. He has to understand my need for balance.

e⁓

My alarm wakes me at 5:43 in the morning. I've always been a fan of waking up at nonfive increments. Those extra two minutes sometimes mean the difference between hot coffee and no coffee.

Ethan snakes his arm around my waist and pulls me back against him before I can roll out of bed. "Why is your alarm set so early?"

"I have to take Merk for a walk."

"I'll walk him later. Stay for a few more minutes. I missed you."

"You missed rubbing your morning wood on my ass." I'm on point with the sassy quips for only having been alert for mere seconds.

He nods into my neck, lips finding my shoulder. "I did. So

much. I tried snuggling with a pillow, but it wasn't the same. Cotton is a poor substitute for your ass." He rolls his hips, his erection sliding between my cheeks. He cups a breast, pinching my nipple between his fingers, making me arch. His low groan vibrates along my throat.

"I didn't get enough of you last night." He grazes the column of my throat with his teeth, and he smooths his hand down my stomach. When his fingers find my clit, I spread for him, hooking my foot over his calf to give him better access.

Shifting my hips, I press against his erection, letting his fingers and his mouth dominate sensation. He throws off the sheets and adjusts his cock, sliding it along my slit until the head passes over my clit. I watch him ease back and forth a few times and then he's pushing in, slow at first, and then faster, harder. Holding me to him, he slips an arm under me and turns my head toward him, his gaze fixed on mine as he pumps into me, telling me I should never leave his bed, that this is what he needs, that I'm what he needs.

That I'm the reason for everything.

So after, when he tells me he'll see me later, I don't mention not being able to go to the game.

chapter eighteen

PAUSE

Lilah

I go to the game, even though I shouldn't. I knew if I stayed home, I'd still have trouble focusing anyway, aware Ethan would be so disappointed. But I tell him I can't stay afterward and that I must sleep in my own bed tonight. He doesn't like the last part, but I placate him with promises of a sleepover tomorrow. It's easier to stick to my plan since Jeannie and Martin came with me, and I drove.

Ethan's moved from second to first line thanks to his outstanding performance this season. Watching him race down the rink, the puck shifting under his blade as he navigates around the opposing team with single-minded focus, is enthralling. It makes me wish I didn't have to work in the morning and that the sleepover Ethan wants tonight was possible.

Minnesota wins the game three to one. Ethan scores a goal and manages an assist, adding points to his consistently increasing stats. I stop to congratulate a sweaty, happy Ethan on the win before I take his parents home. The sportscasters clamor around him, seeking commentary on his performance. We're surrounded by people, players, reporters, and screaming fans, but the only person he seems to see is me. It's heady, watching his confidence soar like this and feeling like I have some small part in it.

"I can't persuade you to come back to my place tonight?" he says in my ear, his damp, hot fingers trailing along my throat.

I want to say yes, but I already need to catch up on my sleep after last night. I can't afford to be more tired than I already am. "It's almost eleven, and I have to work in the morning."

"I need you beside me, though. I promise I won't bother you."

Based on the way he's looking at me, that's a total lie. "To-morrow night I'm all yours."

"Only mine." He tilts my head back, lips brushing over mine gently at first. His groan buzzes across my skin and his tongue slips inside, seeking out my own. It's the high of the win making him like this. My body already regrets that I have to deny us both. But I need to draw some lines or I'm going to put more at risk than just course work.

Cameras flash, and catcalls and shouts have me pushing on his chest, so Ethan finally disengages from my mouth. I'm sure I'm the color of a tomato as he tips my chin up and places a chaste, somewhat-but-not-really-apologetic kiss on my lips. "I love you, baby." He follows it up by dragging a finger down the slope of my nose.

Microphones are shoved in his face. I step back, and even as he reaches out to keep me with him, I'm swallowed by the crowd. He has no choice but to turn his attention back to the media after that little stunt.

Avoiding the cameras as best as I can, I find Jeannie and Martin and escort them to the parking lot. It's never been like this before. Ethan was always a local star, but this is a whole new level. This is the success he always wanted, though not necessarily the media frenzy that comes with it. But reaching this caliber of performance garners a lot of attention, and I'm on the fringe of it all, watching his rise, wondering how long I get to be a part of it.

Martin is tired by the time I drop him and Jeannie at home. Fatigue makes him uncoordinated, so getting him upstairs isn't realistic, even though he's been managing for the most part lately. He protests at first but finally agrees that the main-floor bedroom is a better place to sleep.

By the time I arrive home, it's well past midnight, and although those essays need my attention, I'm barely awake enough to brush my teeth, let alone focus on a textbook. Tomorrow, when I'm fresh, I can tackle the assignment.

I fall asleep within seconds of my head hitting the pillow.

e⌢

I'm jostled around, and a heavy arm comes across my stomach, pulling me in tight against a huge, hard body. I startle awake and it takes me a moment to realize this isn't a dream, and I recognize the smell and the feel of the body in bed with me. "Ethan?"

"Shh. Go back to sleep. I just want to sleep with you. Beside you. I just want to hold you." He fits himself around me, his erection pressing against the small of my back.

I'm disoriented and irritated that I've been woken up at God knows what hour. "Are you serious with this?" I elbow him in the ribs and try to squirm out of his hold.

"I'm sorry, I'm sorry." He runs his palm down my forearm. "I didn't mean to wake you up."

The length of his erection—his bare erection; I know this because my sleep tank rides up—rubs against my low back, silky and hot. I'm angry that my body responds in his favor, nipples hardening, back arching reflexively. "Then why the hell are you naked?"

He tucks his knees into the back of mine, shifting against me. "I was hot. Just ignore it. It'll go away." Even as he says it, his fingers dip under my tank, finding bare skin.

I elbow him in the side again and he grunts, his hold loosening enough that I can roll away. "What part of no sleepover tonight did you miss, Ethan? You can't just show up in the middle of the night all liquored up and crawl into bed with me. How the hell did you even get here, anyway?"

He blinks and frowns, eyes hazy with lust and dimmed with

booze. "I took a cab. Don't be mad at me. I don't want you to be mad at me. I missed you. I have to go away again in a few days. I just wanted to sleep beside you, but you feel so good and then my body just reacts." He bites his lip. How a grown man manages to look so ridiculously contrite and innocent when he's clearly not is beyond me.

"I need sleep, Ethan. When I tell you I need a night off, you have to respect that."

"I know. I promise I won't do it again. Please don't be mad." He drags a single finger down my nose. "If I lie on my back, I can tuck you into my side and you can go back to sleep. I won't bother you."

"Really?" I arch a brow, glancing at the tent in the sheets.

"I'll just go to the bathroom and take care of my problem?" It's a question.

There's no way I can let him jack off in the bathroom while I lie here in bed thinking about what he's doing on the other side of the door. I close my eyes on a sigh.

I grab his wrist, eyes darting to his heavy, thick erection. "You don't have to do that."

"You need sleep." He bites his lip, his eyes full of apology even though his lids are heavy with desire.

"Well, I'm awake now."

"I'll make you feel good. I'll tire you right out if you'll let me. Show you how sorry I am for waking you up." His mouth is on mine, unrelenting, demanding, and then his hands are roaming over my body, peeling off the tank top and shorts, kissing his way down my stomach. He makes good on his promise, licking me until I come.

"I love you. I need you," he says as he fits himself between my legs, entering me.

Deep down a part of me worries this isn't good for me, for either of us, that his need for me and how much I love it is dangerous. But the fears dissipate like smoke as I get lost in the feel of him moving inside me, taking me higher with every stroke.

He's slow and careful, he's sweet and gentle. He's the boy I fell in love with as a girl, grown into a man I don't think I ever fell out of love with, between then and now.

Morning comes way too fast. Ethan doesn't so much as twitch when my alarm goes off at 5:43. I hit Snooze twice, but Merk is breathing in my face, so trying to sneak in a few extra minutes of sleep is impossible. I'm beyond tired; parts of my body ache that really shouldn't. While the first round of sex was gentle, it was like the lead-up to a thunderstorm, a soft breeze that suddenly changed course and became aggressive, sweeping in and dominating. Round two followed minutes after round one and lasted a hell of a lot longer.

I'm going to require so much caffeine to get through this day. I'm not sure what time Ethan arrived, but I do know the last time I looked at the clock it was after three in the morning. I throw glares at his peaceful form while I stumble around in the semidarkness trying to get dressed. I stop worrying about being quiet and throw on the bathroom light so I don't end up wearing mismatched everything. And still, he sleeps like the dead.

I bang around in the kitchen, working out my frustration on the coffee maker. I let Merk out into the backyard, too tired to manage the walk business this morning. I need to talk to Ethan about this, about the way it impacts my job and my schoolwork. I have to tell him about my failed midterm. I don't want to invite conflict, or put him off his game with playoffs so close and so much riding on the next few weeks, but I need him to respect my boundaries.

I glance up at the ceiling, aware he's above me, sleeping peacefully while I have to go to work and be productive. I run a finger down the bridge of my nose, trying to ease my frustration. Last night—or this morning, I guess—he'd been so remorseful for waking me, apologetic, needy, wanting. Ethan has always been good at making me feel needed—maybe too good. Back when we were teenagers, there was so much less at stake than there is now, for both of us.

I pour coffee into a to-go mug as a tide-me-over until I can get a double espresso at the café on the way to work.

I open the fridge to grab the cream and find a paper bag from a local bakery that wasn't there last night. I check the contents and find my favorite muffin inside. When Ethan would have had the time to pick this up, I have no idea, but the sweet gesture only fuels my annoyance.

On my way out the door, I note a bouquet of flowers left on the table at the entryway that I must've missed on my way to the kitchen in my caffeine-deprived haze. I pluck the card from the envelope. It's simple and to the point:

Lilah,

I love you more than Hot Lips.

Ethan

The romantic gestures are lovely and considerate, but it doesn't negate the fact that he's steamrolling my life and I'm letting him. Merk whines, giving me sad eyes as I head for the door. I give him a pat on the head. "Go breathe in Ethan's face until he wakes up and takes you for a walk."

By the time I arrive at work, I'm slightly more alert and definitely more caffeinated. I worry I'll end up jittery on account of how much coffee I've already consumed, but it's better than falling asleep standing up. I drop my things in my locker and head to the nurses' station.

"Hey! Should I be asking for your autograph this morning? Oh...wow...You must've had a night." Ashley's eyes go wide as she takes in my appearance.

I'm dressed in scrubs, and my hair is pulled into a ponytail, which is typical, so I'm not sure exactly what's different about the way I look, other than my bloodshot eyes. I'm guessing the drops I put in before I left for work have worn off already. "What're you talking about?" I set my extra-large coffee on the desk and flip through the morning case files.

She gives me a funny look. "What am I talking about? Your

face is all over the local media, newspapers, Facebook, Insta—
you name it."

I pause my leafing. "I'm sorry, what?"

"I love that you're his good luck charm. It's just so cute."

I rub my temples. "I'm whose good luck charm?"

"Ethan's. Jeez." She drops her voice. "Are you hungover or
something?"

"Absolutely not!" I snap. I raise a hand in apology. "Sorry. I
didn't have the most restful sleep. I went to the game last night,
and it took a while to settle when I got home."

"I bet." She gives me a commiserating smile. "Based on the
way that man kisses you, I can only imagine the other things
he can do with that mouth of his."

"Ashley! Can we keep this PG? And since when have you
seen Ethan kiss me?" I try to think of a time he was anything
but appropriate when stopping by my work. Sure, he's stopped
by to steal a kiss, but it's always been in private, not in front of
my colleagues. In trucks on private property is one thing; in
the middle of my place of employment is entirely another.

"Um...the whole hockey-watching world has seen him
kiss you, live, on TV."

I set the files down. My stomach drops and my cheeks
flush. "No."

"Oh yeah. He really laid one on you."

I slap a palm over my mouth because I'm incapable of
closing it. Last night, after the game, before I left with his
parents, he kissed me. There'd been camera flashes, but I

hadn't considered that there would be video footage as well, or that it would end up splashed all over the godforsaken interweb. Up until now, any PDA caught on camera has been very family friendly. That kiss last night was not. "Oh my God."

"Right? And then that interview. It's totally understandable that you're tired today. I tried to give you the easiest cases this morning."

"Thanks." I'm genuinely grateful but still so confused. "What interview are you referring to?"

Ashley frowns. "You didn't see it?"

"Uh, no. I didn't even know there was one." Ethan didn't mention an interview, although there wasn't much talking last night, apart from his initial apology.

"I have it bookmarked. It's so sweet."

She pulls up a hockey blog on the computer, scanning the area to make sure no one is around before she hits Play. She lowers the volume, the sound of cheering fans far too loud not to draw attention.

"Ethan! Ethan! Can you tell us about your girlfriend? Rumor has it you're high school sweethearts!"

"Ethan! How'd you feel about your performance on the ice tonight?"

"Ethan! Is this the year Minnesota is going to bring the Cup home?"

The questions keep flying, and Ethan holds up a hand, pointing to one sportscaster. "I'm glad I can be an asset to my team this season. I'm proud to be back home and playing well."

"What do you attribute your success to this season?"

Ethan ducks his head and rubs the back of his neck. His hair is damp, curling at the ends. He runs his fingers through it, making a mess. "Great teammates, a fantastic coach, and serious determination all help, as well as a little bit of luck."

"Do you have any superstitions? Anything you do before a game? Rituals?"

"Where do you think that luck comes from, Ethan?" another reporter shouts.

His head whips around, seeking out the asker of the last question. "Lilah." It's the first and only word out of his mouth.

My skin prickles, but I'm not sure if it's in a good way or not. A volley of questions follows that's hard to keep track of.

"Is Lilah your girlfriend?"

"Is Lilah the woman who was here tonight? Where is she now?"

"You laid one hell of a kiss on her!" Several catcalls follow that remark.

"Would you call her your good luck charm?"

Ethan rubs his bottom lip with his thumb. "Among other things, but yeah, definitely."

"Does Lilah know she's a factor in how well you play?"

"Is she part of your pregame ritual?" one saucy reporter asks.

Ethan laughs, maybe a little high on the win and the attention. "I don't rub her like a genie in a bottle, if that's what you're getting at, but I see her before every home game, and I talk to her before every away one."

"And you think she's the key to your successful season?"

Ethan shrugs but smiles. "Every game she's been at has been a success. I play better when I know she's with me."

"Isn't that the sweetest?" Ashley sighs.

"Yeah, totally." Except *sweet* doesn't seem like the right word. I want to be flattered, but the reality is, I'm not sure I am—not the way it's intended. Because if what Ethan is saying is true, if he believes I'm some kind of charm that's making him play better, how much of what's happening between us is real, and how much is based on superstition and pregame rituals? He's carried them through his entire career, and he's had them since high school rep hockey, and back then I was a part of it, too. Even if it is authentic, how am I supposed to cope with being the center of his success?

Panic makes my chest tighten, like I'm trapped in a small space with no exit. What happens if the team shits the bed come playoffs? What if the pressure is too much and it all falls apart, or they don't even make it into the first series, let alone past it? Will that be on me? Will he harbor resentment? Will I feel some level of culpability, especially if I can't be there to attend games, to give him what he needs and be what he needs? But what about what I need? How much of myself am I supposed to give up?

In an instant I'm transported back in time, to those nights when Ethan would stop by to see me before a game for a good luck kiss. Or when he'd beg me to come to a practice, saying he played better when I was there.

I hadn't connected it until now, or maybe I hadn't wanted to—how he's been doing the same thing for home games. We're always together the night before. It doesn't matter if I'm out with Carmen, or at class, or whatever; as soon as I'm home, he shows up at my door.

Sometimes he's even there before I get home, having taken Merk to the dog park so we'll have more time together. Inevitably there's sex. And I've fed right into it, encouraged it even, high on being needed this way. He's made me feel special, wanted, essential.

I run a hand down my face, scared to look too deep. Like a lot of players, Ethan is a slave to his pregame routines and rituals. And now I worry that I've somehow become part of that routine in a way that's no longer innocuous but unhealthy.

I tune back in to the interview in time to hear the next question from a male reporter, who seems far less interested in Ethan's relationship status.

"Trade talk has started and a lot of rumors are flying. You're on the top of the list as a valuable trade player. Do you think you'll be moving teams again, or staying with Minnesota next season?"

"That's hard to predict. There are some great players on the team and some amazing talent moving up the ranks, so we'll see how it all comes out in the wash. I've been traded the last three years, so I'm ready for that possibility."

My throat constricts. We've skirted this conversation up until now, and here he is talking openly about it in a very public forum. My head aches with the sudden slap shot of reality, and my anger balloons. I feel like a crutch he's using to get through the season.

"Lilah?"

I realize the interview is over. "Hmm?"

"Will you go with him?"

"What?"

"If he's traded, would you go with him?"

"I don't know."

"I'm sorry. That's none of my business."

I smile. "It's fine. It's not something we've talked about. Anyway, I should start my rounds."

"Okay, sure. I'll see you at lunch?"

"Yeah. Definitely." I take my stack of files with me, flipping through the first one, not really processing anything through my anger.

If Ethan had done this interview eight years ago and said all of the same things, I would've been ecstatic. Being his good luck charm would've been romantic. But I've spent the better part of a decade trying to get past the fact that I wasn't important enough for him to keep in his life the first time around—so much so, that I pushed the man I married away and ultimately destroyed that relationship.

Being on the flip side of this coin is just as stressful, if not more so. If he fails, if things don't go the way he wants them to this season, where do I fit in? Do I cease to be important again? More than that, do I want my entire identity wrapped up in what I am to someone else? Being needed is one thing, but it has to be for the right reasons.

I spend my entire day bombarded by coworkers and colleagues talking about the interview and how sweet Ethan is, and aren't I lucky to be dating an NHL player. All it does is frustrate me more.

The highlight of my day is a checkup with Emery, who's become my new favorite patient. Unfortunately, she's also seen the media circus and can't stop mooning over how romantic Ethan is. I don't rain on her romance parade, because her naïve joy is the only positive to my day.

She claps her hands as soon as I peek my head in the room. "You're pretty much famous! Should I ask for your autograph? Oh! Can you get Ethan to sign something for me? He's soooo swoony!"

I roll my eyes. "Not you, too."

She scrunches up her nose. "What do you mean not me, too?"

"Everyone's all over me today about the—" I glance at the TV screen, where that kiss plays out on an entertainment reel recap. "Oh, for fuc—" I cut off the swear before I can finish it.

"Well, someone was all over you, that's for sure." Her grin is wide. "You failed to mention how hot he is. I mean, dude was super sweaty and still smoking."

I laugh. "It's the uniform, I'm sure."

"Not hardly. That man is crazy hot. Like, way hotter than Dr. Lovely, and that's saying something, because he's a smoke show, for sure. Is he super romantic, too? I bet he is. Does he bring you flowers all the time? Do sweet things for you?"

"He can be, when he wants to," I admit, thinking about breakfast and the flowers he left for me this morning and his sweet notes that are always encouraging, whether they're wishing me luck on a test or assignment or just telling me he's thinking about me. Most recently, he hired a housekeeper to stop by every week to clean from top to bottom so I don't have to. But his not respecting what I need and want is definitely the opposite of sweet.

"My parents are like that. Like, my dad buys my mom flowers all the time, and sometimes he'll pick wildflowers and bring them home for her. They are, like, always snuggling and cuddling and making out. It's kinda gross, actually. But still sweet, right? But so much PDA. They hold hands wherever they go."

"They sound sweet."

"Gross, but totally," she agrees. "I guess that's kind of what I want. Someone to love me that much."

I smile but don't say anything as I check the most recent X-ray.

"Oh! Does Ethan have any brothers?"

I laugh. "He has two. One is married with children."

"And the other one?"

"He's single."

"Oh my God. That's awesome news."

"He's also thirty-five."

She flops back on the bed with a pout. "Bummer."

"Total bummer," I agree.

By the time my shift ends, my stomach is in knots and I feel like I'm going to vomit. I have an essay due tomorrow and chapters to read. I need to go home and find the energy to finish it, and not in a half-assed way.

I have messages on my phone from my sister and Ethan, and a voicemail from Jeannie. I check the voicemail first. The knot in my stomach tightens a little. Martin has been doing so well recently. I don't want that progress interrupted, worried how it will affect Ethan and me. The concern is unwarranted, though, since it's just an invitation for dinner.

Typically I go there on nights when I don't have class or other engagements if Ethan is away—which means I'm there a couple of times a week. When Ethan's home and not playing a game and we don't have plans, he invites them for dinner. It's been strategic on Ethan's part, getting them used to his new house—giving his dad that extra beer so getting to the car and going home is too much of a chore, meaning he and Jeannie have to spend the night, which they've done a couple of times.

Ethan had the pool house renovated so they can have their privacy and we have ours.

I call Jeannie back on my way to the car and tell her I'll have to take a rain check.

"Ethan's already here, dear. We'll have a quick meal and you two can be on your way."

"I would love to, but I have to work on an assignment due tomorrow. Can we try later in the week?"

"Certainly. Of course. Is everything okay?"

"I'm fine. Just a little preoccupied." I slip into the driver's seat.

"Okay, then. I can send Ethan home with something for you. Oh, he'd like to speak with you."

"Sure." I get that tight feeling in my throat. I brace myself. Saying no to Ethan has never been easy, and I recognize it won't be any different this time around. In fact, it might even be harder.

"Hey, baby, you're not coming for dinner. You not feeling well?"

"I have an assignment to finish tonight, and I've barely started it, so I need the time."

"Dinner won't take long. You can't go without a meal."

"I'll grab something on the way home."

There's silence for a moment. "Are you okay?"

"I'm fine." Two of the worst words in the history of speaking.

"You don't sound fine."

"I'm tired and stressed about getting this done." I bang my head against the back of the seat. Why can't I come out and say what I need to say? Maybe because I don't know what exactly it is I need to say. Or maybe I do and I just don't want to. I'm too much of a pushover for him. It has to stop.

"I'm sorry about last night. I should've gone home, but I was just so amped from the game. It seemed like a good idea at the time."

I grip the steering wheel as that sick feeling in my stomach grows. "I think it's something we need to figure out, though. I can't be up that late when I have to work the next day and not with this course winding down for the semester."

"I'll be better about that. I promise. Maybe I should skip dinner and come to your place? Then we can talk it out?"

It's like he's listening but not actually hearing me. "Don't skip dinner, please. I need the time."

"So I'll come over after dinner, then? I can bring some for you so you don't have to worry about picking something up." I can almost feel his panic like static on the line.

I should take the night for myself. Focus on the assignment and getting sleep.

"Lilah? After dinner is good? I'll bring you food."

I pinch the bridge of my nose and fight with myself not to cave, but I do anyway. I need to set boundaries, and it needs to be tonight. Hopefully having a clock on my free time will help me be more efficient in finishing my assignment. "Come over around eight thirty—that should give me enough time to get this assignment finished." *I hope.* I feel like I'm losing my grip on myself and my entire life.

"Sure. Okay. I can do that. Are you sure you're all right? You sound...I don't know."

"I have a lot on my mind."

"Because of the assignment, or is it something else?" The sharp edge of anxiety makes his voice thick.

"The assignment, work, the media stuff."

"I should've warned you about the interview last night, but it wasn't on my mind. Is it the PDA stuff? I hope you're not upset about that. I wasn't thinking. We can figure out how to deal with that, too, when I come over."

"We'll talk about it all later. I'll see you at eight thirty, okay?"

"Yeah. Okay. Lilah?"

"Yeah?"

"I love you."

"I love you, too, Ethan." But loving him doesn't mean I should bend for him every time he thinks he needs me.

$\backsim$

Merk rushes to the door before there's even a knock, his customary one-bark greeting signaling Ethan's arrival. I check the clock. It's barely past seven thirty. I've managed to finish all but one question on the assignment, but I'm still annoyed by his early arrival.

I stay where I am, seated at the kitchen table, books and papers arranged around my laptop.

Ethan comes around the corner, Merk on his heels, sniffing the bouquet of flowers in his right hand and then the bag in his left. He sets the bag beside my textbook. "That's dinner for you." Ethan wears a sheepish smile. "Sorry I'm early. I was antsy. I brought you flowers."

He holds them out, so I take them. I know he's trying to be sweet, but he's got to understand flowers aren't the answer to everything.

"I feel bad about keeping you up last night and about the media circus. Were you okay today?"

If I get into this now, I'll never finish this fucking assignment. "I'm not ready to talk about that yet. I still have to complete this." I gesture to the spread on the table.

He rubs the back of his neck, eyes shifting around the table, expression chagrined. "Do you have a lot left? Can I do anything to help?"

"You could not be a distraction—that would be helpful," I snap and then sigh. "Could you take Merk for a walk?" Merk perks right up, tail wagging excitedly as he pushes his nose into my lap.

"Sure, I can do that," he says slowly. "Are you still angry with me? For last night?"

I run my hands down my face. "I really need to finish this assignment, Ethan. We can talk when I'm done."

"Right, okay." He chews on the inside of his lip, not

moving. "I really just wanted to sleep beside you, but then you were wearing those shorts and I was all jacked up from the win..." He grins a little, which irks me even more. He thinks it's funny. Cute even.

"For fuck's sake." I slam my laptop closed. Obviously this conversation isn't going to wait. "Are you really sorry, or are you just saying that because you know I'm pissed off?"

That wipes the smile off his face. Maybe he's finally getting it.

"I'm honestly sorry. I didn't realize you were so upset about it." He takes a step back as I push out of my chair, moving around him. "Maybe you could stay at my place when I have home games. That would probably make it easier, right?"

"That's not going to solve the problem." I'm edgy now, my frustration having festered all day. "It's not just you showing up in the middle of the night that I'm upset about, Ethan."

"What else is it, then?" His fingers graze my wrist and I step out of reach. "Talk to me, Lilah. I don't like this feeling."

"I told you last night that I needed sleep and you still showed up. I told you today that I needed time to work on an assignment and you're here almost an hour early anyway. You can't just show up and expect me to drop everything for you. I have priorities and obligations that are important, too."

"I know that."

"Then why show up early when I asked you not to?"

He jams his hands in his pockets. "Because I knew you were upset with me and I wanted to smooth things over."

"By doing exactly what I asked you not to."

"I won't do it again—show up in the middle of the night like I did or come over early if you ask me not to. I'll take a step back if that's what you want."

I don't know if he can actually follow through with that, though. Ethan is so driven by compulsion. I fear he'll tell me what I want to hear to placate me, but when it comes down to it, he won't be able to give me what I need, and I won't be able to make him adhere to my boundaries. Unless I force us both to.

My throat is so dry right now, my anxiety spiking just like his. "We need to talk about the interview."

He blows out a breath. "I'm sorry about that, too. I wasn't thinking when I kissed you like that. And I didn't expect all the questions, but maybe I should've. Don't worry about the trade talks. Whatever happens, we'll figure it out."

And here he is, glossing over all the issues. Placating as he does. In the past I would let him. But I'm not a teenage girl anymore, and I can't keep sacrificing myself for him.

I cross over to the couch, dropping down because my legs feel watery. "I think I just need . . . some space."

Ethan's eyes flare and his brow furrows. "Wait, what? Where is this coming from?"

I can't look at him, unable to see his confusion, which I share, because as the words come out, they're as much a shock to me as they are to him. "I can't keep doing this."

"Can't keep doing what? This? Us?" He crosses over to sit beside me on the couch.

"That's not—" I have to pause to gather my thoughts and not backtrack. What I want and need seem to be at such odds with each other. "I don't want to lose you again, Ethan. It was so painful the first time." I shake my head. "God, I just...lost myself for such a long time, or got lost in myself. I don't know. And then you come back into my life and it's so familiar and easy. I don't want to be without that again. And that possibility scares me, so I've been putting you ahead of me, in front of my own goals and needs. I see how it's affecting my life, and I don't like it."

His anxiety makes his knee shake. "I don't want you to sacrifice your goals for mine. I promise I'll back off. I can give you more time to work on your course if that's what needs to happen."

"That's already going to happen when you make playoffs, which is inevitable based on how the team is doing. That's what you want and exactly what I want for you. But I can't be responsible for your success any more than you can be responsible for mine."

He shakes his head as understanding registers. "That's not what I meant in that interview."

"I know you guys all get sucked into the superstitions and your rituals, especially around playoff time, but I can't be a good luck charm. I don't think you honestly believe I'm the reason you're doing so well, but even the idea is too much pressure. I can't be that for you. I don't *want* to be that for you."

Ethan swallows, his Adam's apple bobbing heavily as he searches for a way to rationalize this. "You were the best thing in my life for years, and then you were missing and my career went to shit. Now you're back in my life and it's better again. Everything is better with you in it. Don't take that away now, not when things are finally going well for both of us."

"That's the thing, Ethan—they're not going well for both of us. Things are going well for *you*."

"How can you say that? You can't tell me we aren't good together." He gestures between us. "You can't tell me this isn't good."

I wish I didn't have to say it, but I know I do, and the words cause a physical ache in my chest. "It's not the *us* part that I'm talking about."

"What is it, then? Because if it's not us, then I don't get what the problem is."

"I failed my midterm."

He blinks a couple of times. "That's not possible." His shock is reasonable. I always performed well in school, particularly on tests, which were his weak spot. He'd get anxious and then blank out or choke. "You never fail anything."

"I did this time."

"What happened?"

"I've been so focused on you, and keeping you in my life, that I've stopped considering what I need." The reality of this breaks my heart. I've spent so much time being independent and self-sufficient over the past eight years. And the first time

I feel truly needed by the one person I love unconditionally, who left me, I abandon my own dreams for his.

"I'll give you more time to study. I'll help you."

I smile, but I know it's weak at best. "I've never been good at saying no to you, Ethan. And I want to make sure you understand that I'm not saying it's your fault I failed. That's on me. I made the choice to put you ahead of me, and this is the consequence. For now I need to focus on this course and my own goals, and you need to focus on getting through the play-offs and having a shot at the Cup. Between work, this course, and us, something has to give."

Ethan runs a frustrated hand through his hair. "So what does this mean? We're what? Taking a break?"

Every part of me wants to wrap my arms around him and hold on. It's not healthy, it's dangerous, and it's setting me up for a world of heartbreak I'm not sure I'll escape anyway. "I have less than a month to get my mark up. If I don't, I risk not getting into the master's program at all. Playoffs start soon and Minnesota is going to make it, which means you need all your time and energy channeled into your game."

Ethan's eyes are frantic; his fingers tap in distress. "This sounds like a breakup speech, Lilah."

I want to take away his fear, but I can't. "I didn't plan this, not any of it, especially not the part where I fall in love with you again. I can't take this on for you. I can't be the reason you succeed or fail. You have to believe in you as much as I do."

"You don't want to do this," Ethan says softly.

I run a finger down the bridge of his nose, wishing the action could calm us both. "Of course I don't. But I need some time and space to focus on my own life, independent of you. It doesn't do me any good to lose my own dream so you can have yours. It just sets us up for failure all over again."

chapter nineteen

CULPABLE

Ethan

Breaks are the beginning of the end.

At least that's what every single break I've ever initiated led to. So it makes sense that I'm panicking, because as much as the good luck charm comment wasn't meant exactly how Lilah took it, I can understand why she did. And now that I'm being forced to reflect on my own actions, I see why she interpreted it that way.

I've spent the months we've been dating re-creating every single good memory as a reminder of what we used to have in an attempt to rebuild this relationship. And it worked. I love her. She loves me. This is the best season I've had since I was drafted. So I don't want to accept her need for space.

"I need you." The words are out before I can consider their potential damage and how they affirm exactly why she's asking for space.

Her hand lifts and then falls to her side, fists clenching and releasing. "You don't. At least not to play the way you have been. It's not me, Ethan. I'm not the reason. I can't be. I won't take that on for you."

I backpedal, trying to rephrase it in a way that's less overwhelming for her. "I need you in my life."

"This"—she motions between us—"it's consuming. When I'm with you, nothing else matters. I can't find balance, and that's what *I* need right now. I need to find a way to have you in my life without losing myself again."

"I want to fix this." I'm worried about not sleeping beside her, not kissing her before a home game, not speaking to her before an away one. She's right. I've built her into my pattern of pregame rituals, at home games and away ones. I've dominated her life and made her the center of mine. But not in a good way, if she wants this space.

She strokes my cheek, eyes shining with the promise of tears yet to fall. "I know you do. There aren't any magic words, Ethan. I need time to focus on what's important to me, outside of you. This can't be like last time, where my whole world seemed like it ended when you went away, and then again when we broke up. I'm not that girl anymore, and I don't want to be her again."

"I loved that girl." I run a finger down the bridge of her nose. "I love this woman even more."

She smiles sadly and ducks her head. Two tears wet the cushion in front of her. I draw her to me, wrapping her in my arms. She doesn't fight me, so I keep her close, dropping my face into the crook between her neck and her shoulder.

"I want to find a way to change your mind," I murmur.

She laughs and then sniffles. "I know."

"But I also understand doing that won't make things better for you."

She disengages from my embrace, swiping away her tears. "Not for either of us, Ethan."

I curve my palm against her cheek, wiping away the ones that follow. This feels wrong. I don't want to lose what we have. I don't want to give her up for any length of time, but she's resolved. I'm still selfish enough to take one more thing from her before I leave.

"Ethan." Her trembling fingers wrap around my wrist.

"I'm just going to kiss you and then I'll go, okay?"

The sound she makes is more whimper than word, but she doesn't pull away as I slide my fingers into her hair, cup the back of her neck, and angle her head to the side. I stroke inside her mouth, memorizing the taste of her, afraid this is going to be the last time I ever get to do this. I need her more than she understands, but I can't tell her that or I'll make things worse.

I wrap an arm around her waist, pulling her tight up against me, and she comes willingly. Her moan is despondent, and her grip on my shoulders tightens as I deepen the kiss, my own fear channeling into this connection I've fought so hard to bring back and keep in my life.

But I realize she's right. In a way, I believe I can't succeed without her. I also know that if I push, she might relent, but it will come with a price. I can't risk her putting all the walls back up that I've torn down, one brick at a time. So I slow the kiss, loosen my grip, and release her, even though it makes my chest feel like it's splitting open.

"I should leave now?" I mean for it to be a statement, but it comes out a question instead.

Lilah nods, fingers at her lips, eyes still full of tears. It goes against every inclination I have to show myself out. But I do. Because I love her enough to give her whatever time she thinks she needs.

ᘓ

I've been sleeping like shit post–Lilah break. Days creep by in reverse. Time drags and life tastes plastic without her. Last night I drank too many beers so I could crash, which means I'm sloppy on the ice during practice. I'm trying to get my head out of my ass and gain control of the puck, but I'm all over the place, missing stupid shots. In my frustration, I take a turn too fast and roll my ankle, slam into the boards, and land on my ass.

"Shit. Fuck." I lie there, staring up at the steel beams above me, hating life.

Josh comes to a stop beside me, ice spraying out beside him. He holds out a hand. "You all right, man? You're off today."

"Tell me about it." I take the offered palm, testing my ankle as he pulls me up.

"Kase. Hit the bench," Coach calls out.

"I'm fine."

"Bench, Kase. Now." He points to the empty space beside him.

Josh claps me on the back of the neck and knocks his helmet against mine. "You need to check your ankle out. We're too close to the playoffs to lose one of our best players, yeah?"

I nod and skate over to the bench, testing the ache. It's the same ankle I rolled a while back. I'm suddenly terrified I've fucked it up and that I'll be out for the rest of the season and everything will be screwed. I'll lose my whole season. All because Lilah broke up with me. Because I suffocated her. Because I forced her to need space.

I drop down on the bench, gritting my teeth against my frustration.

"Let's have a look at the ankle."

"It's fine. I just rolled it."

He arches a brow. I don't say anything else. Instead I unlace my skate and let the team doctor do his job. "Looks fine, but I'm going to suggest cold and heat therapy tonight, and no more ice time today."

"It's really fine. I'm good to play."

Coach's lips flatten into a line. "I'd rather have you warming the bench during practice than on game day, so enjoy a few minutes of downtime. It looks like you need it today."

Realistically, I haven't done any damage to my ankle, but this feels like an omen. I fucked up with Lilah, and this is the start of the downslide. I'm agitated and anxious as I watch practice. I want to call Lilah, to tell her I was right, that I need her. I can't do this without her, but if I do, I'm going to ruin any chance of getting her back, so instead I stew. Like I've been doing for the past week.

"Kase, a word." Coach motions me over as I'm leaving the locker room after practice.

Josh pats me on the shoulder as he passes. "You want us to wait?"

"Nah, I'll catch up with you." I expected this, the being pulled aside for a one-on-one after my performance on the ice today. At least it was just practice, but tomorrow night we have a crucial game. If we win, we start the playoffs against a team we've never lost to this season. But if we lose, we play a team we've struggled to beat. Obviously a win would put us in a far more favorable position.

"Follow me." Coach leads me down the hall to his office.

I expect him to sit behind his desk, but he doesn't. Instead he takes the club chair and points to the one across from him.

"I promise I'll rest tonight and I'll have my head in the game tomorrow. And I know I was off a bit the last game, but it won't happen again." I only managed an assist and fumbled a potential goal. Thankfully, we still won the game.

Coach raises a hand. "There's a lot of pressure on the team to do well, and I'm aware you're feeling that. You've had an excellent season, and I have no doubt you're going to give us your best going into the playoffs, but you need to ease up on yourself out there. You don't have to be perfect every play. It's not a failure if you miss one shot or a pass. Or if you have one bad practice."

Of all the things I anticipated, a lighten-up speech certainly wasn't it. "I just want to do my best."

"Your performance this season has made that very clear. I know there's been a lot on the line for you career-wise, and bringing you home could've gone one of two ways. I also know trade talks are coming, and you're going to have to make some tough decisions once the playoffs are over."

I drum my fingers on the arm of the chair. "I don't want to ruin it all by messing up the playoffs."

"That's not going to happen."

"Look how I performed today. What if that happens again? What if I choke?" Shit. I shouldn't be voicing this to my coach. But it's what happened every time I was traded to a new team, until I came back home. Until Lilah came back into my life.

"Come on, Kase, you're a commodity. You're playing like they expected you to when you were first drafted. People are noticing, and I'm aware of how much pressure that puts on you to perform well all the time. Just remember, how you played during the season isn't wiped out by one bad game or one bad practice, so don't put yourself in a negative headspace before you've even started the first playoff game."

"I'll do my best to go in with a positive frame of mind." I don't know how I'm going to manage that, though, unless

Lilah miraculously decides she doesn't want to be on this motherfucking break anymore. With my luck, she'll probably decide she's done for good, and then I'll be fucked for the rest of my goddamn life. So far I'm sucking with the positive attitude shit.

He taps on the arm of his chair. "How's your father? He still doing okay?"

"Oh yeah, much better. His stubbornness has been as much a pain in the ass as the reason he's pretty much himself again." Or as much himself as he's ever going to be. Some things are harder than others and probably always will be now, and his speech has never fully recovered. A barely noticeable slur affects certain letters. His lack of censor can be tough to take at times, especially when he's frustrated, but otherwise, he's good.

"Everything else is okay?"

I look down at my bobbing foot, crossed over my leg at the ankle, and will it to stop shaking. "Everything's fine."

He observes me for a moment. "Okay. You let me know if there's anything you need—extra tickets for tomorrow night's game, one-on-one with the trainer, physio, massage. We can make it all happen."

"Thanks, Coach."

I meet up with the rest of my team at the buffet close to the rink so I can carb-load. Going home hasn't been all that exciting, not when there's no one to go home to. That big, empty house feels even emptier without Lilah in it. I've woken up the past two nights on the couch in the living room, uninterested in sleeping in the massive king bed without her.

In the morning I wake up to find a text from Lilah. It's the first time she's reached out since she asked for the break.

Lilah: Check the front porch. I'd wish you good luck tonight, but you don't need it.

I roll off the couch and trudge to the front door. Thankfully, my ankle feels fine. I did what I was supposed to last night—soaked in the hot tub, iced it while I drank a beer, got a semidecent sleep. I almost expect to find Lilah standing there when I open the door, but the message was sent two hours ago, and Lilah's at work.

A small box sits on the stoop, a notecard attached to it. I turn it over.

It's not quite what you're used to, but know I'm rooting for you tonight.

~Lilah

The box is full of Hot Lips. I smile and pop one in my mouth, despite the fact that sugar is not on the menu today. I snap a picture and send it to her along with a thank-you. Her response comes a few minutes later, while I'm brewing a fresh pot of coffee.

Lilah: You're going to be great.

I want her to be there with me, so I put it out there, even though I can already predict the response.

Ethan: I still have an extra ticket if you want it.

The next message takes a while longer to arrive. The hope I tried not to give in to deflates like a balloon.

Lilah: I have class tonight, but thank you. I'll either catch the end at home or the closest pub on campus with all the twenty-one-year-old lushes. **eyeroll.**

I'd prefer no twenty-one-year-olds get anywhere near Lilah, but there's not much I can do about that. I don't know how to navigate the new boundaries, so I let her lead.

I get why she needs this time, even if I don't like it. I know what we're like when we're together, because she consumes my world just as much as I seem to consume hers.

I fire off a quick thank-you, tell her to have a good day, and pour myself a coffee, feeling lighter than I have since she asked for space. I need to stop by my parents' place this morning to drop off the tickets for tonight's game before I head to the arena for the pregame skate.

My mom's car isn't in the driveway when I arrive, which I assume means she's out buying groceries or something. I find my dad sitting on the screened-in porch with a travel mug of coffee in his hands.

"Hey, where's Mom?"

"We ran out of cream. Coffee tastes like shit with milk unless it's one of those expensive latte things." He pats the arm of the chair beside him and inclines his head, an invitation to sit. "What brings you by?"

I drop into the chair. "I have tickets for tonight's game. Row two, center ice."

He lets out a low whistle. "Pays to have someone on the inside, doesn't it? It's going to be a good one."

"I hope so." I tap on the arm of the chair, restless. I wish I had the same faith in myself as everyone else seems to. "I got benched during practice yesterday." Okay, now I'm being a little overdramatic.

He raises a brow. "What'd you do?"

I chuckle. "I rolled my ankle."

He nods knowingly. "Pushing too hard, like you've got something to prove."

"I do have something to prove."

He gives me a wry smile. "I think you've already proven it, son. You'll be fine. You know what you're doing out there on the ice. Just keep your head in the game and stay focused on the goal." He takes another sip of his coffee and grimaces. "Lilah stopped by this morning on her way to work."

I glance over at him, aware the segue is meant to throw me off.

"Give her some time. This is hard on her in ways you can't understand, Ethan."

"I don't know what's going on with us," I admit.

"She's scared. This year has been full of struggle, for both of you, but mostly for Delilah. She ended a marriage that wasn't right for her, and I had a stroke and we had no idea if I was going to be okay. Those two things alone would've been difficult for her."

"And then I came back into her life."

He nods. "You did, and without warning, at a time when she was vulnerable."

"I don't know if that's good or bad, considering how things are right now."

My dad smiles with a serenity I don't share. "You two fought against what you have for a long time, and then when you finally figured it out, there was no separating you. Your mom and I worried about what that would be like with you being a year ahead and going away to college while she was still here."

"That first semester wasn't easy."

His expression turns somber. "I remember."

"My marks were shit."

"Well, Delilah was the one who kept you focused on school, wasn't she? She was always the level head between the two of you. You'd go off half-cocked with these ideas of what things were going to be like, and she'd be over there planning things out."

"She was a drill sergeant with the studying." And the rewards for correct answers were a real incentive to do well, not that I'm going to mention that to my dad.

He sets his coffee down and shifts a little so he's facing me more than the view. "You two can be a good balance for each other. Delilah is grounded and logical, and you're an idealist." He raises a hand when I open my mouth. "Now, before you take that as an insult, hear me out. That idealism is exactly why you're where you are in your career, so it's not a bad thing. Delilah made safe, strategic choices, and you made the ones you felt were right, at least most of the time, when I wasn't interfering."

"You were right, though, about us breaking up when I was drafted—whether you meant it or not. That was the right thing to do. I just should've found a better way to do it." I look at the lake, watching the waves lap against the shore. In little more than a month it'll be warm enough to swim. Eight more weeks and it'll be perfect. I wonder if Lilah and I will be together by then, if this break will be enough time for her to figure out what she wants. I hope so. I hope I don't fuck my career without her.

"Maybe. But you were kids. You both need to let that go. I told her the same thing this morning. That we make decisions based on what we think is right at the time, and those consequences can follow us, but they don't govern the path we're on forever. It's what we take from that experience and how we allow it to impact the choices we make as we move forward that mean the most."

"I'm worried I've screwed things up and pushed her away again."

"You two were never good at moderation. She's trying to find a way to piece herself back together and fit you back in at the same time."

That makes sense. "The interview didn't help. She said the pressure is too much."

"For her it is. Imagine if you'd been the one to lose her."

"I did lose her."

"But you had time to prepare for that loss. You had weeks, Ethan. We had those conversations where you'd idealized how things would go. You had your future all mapped out, but there were too many uncertain variables. Just like Delilah can't handle the pressure now, she was less prepared to handle it then, but she would've tried for you."

He's right. She would've followed me wherever I went, and if I'd failed, she would've owned it, internalized it. As much as I hate it, she was right to ask for space. I've dominated her life these past months, forced myself into every spare moment I could, and pushed down all the boundaries she tried to set for me, for herself. When I really think about it, I've kind of been an asshole.

"She needs to be your equal, not a charm you stick in your pocket and carry around with you. She's not the reason you're playing the way you are, Ethan. You've always had the skills and the drive. You just needed the variables to line up."

"But Lilah's a big part of that."

"She doesn't have anything to do with your ability to play hockey. You've always been an excellent player. I remember the first year you played professionally. You were amazing to watch, all that anger channeled into the game. Professionally it was a great season for you, but emotionally, you struggled. And the further you got from the things that made you comfortable, the more your game suffered. You have all the things that make you comfortable right here."

"Not Lilah, though."

"She's nervous about the trade talks. She's afraid to lose herself again, especially when she's finally on the path she set for herself."

"I want her to come with me this time if I get traded."

"Have you talked about that with her? Does she know that's what you want? Is it what she wants?"

"I haven't brought it up because I don't know what next year is going to look like." I know exactly what I want, but I honestly don't know if she'll want the same, which is why I've avoided the conversation, and maybe that wasn't a great idea.

"Well, if it's what you want, then you need to fight for that, son. For her. I think her biggest fear is that you want her for the wrong reasons. Her needing this time apart is as much about what she thinks you want as it is about her trying to put herself ahead of you. She was never good at that, just like your mother was never good at putting herself in front of me. They're caretakers, sometimes to a fault. That's something you'll need to be mindful of in the future. It'll be up to you to make sure you're not always the first priority."

I consider this for a moment, the dynamics of my parents' relationship, how my mother's world has always revolved around my dad, and his around her. I see now what he's talking about. For eight years Lilah learned to live without me, and I her. But since I've returned to Minnesota, I've made my world revolve around Lilah and hockey. What I failed to consider is the life she built without me in it. In trying to make her mine again, I've upset her balance and her life, pulling her away from the things she loves outside of me.

"I'm not sure I know how to do that."

"You put aside your own needs. You do what you're doing—you give her the space she's asking for."

"That's not easy."

He chuckles. "No, but you'll do it because you love her and you want to keep her in your life, like she wants to keep you in hers. For as strong as she is, she's afraid of being let down again."

"You're really close to her, aren't you?" I'm almost jealous of their relationship, because I've never been that close to my dad. This year has changed that to a certain extent. I'd always felt as if his disapproval over my career choice made it impossible to get close to him, that if I'd gone into medicine like he'd anticipated, we might've been closer. Or maybe not. Maybe this is just our time.

"She might not be my blood, but she grew up in this house,

and she's like a daughter. Lilah's always been a big part of all of our lives, but as much as we love her, I don't think she's ever felt like she truly belongs anywhere."

"She belongs with me."

My dad laughs, his smile full of a knowledge that only comes from life experience and observation. "So I guess you need to make sure she understands that she's the other half of your soul, and that you need her because you love her, and no other reason."

chapter twenty

FAMILY SECRETS

Lilah

How much longer are you going to make me do this?" Carmen asks as we toss our yoga mats into the trunk of her car. Tonight I walked to yoga for some extra fresh air, but I'm happy to catch a ride home.

"No one is forcing you to come to yoga with me."

"Someone has to keep you from moping all the time."

I give her a look from over the hood and wait for her to unlock the doors. "I haven't been moping."

"You've been replacing sex with exercise, and that's almost as bad. I'm constantly sore, and not in a ridden-hard, bent-into-a-pretzel, and highly satisfied kind of way."

"Well, it's not my fault you've made yourself available. You can always opt to hang out with me after I'm done with the yoga."

"What kind of sister would I be if I didn't come with you and then complain about it?"

"I feel so honored by your sisterly dedication." I adjust the seat so I'm not eating the dashboard and buckle myself in. She keeps it close to the dash so Barkley won't try to sit in the front seat with her, since he's huge and can be a distraction.

Another reason I'm so intent on all these yoga classes is to keep myself occupied and not focused on Ethan and the playoffs outside of work and exam prep.

His away games have been easier to manage than the home ones in some ways. In others, they've been more of a challenge. Missing the game that secured their place in the playoffs was difficult but necessary. As much as I wanted to be there to support him, my own life needs my attention. The time has paid off. I've managed to earn exemplary marks on the last three assignments, and my grades are up as a result. I'll be in a much better place going into this exam than I was when everything blew up between Ethan and me.

He's currently in LA, and tomorrow they play the second away game of the series. Minnesota lost the first game two to one. That they're playing against the team he used to be part of when he was first drafted makes his anxiety worse. The opposing team was chippy last game, and they'll have inflated egos from the previous win, so hopefully Minnesota can use that to their advantage. Ethan flies back later this week, and they'll have home ice advantage for the next two games. They're getting so close to securing a place in the finals. I want this so much for him, so he can see how good he is, with or without me.

"You know what would be nice?" Carmen asks.

"What's that?"

"If you'd figure out what you're going to do before the season is over—like, it'd be great if we could go to some of these playoff games."

"You've never been into hockey."

"I'm not. It's the players I'm into. Those boys are in seriously good shape. And those playoff beards. Sweet lord. How good does that feel between your thighs?"

I can't answer that question because I haven't had Ethan's beard between my legs. I'd like to say I'll have that experience before he shaves it off at the end of the season, but I'm not so sure that's going to happen.

"I can get you tickets if you want them."

"Not if you're not coming with me."

"I can't go."

"What's one game, Lilah?"

"It doesn't send the right message."

"What message are you looking to send? What are you going to do?"

"I don't know yet." I truly wish I knew what the right decision is. In these weeks of separation, I've come to see how much I've allowed this relationship to take over every single part of my life. I don't know if I'm capable of finding balance with Ethan.

When I get home, I find a small box on my front porch. It doesn't have a return address, and it was sent Priority Mail. I drop my keys on the side table and absently pat Merk on the head. He's been for a walk already, so I cross through the house and let him run around in the backyard while I open the box.

Inside is a bag of Hot Lips and an envelope. I pluck the envelope from the bottom of the box. It's lumpy, something hard sliding around inside. I flip it open to find a card inside, and as I slip it free, something silver falls to the floor. I bend to pick it up, and a lump forms in my throat that's hard to swallow around.

It's a set of dog tags. Ethan's dog tags, to be specific. The ones I gave him all those years ago when we started dating. He doesn't go anywhere without them. They're either hanging from the rearview mirror of his truck or tucked into the pocket of his jeans. In all the time he's had them, he's only misplaced them a couple of times, at least that I'm aware of. He tore apart his room to find them both times.

I finger the smooth, worn metal and press them to my lips. They smell faintly of his cologne, or maybe that's in my head. That they're here with me and not with him on the other side of the country seems incredibly significant.

The card clutched in my other hand reads *Good Luck!*

I flip it open and smile at his messy scrawl.

Lilah,

You got this, baby. I just want you to know I'm thinking about you tomorrow while you're kicking stats ass, wishing I were there to cheer you on like you've always done for me.

I love you,
Ethan

It's been weeks since I asked for a break. Ethan hasn't pushed at all, but he's been constant in his quest to show me that he's thinking about me. Groceries magically appear in my fridge twice a week, along with prepared meals so I don't have to cook. He'll stop by in the afternoon when he's not at away games and take Merk for a long walk so I can focus on studying. He's never there when I get home, but he leaves notes and flowers.

I take a few selfies—something I don't usually do—first of me kissing the dog tags and another of me wearing them. The chain is long, so they sit quite nicely in my cleavage, which is pretty great at the moment, considering my yoga top. I send the pictures to Ethan along with a thank-you.

My phone buzzes less than a minute later, my stomach knotting as I answer the video call. "Hi."

"Is this okay?" He's in a hotel room, shirtless.

"The view you mean?"

He grins and laughs. "I meant me calling. I'm glad they got there. I was worried they'd be late getting to you."

"Thank you for these." I finger the dog tags.

Ethan's eyes are soft. "They look good on you. You're gonna rock that exam tomorrow, baby."

My stomach dips over the endearment, his sweet expression, his thoughtfulness. "It's been nonstop studying around here the past week, so I have my fingers crossed. How's every-thing there?"

"Good. Just getting ready to head to the rink for practice."

"I should let you go, then." There's awkwardness for a mo-ment. "Good luck out there tomorrow night if I don't talk to you before then."

"Thanks, baby, but you don't need luck if you've got skill." He winks and we both laugh.

I end the call feeling both lighter and heavier. I miss him and now I have this piece of him.

Even though I don't buy into superstitions all that much, I find myself touching the smooth steel of the dog tags the next evening during my exam. I press them to my lips as I answer question after question. I only struggle with one problem; the rest I seem to breeze through. I leave the exam feeling con-fident that I've done well, and I'm finishing the semester and the course on a high.

I get home in time to watch the last period of Ethan's game. I pour a well-deserved drink and settle in, excited to see that Minnesota is up one goal. They keep the lead and Ethan man-ages an assist with three minutes to go. LA can't catch up, and Minnesota takes the win. I send Ethan a quick message:

Lilah: Nice work on the ice tonight—no good luck charms necessary.

It's a long while before I hear from him, likely because of

postgame interviews and time spent in the locker room. I'm already cozied up in bed and half-asleep by the time I get a response.

> **Ethan:** Mad skills here. You kill the exam?
> **Lilah:** You know it.
> **Ethan:** That's my girl. What're you up to now?
> **Lilah:** In bed. Early morning for me.

I don't get a response right away, which is a bit of a surprise all considering, so I fire another text off, second-guessing myself as soon as I hit Send.

> **Lilah:** No innuendo about me being in bed?
> **Ethan:** I kept those all in my head. I'm trying to be good over here, and you baiting me is unhelpful. Go to sleep so you don't mess this up for me.
> **Lilah:** Night <3
> **Ethan:** Sweet dreams, baby.

When Ethan comes home the next day and stops by with flowers, I suggest we go out for a postexam, game-win celebration drink. He doesn't invite himself in afterward, and he doesn't try to kiss me—well, not on the lips. All I get is a peck on the cheek, and when I try to give him back the dog tags, he tells me to hold on to them until my exam results come in.

Even without the tags, they win the next two home games

and head back to LA, hopefully to finish out the series and move on to the finals.

℮

Wednesdays have secretly become my favorite day at work because that's when Emery comes in for her weekly PT and a checkup. She's a bright light in my week. It's been long weeks of hard work for her, but she's recovered well, and based on her progress, she'll be able to return to the soccer field soon.

I peek into the physio room, taking a moment to watch her as she goes through the exercises, determination making her push hard. As happy as I am to see her doing so well, I'm a little sad that she'll be done with treatment soon and I won't get to see her anymore. I've grown attached to her, which isn't something that usually happens with patients, but then I don't often see them on a weekly basis like this. Which is maybe why becoming a practitioner is so appealing, especially if I get to work with families. I'll be able to see progress as it happens, as I have with Emery. I feel like I can really make a difference.

She waves when she spots me at the doorway. "Check this out, Lilah!" She does some kind of move that would probably pull all sorts of muscles if I were to try it.

"Looking good."

"Right? Dr. Lovely said one more week and he thinks I'm

clear to play summer league. Took forever, but it's been so worth it."

I mirror her enthusiastic smile. "That's fantastic news."

"I know." Her grin falls a bit and she fiddles with her ponytail. "I'm kinda sad I won't have a reason to come here anymore, though."

"Miss checking out the lovely doctor?" I cross over to where she's standing.

Her smile returns, impish this time. "It really is too bad he's so old. Maybe when I'm of legal drinking age, he'll be interested."

I laugh at the idea that midthirties is old to her. "May I request that you don't break anything else in order to test that theory, please?"

"Uh, yeah. I have zero plans to break any more bones. Um, I don't know if this is, like, allowed or whatever, but maybe, I don't know . . . we could keep in touch once I'm not a patient here anymore? Or you could, like, come see a game or something if that's not allowed."

"I would love that." And honestly, I probably would've found myself at a game even if I hadn't had a direct invitation, but this certainly makes that easier. "Actually, I might be taking some courses there in the fall."

"Really?"

"Yup, so maybe we can meet up for coffee, or something."

She claps her hands and does a little jumpy thing before throwing her arms around me. She releases me before I can return the embrace. "Awesome. I'm staying to take extra courses this summer, and it looks like I get to keep my lifeguarding job, so I'll be around."

"What's the boy situation looking like?"

She makes a face. "I went out with this guy last week, but he thought coffee would get him an invitation back to my apartment. There's a graduate student in my building who offered to help me study for my human biology final, and I totally wouldn't mind if it ended up being hands-on." She nudges me with her elbow and gives me an exaggerated wink.

I laugh at that. "Just make sure you're safe about the hands-on part."

"Oh my God! Do not do that parent thing with me. I already have a mother who is way too interested in having those kinds of conversations. Oh! Speaking of parents, you'll probably meet them. They're picking me up today."

"Are they here for a visit?"

"Yeah. They're driving across the country in an RV for fun. They've already done the entire West Coast, so they figured they'd head this way before they go south again. I swear, my dad has no idea how to relax. They've gone on, like, four trips already, and he's only been retired for four months. Anyway, they're stopping here for a few days. Personally I think my parents are kind of having a hard time with me not coming back for the summer and this is their way of managing, since I'm pretty much their only kid."

"That makes sense. There's not really a reason for them to

stay put all summer if you're not going to be there, so they might as well come see you, right?"

"Yeah. So I try not to get all uptight about how much they call, or that they want to know every detail of every little thing."

"That's a mature attitude." I had the opposite experience as a kid with my own mother. She was too busy juggling jobs and trying to put food on the table for all of us to be interested in the details of my life.

She shrugs. "I'd rather have parents who want to know everything instead of nothing, I guess." Her phone buzzes in her pocket, and her eyes light up as she checks the message. "They're here! Want to come meet them? I kind of told them about you..." She scrunches up her nose, like maybe she's embarrassed. "Except—and don't be offended—I called you Nurse Ratched. I meant it as a joke, though, because, like, clearly you're the opposite of a manipulative psychopath."

I bark out a laugh. "I should probably get an introduction, then, just so they're not worried about your medical care."

"My dad says they're waiting by the front entrance. I hope they didn't bring the RV, 'cause that'd be kind of embarrassing." She bounces with excitement as we walk down the hall. A couple in their fifties stand close to each other by the main doors, heads bent together as they check a phone. They lift their gaze as Emery calls out, "Mom! Dad!"

She breaks into a jog, throwing herself at her parents, and my heart aches a little, but in a good way, as they wrap her up in their arms, the three of them parts of a whole. I stand back, a silent observer, and wonder if I'll ever have a family of my own. And if Ethan will be a part of that or not. Regardless, it would be nice to have someone who loves me as much as Emery seems to love her parents.

"Mom, Dad, I want you to meet my friend, or my nurse." She flails as if unsure how to introduce me.

"I think I'm safely both of those things."

I smile at her mom and then shift to greet her father.

"Delilah Jane?"

I stare at him, openmouthed and unable to speak. It's been twenty years, but even with the lines on his face and the receding gray hair, I couldn't ever forget him.

"Dad?"

chapter twenty-one

FORGIVENESS

Lilah

I open my eyes and find myself surrounded by medical staff. It takes me a few seconds to process what's going on until I see the concerned face of Emery, arms crossed over her body as if she's hugging herself. Beside her, twenty years older than he was the last time I saw him, is my father.

"I'm fine." I brush away the hands of my colleagues, embarrassed. I've never fainted in my life.

"You hit your head pretty hard," Emery says.

"Let me do a quick assessment, Lilah." Dr. Lovely isn't asking—he's telling.

I acquiesce because there's no way I'm getting out of an exam to check for a concussion at the very least. "Okay. Fine."

I ignore his offered hand and manage to get to my feet on my own, but I'm a little off balance. Still, when a wheelchair appears, I balk. "I can walk to an exam room."

"You will take the chair, and you will be a gracious patient, Delilah," Dr. Lovely replies evenly.

I purse my lips, give him a glare that would wilt a lesser man, and drop into the chair.

"Lilah?" Emery's soft voice brings my attention back to her. She looks so confused and maybe a little scared.

I give her a small smile. "I'm fine. It's okay if you have to go. I know how to get in touch with you."

She bites her lip and rushes over, throwing her arms around my neck in an awkward hug. "I hope you really are my sister, because that would be the best ever." She lets me go and steps back, using the sleeve of her shirt to wipe at her eyes. I feel my own pricking with an echo of her emotions.

I don't look at the man responsible for providing half of my DNA as they wheel me away.

Despite assuring everyone I'm physically fine, a thorough assessment is done before I'm given the all clear. The whole thing takes an hour.

"I'd like you to call your sister and have her pick you up," Dr. Lovely says when he's finally satisfied I don't have a concussion, just a bump on the back of my head.

For a moment I'm confused, and he must read it on my face, because he adds, "Carmen. Is she available to take you home?"

"I'm fine. I don't have a concussion, and I have three hours left in my shift."

He crosses his arms over his chest. "You're not finishing your shift with a head injury, Delilah."

"Stop calling me Delilah, and I fainted—it's not a head injury."

"You fainted and hit your head on a cement floor. That's a minor head injury, and while you may not have a concussion, I'd prefer not to take any chances with you, or with any of my other patients. You also have the next two days off."

"For a bruise?"

"I think your headspace might not be the best right now."

When I begin to argue, he gives me a look. "Lilah, that man out there said he was your father, and he hasn't seen you since you were six. You've been treating your half sister for weeks because of a shattered ankle. Now, I'm just guessing here, but I think you may need a couple of days to get your head around that."

"I thought you were a physician, not a psychiatrist."

His cheek tics with a suppressed grin. "Call Carmen, please."

I slide my phone out of my pocket with an irritated sigh. "You know, you might think you have a great bedside manner, but really it's just your face that allows you to get away with ordering people around like this."

He smiles. "I'll take that as a compliment."

Carmen answers on the third ring. "Are you busy?" I ask.

She snorts. "That's your greeting?"

"Hi, Carmen. How's your day going? Are you busy?"

"Tell your sister hello for me," Dr. Lovely says as he removes his gloves and tosses them in the trash.

I give him my WTF face but do as he says. Otherwise I'm sure he'll take the phone out of my hand because that's the kind of mood he seems to be in. "Dr. Lovely says hello."

"Noah Lovely?"

"Yeah."

"Oh, uh, I guess tell him I said hello back? Why're you calling me?"

I address Dr. Lovely. "She says hi back. This feels very eighth grade, by the way."

All he does is grin. What the hell? I shake my head, which is starting to ache, and return to my conversation with my sister. "I fainted and hit my head and Dr. Lovely would like you to pick me up because he feels I'm unfit to drive."

"Are you okay? Why did you faint? Is something wrong? Did something happen? Is Martin okay? What about Ethan?" Her voice continues to rise as she peppers me with questions.

"I need you to calm down, or I'll have to call someone else for a ride. I'm fine and so are Martin and Ethan, as far as I know. I'll explain everything when you get here, if you're available to pick me up, that is."

"I can be there in half an hour. Is that okay?"

"Half an hour is perfect. I'm sure there's some workplace accident report I need to fill out in the meantime."

"I'll be there as soon as I can."

I end the call and sigh. As if I need any more complications in my life. The Ethan situation is more than enough all on its own. Now I find out I might have another sister. Not might, I *do* have another sister. And I like her. Except right now I feel nothing but jealousy. My father left us all to start a new family. From Emery's accounts, he's a fantastic dad and completely head over heels in love with her mother.

I rub my temples and hop down off the hospital bed. "I need some air."

"I'll walk you out, then."

I'm too exhausted to argue that I'm fine and don't need a babysitter. I could use a nap more than anything else, but fresh air will have to do. We stop at the hospital cafeteria for a coffee before he escorts me to the front entrance. I guess he's serious about walking me out of the building.

As I'm approaching the doors, I hear my name. I freeze, then turn as my father pushes up out of a chair and smooths his hands down his thighs. He looks nervous and uncomfortable. I should hope so.

He takes a few halting steps toward me, stopping about four feet away. "Are you okay?" He turns to Dr. Lovely. "Is Delilah okay?"

"She's cleared to leave but not to drive."

"I could give you a ride home. We could talk."

I bark out a disbelieving laugh. "You're about twenty years too late for father-daughter bonding, Darryl. Besides, Carmen is coming to get me."

"Carmen still lives here?"

I hate that this is a question he legitimately doesn't have an answer to. "Where's Emery?"

"I sent her home with her mother. She's very...confused."

"Well, that makes two of us."

"It would be good if we could talk, somewhere private. Emery isn't at fault for any of this." He gestures between us.

I realize Dr. Lovely is still standing beside me, bearing witness to this family drama. I turn to him. "It's fine. I'm fine. You have real patients with real emergencies."

"I have a private lounge you can use if you'd like to have a conversation," he says, not to me, but to my father.

"That would be great," my father replies.

Again, I don't argue. I'm too shell-shocked, so I follow along dumbly to the lounge, usually reserved for families of patients in critical surgery.

"I'll check on you in a bit," Dr. Lovely says before he closes the door.

"You look so much like your mother," my father says once we're alone.

I give him a disbelieving look. "Really? That's your lead-in? That I look like the woman you abandoned along with your six kids, so you could what? Have a do-over? Start a new family that was less inconvenient than the one you had? It's been twenty years. Where the hell were you when I was growing up?"

He blows out a breath and drops his head, hands clasped in front of him. "It was complicated, Delilah."

"That's a cop-out. Why did you bother to wait for me if you're just going to tiptoe around answers? Or is it because of

Emery? Jesus. Did she even know you had a whole separate family?"

"She knew I had children from another marriage."

"Does she know you haven't seen any of us in the last twenty years since you abandoned us?"

He lifts his hands, contrite. "I understand why you're angry."

"Do you? Do you *really* understand? I don't think you do. One day you were part of my life and then you disappeared." I snap my fingers. "And I always wondered, why weren't we good enough? What did we do that was so bad that you erased your existence from our lives?"

"I tried to contact you."

"Bullshit," I spit.

"I know this is a shock, Delilah, but please, let me at least explain my side. I'm sure you have your mother's, but you're missing mine. I never wanted it to be this way. I didn't want to lose contact with my kids. It was devastating. Things with your mother and me were never easy. We were married before we were even out of high school. We were kids with ideas of what life would be like, and she wasn't even eighteen when your oldest brother was born.

"We struggled so much, our parents weren't much help, and it was . . . day-to-day for such a long time. Just when it felt like things were starting to balance out, your mother got pregnant again. Babies became Band-Aids for us. Every time something went wrong, or we'd have a disagreement, we decided another baby was the answer. I loved her and I wanted her to be happy, and babies made her happy."

"Did they make you happy? Was that what you wanted?"

"I wanted a family, and I loved all of you. After you I thought maybe it was time to stop. We pretty much had our own hockey team." He laughs a little at that but quickly sobers when I don't join in. "Six was a lot of mouths to feed on one salary. I was working two jobs and trying to finish college so I could be a better provider. When I scheduled a vasectomy, your mother was upset."

"So you left?"

"No. Of course not. But that's when things started to unravel. I don't want to demonize your mother. I don't think that's helpful, and I'm not sure exactly what she told you, but she was the one who kicked me out. I applied for custody but was denied because I had left the home. Things worked differently back then. She made it impossible for me to see any of you, and she stonewalled any of my attempts to contact you and your brothers and sister. I should've tried harder—I know that. But I met Renee and she was just"—he sighs—"I had a chance to start over, so I took it."

"Does *she* know about all of us?"

He nods and looks at his hands. "She does. She suggested I reach out, and I tried, many times, but by then your brothers had moved out, and your mother threatened a restraining order if I tried to see you and Carmen. I didn't want to make your lives more difficult, so I stayed away."

"Do you have any idea how horrible it was to grow up thinking I was unwanted and unloved by one of the two people who were supposed to love me unconditionally?"

"I can imagine—"

I cut him off. "No you can't. Not even a little bit. You can't imagine what it was like growing up in a house so full of chaos that I was forgotten about most of the time."

He stiffens, and his fingers curl around the arms of his chair. He seems legitimately shocked and saddened by this revelation. "I'm very sorry, Delilah."

"I'm not sure I can accept your apology. That damage was done a long time ago. It's rooted in who I am, and it's impacted all of my relationships. I don't know how to forgive that." As I watch my words sink in, causing fresh pain I share, I realize the truth in what I've just said. For the first time I see with real clarity why Ethan's leaving was so devastating, and why I've been so tentative and reluctant to fully embrace this second chance with him—because I'm convinced that no matter what, I'll lose him again. Deep down I fear his love for me has an expiration date attached to it, like I believed my father's did.

"I know I may never be able to earn your forgiveness, but don't take this out on Emery. She'll be crushed if you don't want a relationship with her."

"How much of your version of the truth does she know?"

"I tried to do better the second time around."

"Well, she loves you and thinks the world of you, so I guess your second family won out, didn't it?" I blow out a breath, trying to manage the overwhelming anger and shock. "I'd like a relationship with Emery. She's a good person, and I'd like to know her better."

"She'll be happy to hear that." His smile is eclipsed by his pain, but I won't own that because I'm not the reason for it in the first place.

My phone buzzes, and I check the message. "I need to go."

He stands along with me. "Is Carmen here? I'd like to see her."

I hold up a hand. "I don't think that's the best idea right now. It would be better if we arranged something after I've had a chance to talk to her. She doesn't deserve to be blindsided like I was."

"Right. Yes. Of course. Should I give you my contact information? We're staying in Minneapolis for a few days and I'm happy to extend our visit if she needs time to consider it. I hope I'll have the chance to speak with her."

"I'll talk to her and she can decide if that's something she wants."

He recites his number, and I add it to my contacts. This whole thing is like an out-of-body experience.

"Delilah."

I open the door and look over my shoulder. If he tells me he loves me, I may lose it on him. I've been pretty reasonable up until this point. I need to get away from him so I can think, process, wrap my head around this.

He stuffs his hands into his pockets. "I wish I'd made different choices."

"Me, too."

On my way to the front entrance, I run into Dr. Lovely again. "I was coming to check on you."

"Wanted to make sure you didn't have another head trauma on your hands?"

He falls into step beside me. "Something like that. How *is* your head?"

"Other than sore and full of more crap than I'd care to deal with in the next lifetime, fine. Carmen's waiting for me in the parking lot, so now I get to tell her we have a half sister we didn't know about, and our father is in town."

The automatic doors slide open and we step outside into the crisp afternoon. "How do you think she'll react?"

"I have no idea. Hopefully she doesn't faint like I did, or else no one will be able to drive. What're you doing?" He's still walking with me. It's starting to feel a little weird.

"Making sure you get safely to your sister."

I can't decide if it's his medical duty making him so ultra attentive, or if I'm just hypersensitive to it. Carmen's car is parked at the emergency entrance in the no-parking zone. "She's right there—I'm good. You can go back to doctoring now."

He ignores me and strides over to her car, opening the door and ushering me inside. He takes it upon himself to roll my window down from the inside, which is also strange. I buckle myself in while he closes the door and bends down so he can see into the car.

"Hello, Carmen." He smiles placidly at my sister.

"Noah."

"Thank you for coming to pick up Lilah. She's had a bit of a rough afternoon. If there's any nausea or vomiting, or if the headache gets worse, please call my pager." He extends his arm through the window, bypassing me to hand his card to my sister.

"Do you have a concussion?" Her eyes are wide, her gaze moving to Dr. Lovely. "Does she have a concussion?"

"It doesn't appear that way. However, I would prefer not to take any chances with my staff."

"Right. Okay."

"Please don't hesitate to contact me if you have concerns or questions." She tries to take the card, but he holds on to it, eyes shifting to me. "I'd like an update on how you're feeling tomorrow, Lilah."

I give him an army salute. "Sir, yes, sir."

"Get some rest, please." He lets go of the card. "Drive safely." Then he removes his head from the window and disappears back inside the hospital.

"Jeez, he's intense," I mutter.

"Sure is." Carmen pulls away from the entrance. "What happened?"

"I think it would be best for me to tell you when we get to my place."

"This sounds bad."

"It's . . . complicated."

"Does it have to do with Ethan?"

"No, it has nothing to do with Ethan." Not directly, anyway. But it may impact how things unfold with him from here on out.

"Can I at least get a hint or something? This is seriously stressing me out, Lilah."

I drop my head against the headrest and suck in a breath at the pain, quickly leaning forward again. I run my fingers over the lump at the back of my head. It's practically a goose egg. "Trust me—it'll be better if we're not in a moving vehicle when I tell you."

She sighs but lets it go, for now.

"How do you know Dr. Lovely, anyway?" I ask as she heads toward my house.

"We went to high school together."

"He's a few years older than you, though, isn't he?"

"I was a freshman when he was a junior." She taps the steering wheel.

"Did you have a crush on him or something?"

Carmen rolls her eyes. "Have you seen that man? He just gets better looking all the time. It's totally unfair. Every girl in the entire school had a crush on him. It was ridiculous. Anyway, he tutored me in science when he was a senior." Her face is a little red.

"Want to tell me more about that?"

"There's nothing to tell. He tutored me and I didn't fail my science class. All was right with the world."

I don't buy it, but then who knows with Carmen? Maybe it was that simple and I'm just reading into things. I close my eyes and try to focus on something other than the throb in my head. A few minutes later Carmen pulls into my driveway and cuts the engine. "You need to spill it, right after you make me a margarita."

Once we're in the house, I fix her a drink and stick with water for myself, because alcohol and head injuries aren't a good mix. I take a seat on the couch beside my sister. "You remember that girl I told you about, the one who shattered her ankle?"

Carmen shrugs. "Sure."

I can't tell if she actually remembers or she's just saying she does—not that it matters. I have to come out and tell her—no sugarcoating. "She's our half sister."

She's quiet for a few very long seconds before she reaches for her purse. "I'm sorry . . . How hard did you hit your head?"

"I'm serious, Carm. She's our half sister."

"Okay. And how do you know this?"

"Because our father picked her up at the hospital this afternoon."

She blinks several times but doesn't say anything.

"Carm?"

"You were right not to tell me while I was driving."

"Can I get you a glass of water?"

"A bottle of tequila might be better." She exhales a slow breath. "I can't... This is... I don't even..." She shakes her head and rubs her temples. "Did you talk to him?"

"I did."

"What was he like? Is he still in town?" She looks utterly stunned, much like I was when I first saw him.

"He looked like a much-older version of the dad we knew, I guess. And yes, he's still in town and he'd like to see you, but I wanted to be the one to tell you. I didn't think it would be good to surprise you the way I was—one head-injured Smith at a time and all."

She laughs a little but then grows serious. "What did he even say? Do you think I should see him? God, it's been twenty years. This is so—"

"Weird?"

"I was going to say fucked up."

"I think you should do what you think is right for you. He apologized for leaving us, explained why he did, but it doesn't erase the past, and it doesn't make it hurt any less that he started a new family and left us all behind like we were nothing."

Carmen leans back, running her hands over her thighs. "I was what? Nine when he left? I remember things weren't good right before that happened."

"Not good how?"

"Things were off. I mean, they were off a lot, but I remember Adam saying shit was about to hit the fan or something. I didn't really get what it meant, but then a week later Dad up and left, and Adam wasn't even the least bit surprised. He said he figured it would've happened a lot sooner."

Adam is ten years my senior and the middle child, also a twin. He went to college out of state, and I see him maybe once every two years at best. Carmen is the only sibling I've stayed close with. The rest of them scattered as soon as they were old enough.

It's no wonder Ethan's family has always felt so much more like mine than my own, because they were the only constants in my life, along with Carmen.

"I don't know if I want to see him, Lilah. I'm not sure it's worth digging up all of those skeletons."

"I guess the question is, will you regret it if you don't see him while you have this chance?"

Carmen rubs her forehead and sighs. "Probably?"

"Then I think you should. You don't have to forgive him or let him back into your life, but I think hearing what he has to say firsthand isn't a bad thing. If nothing else, maybe it'll get us some closure."

"I guess. What about this half sister?"

I smile. "Emery. When you're ready, I think it would be great if you could meet her. She goes to college here and she'll be local for a few years, so maybe we can build something there."

"Do you think she'll like me?" I've never heard Carmen sound so unsure of herself.

"I think she'll love you as much as I do. You're a lot alike, actually."

e~

It takes Carmen less than an hour to warm to the idea of meeting Emery. Ten minutes after that, I'm calling our father so I can arrange for us to meet Emery for dinner. He agrees to drop her off and seems understanding, although slightly disappointed, when I tell him that Carmen isn't quite ready to see him, yet.

We arrive at the restaurant a few minutes early. Carmen is nervous, touching her hair, adjusting her shirt. "Maybe I should've worn a dress instead of jeans. Do you think I'm too casual?"

"You're fine. She's a college student. You're not interviewing for a job; you're meeting your sister."

"Oh, shit." She flaps her hands in front of her face. "I don't want to cry."

All hope of holding back the tears is lost when Emery walks through the doors, looking equal parts nervous and excited. When she sees me, she hesitates for a second, so I take a step forward. She rushes over and throws her arms around me, hugging me hard.

After a few long seconds, in which tears threaten and spill over, she lets me go and turns to face Carmen. I can't believe I didn't see the family resemblance until now. Where Carmen is dark haired, Emery is fair like me, but the shape of their faces and the wide smiles are the same.

"Carmen, this is Emery. Emery, this is your sister Carmen."

My heart suddenly is full as I'm pulled into their embrace. I'm fortunate to have this love, and in this short life, it's best not to take it for granted.

Dinner with Emery is exactly what we all need. I would invite her back to my place afterward, but I know her parents aren't in town long and that Carmen and I are going to be here when they're not, so we make plans to get together for a girls' night soon, and Carmen and I go back to my place.

"I really like her," Carmen says on the drive home.

"She's great, isn't she?"

"Do you think that went well? It seemed to go well." Carmen chews her bottom lip.

"It went as fantastic as meeting a half sister you didn't know you had could go."

She laughs a little. "God, we're a messed-up lot, aren't we?"

"At least the new half sister is your only drama," I reply.

As if on cue, my phone buzzes from inside my purse. I haven't checked it since I called to make arrangements for dinner. I rummage around in my purse until I find it and check the screen.

"It's Ethan?"

I leave the message unchecked for now. "It is."

"Does he know yet?" Carmen asks softly.

I shake my head. "I haven't had an opportunity to talk to

him since all of this happened." I don't even know if they won the game.

"Don't you think you should tell him?"

I finger the charm on my bracelet. "I don't think this is the kind of family drama I want to unload over the phone, you know? Besides, I'm not even sure what's going to happen between us."

"You can't tell me you're still on the fence over this." She reaches over to flick the bracelet as if it proves some point.

And I suppose in a way it does. I haven't taken it off. I carry him with me wherever I go.

"I don't even know if he's going to be here next year. What if he's traded again and he ends up somewhere across the country?"

"Then you figure it out. Maybe you quit your job here and live in a new city. Or maybe Minnesota keeps him and he stays here. Either way, I think you've already made your decision."

"I needed him to have faith that he can do this on his own. That I'm not the reason."

"I think he's proved that in the playoffs. And let's be real here—I've said it before, and I'll say it again, you are part of the reason."

"I'm not," I snap. "Ethan's performance on the ice has nothing to do with me."

Carmen gives me her calm-your-ass-down face. "Maybe not directly, but he's happy with you."

"But what if it's only because he's doing well this season?

What if he doesn't get traded and he stays here but then next season is terrible for him? Then what?" I voice the fears that have plagued me these past weeks.

"You're thinking too much in extremes. Imagine you achieve your ultimate dream. Like, say I actually had the balls to open up a bakery, which I have no intention of doing incidentally, because it's the worst investment ever based on the research I've done. Only, like, ten percent of bakeries are successful and making a profit after five years." She must realize she's rambling, because she flops a hand around. "Anyway, for the sake of argument, let's say I'm one of the ten percent and I make that happen, but in order to have that dream, I have to give up something equally as important."

"Which would be margaritas in your case."

"Ha ha. But yeah. I'd be miserable without my margaritas. Ethan has his bakery and you're his margarita, and right now he's not allowed to have margaritas, but"—she lifts a finger signaling for me to keep my mouth shut—"there's the possibility of getting his margaritas back if he can be patient."

"That's the worst analogy ever, Carmen."

"I thought it was pretty damn good. And you better have more tequila at home or I may just un-sister you."

"That's not even allowed to be a thing." Carmen has been a huge support over these past weeks—un-sistering is not an option.

"But seriously, Lilah, you're part of the whole of his success. You're a driving force. He wants to be with you, so he's willing to give you this time because it's what you need. Don't you think it would be better for both of you on an emotional level to just set some boundaries and be together? Hasn't he proven to both of you that he can play hockey regardless? You don't need to keep pushing him away anymore, do you?"

"It's hard to find balance with him," I admit.

"That's because you didn't have as much to balance before. You don't have to sacrifice doing well at your job or at school or spending time with family to be with Ethan. All of those pieces can fit into your life along with him."

"But how? I don't want to lose him again. And I can't lose *me* again, either."

"You can't live in fear of what-ifs."

"I don't ever want to hurt like that again."

"Love has the potential to cause pain. It's a risk, and I think this is one worth taking. Don't you think he loves you enough to want you to be happy? Do you think he'd wait for you for eight years just to bail when you get a case of the nerves?"

"He didn't wait eight years for me."

"Really? He hasn't had one serious relationship since you, even after you married the wrong man. Maybe it wasn't intentional, but he never found someone he could love as much as he loves you, and you clearly feel the same way. Just own it. I promise it'll be better for both of you."

I finger the hockey charm dangling from my wrist. "He'll be home tomorrow."

"So you'll be waiting for him at his house, right?"

"Do you think that's a good idea?"

"Is bacon dipped in real maple syrup a good idea?"

"Um…"

"The answer is yes, Lilah. Yes, it's a good idea."

chapter twenty-two

HOME

Ethan

Success is only as gratifying as the people you get to share it with, so coming home seems rather anticlimactic.

I pull into my driveway, wishing the high I was on last night carried over into this morning. We're up three to two in the series. Tomorrow night could be the game that puts us in the finals. We could be one step closer to the Cup.

I grab my duffel from the back seat and head up the front steps, not all that excited to walk into an empty house. What I really want is to drive over to Lilah's. I understand her need for space and I want to respect it, but I miss her. I may not need her to play well, but I need her in other ways. I need her to feel whole.

I drop my bag in front of the laundry room and pull out my phone. Clicking on her contact, I scroll through the messages she left last night after we won the game. They were positive, excited even, but brief. I want to check in and make sure she's okay. I worry she's gotten her exam results or something and they weren't what she wanted them to be.

I hit the Call button and pause halfway to the living room, confused by the echo of the ring, at least until Lilah rounds the corner. "Hi." She lifts her phone, wearing a small, nervous smile.

I end the call, mouth instantly dry, palms clammy. "This is a surprise."

Her eyes move over me slowly. She looks tired and possibly like she's been crying. "I have some things to tell you."

"Good or bad things?" I cross the foyer and stop when I'm inches from her. I don't know how to read her beyond the obvious exhaustion, and all I can do is spin hypotheticals.

"A bit of both?" It's more question than answer, though, as if she's uncertain herself.

"What happened? Are you okay?" I want to hug her, but I can't be sure how it will be received.

"I don't even know where to begin." She links her fingers with mine and leads me toward the living room. "Come sit with me."

I drop down beside her on the couch and give in to the urge to touch her. I run my finger along the slope of her nose. "You look tired, baby."

"I am. I didn't get much sleep last night."

"Want to tell me why?" I can't decide whether her being here means she's seeking comfort from me or if it's something else.

Any worry I might've had about us is erased as she relays what I've missed over the past couple of days. It's nothing I could've ever expected, and certainly nothing she could've, either. Seeing her father after twenty years, and learning she's been treating her half sister all those weeks, would've been painfully shocking. "Why didn't you call me last night?"

She laughs a little. "Because I was up until three in the morning with Carmen and I didn't want to tell you this over the phone."

"Is Carmen okay? Are you? I wish you had called me, especially with the whole fainting thing." I don't like that she was hurt and I wasn't here to take care of her.

"It's a bruise. I'm fine. My doctor was a super thorough pain in my ass about it."

"You could've had a concussion."

"Dr. Lovely checked for that."

I nod. She works in a hospital; of course she had excellent medical care. "How do you feel about your dad being here? Will you see him again?"

She props her cheek on her fist and sighs. "I don't know. I'm not sure I want to try to rebuild that relationship. He walked away from our entire family once. What's to say he won't do it again? And I just don't know if I can find forgiveness for him. I haven't had much time to get used to the idea, or even consider that it's a possibility."

"Do you think you'll be able to forgive him eventually?"

"I don't know." She fiddles with the hockey charm on her

bracelet. "I know why this has been so hard for me, though, now."

"You mean us?" My throat constricts as I take in her guarded posture, knees tucked under her.

"In my head I connected those two events. My dad leaving our family and you breaking up with me felt a lot like the same kind of loss. But it was so much more painful with you because the way I loved you was so . . . consuming. It echoed a pain I hadn't recovered from. Does that make sense?"

"Yes." It does, in so many ways I hadn't considered. My knowledge of Lilah's father had been limited to her six-year-old perception of events. One day he was there, the next he was gone. And before that, he was rarely ever home since he worked so much, so his leaving hadn't changed much in her day-to-day life. But I can see now how that absence over time would have an impact, and how my leaving echoed that abandonment.

But it was also so much worse because I'd been her everyday, and she'd been mine. And I'd taken that from us both.

I don't want to ask the next question, but I have to, because this state of uncertainty is unbearable. "If you can't forgive him, does that mean you can't forgive me, either?"

"There's no simple answer to that question, Ethan."

I fold my hands in my lap and prepare for the worst. I don't know how I'll manage if this is her ending things between us for good. She carries half my soul, and without her, I don't know how to exist. All those years without her had been like living a half-life.

"In my head I'd forgiven you. It's my heart that's had a hard time forgetting. I let fear dictate my actions with you this time around."

"How?"

"I put you ahead of myself because I was afraid. So every time you said you needed me, I caved. I didn't want to disappoint you, or give you a reason to leave again. And honestly, I like being needed...I felt necessary, essential even."

The conversation I had with my father a few weeks ago makes so much more sense. "You are necessary, Lilah. I won't ever do to you again what I did before. I promise I won't hurt either of us like that again."

Her smile is soft. "I need to find a way to balance my love for you with the rest of my life."

"I'll give you whatever you need. If it's still time, you can have it. Or space. Just know that I won't be selfish with you, even if I want to be. I won't ever take your love for granted, and I won't put my success on you."

She laces her fingers with mine on a deep exhale. "I'm sorry I made you wait."

"For you to forgive me?"

"For me to be brave enough to love you the way I want to."

"I didn't get my head out of my ass for eight years. This past month might not have been easy, but it was necessary. You were right. I can see the pressure I was putting on you, maybe not intentionally, but it was there. I don't want you to ever feel like my love for you has limitations, especially not based on how my hockey season is going."

Her smile is soft understanding. "I wanted to be more than that, for both of us. I had this plan for my future, and then you came back into my life and I lost sight of everything except for you. I became dependent on your dependency."

"You're not just part of some pregame ritual based on superstitions. You know that, right?"

She laughs a little. "I do, although I'm not opposed to all of your pregame rituals. Your boxers are pretty comfy to sleep in, and the taking-them-off part is always fun." She runs her fingers through my playoff beard. "I'm also a big fan of this, but your naked rituals are probably my favorite."

"That's stress relief, not a ritual."

"Call it whatever you want, but I'm more than happy to be the recipient of orgasms in the name of stress relief."

"I'm always up for providing stress-relief orgasms. Actually, I probably have a lot of those to make up for. We could do some of that now, you know, like pre-pre-game stress relief."

She nods somberly. "You really can't overdo it on the stress relief, can you?"

I cup her cheek in my palm and tilt my head to the side. When I'm within an inch of her mouth, I pause. "Does this mean we're not on a break anymore?"

"Do you actually need to ask that question?"

"I want to be clear about what kind of kiss this is going to be."

"Ethan."

"Is this our back-together kiss?"

"As opposed to what?"

"I don't know. Maybe it's a test kiss for you."

"A test kiss?"

"Uh-huh, to see if you're as interested in pre-pre-game stress relief as you think you are."

"I've already expressed my interest."

"But is that all you're interested in? I need to know exactly what's at stake with this kiss so I can strategize my approach."

"This isn't a hockey game, Ethan. It's a kiss, which will hopefully also lead to some scoring." Her luscious lips turn up at her bad pun.

I breathe a laugh as she grabs my shirt and attempts to connect our mouths. I cup her face between my hands and sit up on my knees, tilting her head back. She rises with me, fingers circling my wrists. With my thumb I skim the curve of her bottom lip and watch them part. Her eyes stay on mine as I bend to kiss her chin. She whimpers, annoyed.

"Tell me I'm yours," I whisper.

"You're mine." Her eyes search mine, soft and wanting. "And I'm yours."

"Yes. Mine." I drop my head, lips brushing over hers before I pull back again. "Always."

The sound that falls from her lips is half need, half frustration. I understand it, share it even. I want to wrap my arms around her; I want to feel her body against mine, the softness of her lips, the warmth of her touch. These weeks without her have been a painful eternity. I'm not sure how I survived eight years. But I also want to savor this moment because this is a new first kiss. This is the one that marks the beginning of our forever. Because I'm never letting her go again.

When I close the space between us, Lilah's lips are already parted, so I stroke inside her mouth in a slow, shallow sweep before pulling back. She tries to follow, but I hold her still. "Do you remember when all we used to do was kiss?"

"Why're we still talking?"

"Do you?"

"Of course I remember. I'd be so worked up, dying for something else to happen, but I had no idea what."

I would've humped a tree back then. I'd wanted to put my hands all over her, touch every part of her body that she'd let me, but I hadn't ever wanted to push. Now I do. I want to claim back what's always been mine, and I'm fighting with myself to take it slow. "Is that how you feel right now?"

"Yes, but I know what's going to happen next."

I suck her bottom lip, nipping gently. "You think so?"

She drops a hand, stroking me through my pants. "Definitely."

I bite back a groan, hoping to stay in control a little longer. It's been weeks since I've been inside her, surrounded in the feel, the smell, the taste of her. "Want to tell me?"

"You're going to tease me like you do, get me all excited, and then you're going to love me, probably for several hours, with short intermissions."

"This is one of the many reasons why we belong together."

She grins. "Because I'm sexually psychic?"

I laugh. "I'm taking you upstairs." I lift her and she wraps her legs around my waist as I carry her to the bedroom.

We take our time undressing, touches soft and reverent. Her bra is lacy and pale, feminine and pretty. She's always been such a delicious temptation. That hasn't changed at all with time. I thread one hand into her hair, the other skimming her breast, following the edge of her bra until I can flick the clasp open. I trace her nipple before I trail a path to her hip, memorizing her body all over again. Hooking my fingers into the waist of her pants, I pull them down, exposing the matching panties.

"I missed you. It was hard to give you space."

"It was hard to take it."

Lilah's hands move over my shoulders, one curving around the back of my neck, the other smoothing down my spine. I drop my head to kiss her again. Her tongue meets mine, pushing back, sweeping inside my mouth. This isn't like the sweet kisses of youth, or the desperate reunion after years of separation and lost time found again. This is reacquainting under the promise of something new.

Laying her down on the bed, I fit myself between her legs and stretch out over her. She hooks her ankles behind my back, and tongues and teeth clash as gentleness wanes, replaced by aching need, the fallout of deprivation.

Lilah groans, fingers sifting through my hair and gripping hard. "Roll over."

I push up on one arm. "Why?"

"So I can be on top and you can see me."

I flip onto my back, taking her with me. She uses my chest to brace herself, sliding over my erection through the barrier of satin and my pants. They need to go.

I settle my palms against the dip in her waist, just above her hips, thumbs brushing under her ribs. "God, you're perfect."

"Says the professional hockey player with the body of a god." Her fingertips trail over my chest and down my stomach. The muscles twitch and flex with the touch.

It's only been a handful of weeks, but it feels like the first time all over again.

I pull her closer and lift my head, capturing a tight peak between my lips, swirling my tongue, then sucking.

"God, Ethan." Lilah braces her hands on my chest and tries to push away.

I slide my arm around her back, fingers splayed between her shoulder blades to keep her close, moving higher to grip the back of her neck. I release her nipple and lift my head, my playoff beard brushing the wet flesh. "This is the teasing part you talked about." I gently bite the swell.

Her eyes fall closed on a grin. "Some things never change."

"Mmm." I run a light finger down her side and she jerks.

"Like this ticklish spot right here, or the little sigh I always get when I kiss right here." I press an openmouthed kiss against the side of her neck and she hums. "And the way I love you." I tip her chin down as her eyes flutter open. "You're in my soul, Lilah. That will never change."

Her fingers drift over my lips before our mouths meet. "I love you always."

We touch and kiss, hands roaming. Lilah's fingers dip into the waistband of my pants. Flicking the button open, she slips her hand inside. I groan at her gentle exploration.

Her strokes are slow, unhurried, almost a torment, which I'm sure is part of her plan. I lift my hips, trying to get her to go faster, to squeeze tighter, but she maintains the same even rhythm. "You're not the only one who can tease, you know."

I laugh and bite her neck, getting the squeeze I'm looking for. "I want to be in you."

She brings her fingers to her lips, her smile knowing. "You mean in here?" They drift down, between her breasts, over her stomach, and across the satin and lace between her thighs. "Or did you mean here?"

"I like that option the best."

"I thought there was going to be all this teasing." She's still stroking, pushing me closer to the edge.

"Well, we have hours, don't we? Besides, you're doing enough teasing for both of us."

I wrap an arm around her waist and flip her over. She

shrieks and then moans as I settle between her legs. "I bet I make you come before I do."

"What do I get if you come first?" She arches at the roll of my hips.

"Endless orgasms. As many as you want." I kiss her neck, then shifting down her body, I cover the satin between her legs with my mouth and suck.

She gasps, fingers sliding through my hair. I skim a fingertip under the edge of her panties and get a moan. Then I move the fabric to the side, enough that her clit barely peeks out, and I lick along the edge of the fabric, grazing the sensitive skin.

"Ethan," Lilah groans.

"I like it down here. I'm gonna be here for a while, I think." I circle and tease, taste and torment, driving her higher and higher until a sheen covers her body and she trembles, on the edge of release.

As she comes, I yank her panties down her legs. Before the orgasm ends, I'm inside her, feeling the pulse and squeeze as she surrounds me.

"I think I win." It comes out gravelly and rough.

Lilah's eyes flutter open, lids still heavy. "You can win every time if you want. I really don't mind."

I kiss her chin and then her lips. Staying close, I make love to the first woman who ever owned my heart and kept it until I found my way back to her.

chapter twenty-three

WIN

Lilah

"This is so delicious!" Emery drops down beside me on the couch, and her drink nearly sloshes over the rim of her glass.

I pause in my nail polish application. "What is that?"

"A margarita." Carmen sets a glass on a coaster beside my half-painted toes, then sits in the armchair across from me. Her eyes flutter shut as she takes a sip of her own and releases a contented sigh.

"A virgin one, I hope," I say, knowing full well it isn't.

Not that it matters—we're having a sister sleepover. At Ethan's instead of my place, because he has enough bedrooms. It's great for family events and parties, like the one Ethan threw last week. After my exam results came in, he decided we needed to do something special to mark the important milestone in my life. I passed the exam with a ninety, which bumped my final grade and alleviated my worries about getting into the master's program. The party was ridiculous and unnecessary, but it was nice to be celebrated like that with the people I love. Emery finally had a chance to meet Ethan that night. She's pretty smitten, which is understandable. He's charming and gorgeous and difficult not to love.

Tonight it's just the three of us—me, Carmen, and Emery—so there's a good chance we'll all end up in the same room. One of the five bedrooms in the house has been outfitted with a queen bed and double bunks.

It's supposed to be for Dylan's kids when they visit from out West, but we had a sleepover last week when Ethan was out of town for no other reason than we like spending time together. Emery thinks it's fun to do the bunk bed thing, and since she's never had the sister experience before, Carmen and I are happy to oblige.

Ethan also turned the heat up in the pool so it's warm enough to swim. Plus there's the hot tub and the sauna. Tomorrow is Saturday, so none of us have to be up early for work, including Emery, who's taking extra courses and working part-time.

Emery grabs the remote and turns on the TV. It's already on the hockey channel. "When does the game start?"

"In about twenty minutes." I resume nail polish application.

"Cool." Emery takes another gulp of her margarita. She's already drained most of it.

"Slow down, there, half-pint," I warn. "It's bad enough

we're breaking the law with the underage drinking. I don't feel like taking a trip to the hospital for alcohol poisoning."

"It's so tasty it's hard to stop." She sets her glass down, though, and taps her lip thoughtfully. "But I don't want my next run-in with Dr. Lovely to be while I'm having my stomach pumped."

Carmen raises a brow. "How do you know Noah?"

"He was Emery's surgeon when she broke her ankle," I explain.

"He's so hot." Emery sighs.

"He's a little old for you, don't you think?" Carmen asks from behind the rim of her glass.

"Oh, totally. I think my dad would shit an entire pile of bricks if I brought home a guy in his thirties." Her eyes go wide, darting between us. "I'm sor—"

"Don't apologize," Carmen and I say at the same time.

Emery bites her lip, her smile gone. "It's still kinda weird, this whole thing." She gestures between us. "And I forget sometimes, you know?"

"It's really okay," I reassure her.

Since the discovery that Emery is our half sister, Carmen and I decided to give our father a chance to make amends. I'm not sure I'll ever be able to forgive him entirely, or to call him Dad, since he's never been one to me, but for Emery's sake, I'm willing to at least be civil with him. She's right about it being weird, and sometimes quite awkward, but she's worth the effort.

Commentators for the hockey game appear on the TV, ending our conversation. It's the sixth game in the series and Minnesota is down one game. Tonight they're either going to game seven or coming home without the Cup. I'm crossing everything it's the former, not the latter.

We drink far too many margaritas while we watch the game. It's intense. The score stays close in the first period, but in the second Ethan scores a goal and follows with an assist, giving them a solid lead they manage to hold on to for the rest of the game. My heart swells with a pride so huge I can barely breathe as the final buzzer sounds—though it might also be because both of my sisters are hugging me so tightly. Tomorrow he'll be home.

His dream is right there, within reach. The Cup is almost his.

⁂

"I'm so excited! I can't believe I get to see the championship game live!" Emery's arms are linked through mine and Carmen's as we navigate the crowded arena. It's a challenge to walk straight with how much bouncing she's doing, but her enthusiasm is infectious.

I'm nervous for Ethan. The series is tied three to three. At least his team has home ice advantage.

Martin and Jeannie are ahead of us. I marvel as he takes the stairs at a cautious but competent pace. He's come a long way in the months since the stroke. Once we reach our designated row, Jeannie and Martin allow us to file down it first so they can have the seats closer to the end. Center ice provides the perfect view of the entire rink.

Emery grabs Carmen's shoulder. "Oh my God! Dr. Lovely is here! Best night ever."

Carmen shoots her a look. "I thought we established that he's too old for you."

Emery rolls her eyes. "He's still hot, though."

We make our way down the row. There's some elbowing and whispers as Carmen tries to make Emery sit beside Dr. Lovely but ends up beside him herself.

Emery grips the armrests, vibrating with excitement. She surveys the rows of fans, cringing at some of the outfits the bunnies are wearing. She elbows me in the arm. "Hey! Who is *that*?"

I follow her gaze. "Who is who?"

"That guy standing beside Jeannie." Emery's had an opportunity to meet Ethan's family in the past two weeks, but this is the first time his brothers have been in town since she's been introduced to the Kase family.

"Tyler?"

"Oooh. Ethan's older brother, right?"

"Yup."

Emery narrows her eyes. "How much older is he again? Like, a few years?"

"Try seven."

She slaps the arm of her chair. "Dammit! He doesn't look *that* old. Why am I always lusting after these old guys? Why can't college guys be less jerky and more..." She flounders, searching for a word. When she can't seem to find one, she gestures to Tyler. "Like that."

"You'll get to meet him after the game."

She makes a *pfft* sound. "Whatever. He was in high school by the time I was freaking born." Crossing her arms over her chest, she sighs and then brightens. "Will I get to meet some of the hockey players after this? Most of them are under thirty, right?"

"Yes. You'll get to meet them, and yes, most of them are under thirty."

"Great. Something to look forward to, you know, apart from the actual game."

Drinks are purchased and no one says anything when a beer is handed to Emery. The game is a nail-biter. The score is tied one to one at the end of the first period. Ethan plays flawlessly. While the trade opportunities will be there no matter the outcome of this game, if they win, they'll be far more favorable for him.

At the bottom of the second period, New York scores, giving them the advantage going into the final period. I watch Ethan and his coach strategizing before he returns to the ice.

I fidget with the bracelet around my wrist, fingering the hockey stick charm, saying a little prayer to the hockey gods. Minnesota gains control of the puck at the beginning of the third period, and the team captain scores another goal, with Ethan managing the assist. We're on the edge of our seats, quite literally, the score tied, and no shots get past the net on either side.

It's beginning to look like the game is headed for overtime until Ethan commandeers the puck with only minutes left on the clock. He's lightning fast as he glides down the ice, maneuvering around the opposition, keeping the puck close. Skating around the back of the net, he shoots on the way up the rink, sneaking the puck past the goalie. We're all out of our seats, along with the mass of Minnesota fans; the screams of excitement send a shiver down my spine. New York scrambles for the puck, but Minnesota keeps it out of their reach as the seconds tick down and the final buzzer sounds. The roar of the crowd is deafening as Minnesota streams onto the ice, high on the win.

I'm riding the same wave as everyone else as Minnesota players pass the cup while they skate the rink, celebrating this monumental win.

The game is long over before we finally make our way out of the stadium and head out to celebrate with the team. The wall of flat screens shows game highlights and interviews. Ethan's smiling, sweaty face pops up at the same time an arm slips around my waist and warm lips brush my ear. "Took you long enough to get here."

I turn to face him, wrapping my arms around his neck. "I had to fight through your throng of fans."

"You need to start taking advantage of the fact that you're my girlfriend and throw your special pass around more." He dips his head, lips meeting mine in a gentle, sweet kiss.

"You did it," I say against his warm mouth. He tastes faintly of bourbon. "You brought the Cup home."

He leans back far enough to meet my gaze. His smile is radiant. The only other time I've seen him this happy was when he was drafted. "Well, I can't take all the credit. I have a whole pile of teammates who were in on it, too."

"But you scored the winning goal."

"I'm planning on scoring a lot of those later when we're celebrating alone."

I wrinkle my nose and poke him in the chest. "Leave it to you to ruin a moment by turning it into a sexual innuendo."

"I'm not ruining the moment." He holds me tighter when I try to push away. "Do you know what the best part of winning the Cup is?"

I try not to smile, certain he's going to throw another dirty quip at me. He's half in the bag, I think, despite only having been at the bar for maybe half an hour. "What's that?"

"That you're here to share it with me."

TRADES

Lilah

Merk's ears perk up and he gives his customary single-bark greeting, alerting me to Ethan's arrival.

I sit up in a rush, dropping my book on the wet patio, not caring that I've lost my place or that the pages will be wavy with water damage. I wasn't actually focused on anything I was reading. Ethan is finally home from an all-day meeting with his agent to talk trades. Until forty minutes ago, I was at work. I didn't call or text for information. I want to be face-to-face with him when I find out what next season is going to look like for him, for us.

He smiles and takes off his sunglasses. "Anxious, baby?"

"Immensely."

He straddles the lounge chair I'm half sitting in, slips his hands under my knees, and adjusts my legs to drape over his so we're facing each other.

I slap his left hand when it slides up too high on my thigh.

"Ethan! Do not play this game with me. Tell me what the trade options are."

"We have three."

We. Not *he*. *We*. This has been the mantra in my head all day. Whatever happens, wherever he goes, I go, too. If we have to start over, we do it together.

I take a deep breath. "Okay. Give 'em to me."

"Edmonton offered six million for one year."

"Canada?" I like maple syrup, so I guess that could work for a year, but it means I'll have to either postpone my master's or look into programs out there, which is a little unfortunate considering I just received my acceptance letter to Minnesota last week. I have no idea if my nursing degree is accepted in Canada. It's something we'll figure out if that's where we end up. Or I wait one more year. Either way, doable.

He gives me a cheeky grin. "It's a nice place. The people are friendly up there."

"Isn't it a lot colder than here?" Minnesota winters are cold, but I'm pretty sure they don't need freezers up there from November to April.

"Cold means lots of cuddling, and that's only option one."

"Okay, I like cuddling. What's option two?"

"Nashville offered four million a year for three years."

I try to temper my sigh of relief. That should take Edmonton out of the running. Nashville might be far away from Minnesota, but at least my eyelashes won't get frostbite.

"What's the third offer?"

"Three million a year."

"Where and for how long?"

"Five years, and right here." He tilts his head to the side, waiting for my reaction.

I want to scream my excitement. I want to hug him and celebrate, but there are things he has to consider, and I don't want to push the decision one way or another.

I play it cool, but I'm sure the tremor in my voice is telling. "What does your agent say?"

"He says it's up to me to make a decision."

"Based on?" I prompt.

"What's best for me."

"And what do you think is best for you?" I run my fingers up and down the length of his.

"You."

I glance up, expecting a smile, but he's completely serious. "You can't ask me to make the decision for you, Ethan. I can't do that."

He flips his hands over, lacing our fingers together. "I wouldn't ask you to do that."

"And you can't make a decision based on me. We've already been through that. It's not realistic."

"I know that."

"So you need to make the choice that's going to benefit—"

He cuts me off with a kiss.

As soon as he pulls back, I attempt to finish the sentence: "—your career the—"

His tongue is in my mouth again. I don't fight, and this kiss lasts a lot longer—long enough that he untwines our hands, and his fingers start migrating up the outside of my thighs, and I end up straddling his lap.

"Do you know what benefits my career the most?" Ethan kisses a path down my throat, fingertips skimming along the edge of my bikini top.

"Don't say me."

"Fine. I want to stay here because it's home. You have a life here and people you love and a career path all laid out. I won't disrupt that when you've worked so hard for it, and I refuse to leave you again. So we stay here because that's what's best for us. We both know my career is temporary and you're not. You're forever and I'm not going to put that at risk ever again."

"But what if you went to Edmonton and next year they sign you for five years at five million a year?" I'm playing devil's advocate, not because I want him to change his mind, but because I want him to be sure this decision is the right one and that he's not making it for the wrong reasons. Namely, me.

Ethan runs his fingertip from the bridge of my nose to the tip.

"Hypotheticals don't matter. I want *you*, Delilah Jane. I want what we have right here. I won't give that up, or my team, or my family. I'm willing to sacrifice a few million dollars over the next few years in order to secure that."

"So you want to stay in Minnesota, even though they're offering you the least money?"

"Per year. Contract-wise, it's the best deal. Besides, I'm not worried about the money. Three million dollars a year is more than enough to survive off of for the rest of our lives if we're not stupid about it."

"So you don't want to be greedy?"

"About money? No. About you, definitely. I spent eight years without you, and I had no idea what I was missing until I finally got you back."

"I don't want you to make the wrong choice."

"I'm not. Staying here is the right decision. I do have two important requests, though."

"What kind of requests?"

"Ones you need to hear out before you say no."

He looks serious again and a little nervous. "That's a good way to put me on the defensive."

"Just listen before you react."

"I'm listening."

"I think you should take a year off work—"

"There's no way—"

He puts a finger to my lips. "I said listen, please, Lilah." He waits to make sure I'm going to follow his instructions. I do, but I'm sure I look unimpressed.

"I know you love your job, but even part-time it's going to be a lot to juggle with taking a master's course. Just take the year. I'm sure Fairview will want you back when you're finished. Then you'll be right where you want with your career without anything to get in the way of the goal."

"I can't afford to take the year off. I have a mortgage to pay." Even as I say it, I know it's a ridiculous excuse.

Ethan arches a brow. "Which brings me to my next request. I know your independence is important to you, and I love that about you, but I'd like you to officially move in with me. You're already sleeping here most nights of the week anyway. The off-season is short. These are the only months we have together uninterrupted by constant travel. Financially it doesn't make sense for you to pay a mortgage for a house you barely live in, especially when this is where you belong." He holds on to my hip, smile growing devious. "Right here, in my lap, every single day."

"That would make for awkward family get-togethers."

He ignores my joke. "Move in. Take the time off work so you can have the career you want without sacrificing every other part of your life if you don't have to. Selfishly, I'm referring mostly to myself. You're essential to my survival. You're as important as the air I breathe. You soothe my soul and keep my heart full—you always have. Just be here with me. We've spent enough time apart."

He's right. And more than that, we're ready for this. "Okay. I'll move in."

"And take a year off to focus on your master's."

"I'll start the paperwork for that." I trace the contour of his jaw with gentle fingertips. "I love you."

"Just like I love you."

I grin. "So we stay."

My favorite smile appears, and I get a little lost in the blue sea and amber sunrise shadowing his right eye. "So we stay." He kisses me softly. "This time we only move forward together."